I0602254

EYES OF DARKNESS
BOOK ONE OF THE ASH SAGA

WRITTEN BY
MAX RUSCINSKI

This is a work of fiction. Names, characters, places, and incidents either are the product of the author's imagination or are used fictitiously. Any resemblance to actual persons, living or dead, events, or locales is entirely coincidental.

Copyright © 2021 by Max Ruscinski

All rights reserved. No part of this book may be reproduced or used in any manner without permission of the copyright owner except for the use of quotations in a book review. For more information, address: authormaxruscinski@gmail.com

First Edition: March 2021

Cover art by Hatrobot

ISBN 978-1-7774-2750-4 (paperback)
ISBN 978-1-7774-2751-1 (ebook)

www.maxruscinski.com

PROLOGUE

"When you're hunting with the Wilson's, there'll always be a catch!"

Todd awoke to his brother's voice, but his brother was not there. In fact, he did not have a brother. Well, to the world he had a brother, but Skipper was no brother to him.

"When you're hunting with the Wilson's, there'll always be a catch!" His fake brother said again. Skipper used one assertive hand to point at the camera and the other to hold up the freshly shot deer, blood still pouring down its neck. Todd had woken up to this image every day lately. The blood, Skipper's smirk and wink, the deer's open eyes. It was as if the deer was staring into the souls of all the viewers, condemning them for watching this terrible show. At least that's what Todd's opinion of the show was.

"This is a gold mine!" He remembered the greed-ridden

studio executives giving them a call five years earlier. Apparently, there were a lot of moms and dads who liked to waste their lives watching hunting shows. It had been Skipper's cousin, a big-shot agent in LA, who first got them in touch with the studio. He also thought the show could be a huge success. It seemed everyone except for Todd thought that.

Todd was reluctant to join the show. He had always been a private person and did not enjoy putting himself out there. He never really left his hometown in Northern California, so it was extraordinarily overwhelming for him when he first went to LA. He hated that place and he hated the fake, manufactured people that lived there. But he had to admit, they're good at what they do. They find people who can make them rich, then they reel them in like a fish on a line. They keep reeling and reeling until they finally catch you. And don't think they're going to throw you back in the water after. No, they hold onto you until you've breathed your last miserable breath.

Todd would not have accepted the offer, but the studio was insistent that they needed both of them and Skipper ended up convincing him. After all, him and Skip grew up together. Their fathers hunted together, so they followed in their footsteps and started hunting as well. They were even best friends at one point. But that was many years ago, and those days were long gone.

Once thoughts of the show stopped haunting Todd's mind, he looked over at his wife Marissa, who still slept soundly next to him. Over her shoulder he could see the clock, 4:03am. He had been a hunter for so long that he was used to automatically waking up this early. Years ago, he would have jumped out of bed with a smile on his face, excited for a day of hunting. Today, however, he had a slight frown he knew would not disappear anytime soon.

The studio had sensed some tension building between him and Skipper when they were finishing up the last season. So, before they started filming the fourth season of their hit show, they wanted them to go on a few hunts together off camera. It was as though he was back in high school and his teacher was assigning him homework. The studio had caught him, and just as he thought, they would not let him go until he breathed his last breath. But he wasn't going to let that happen. He didn't plan on dying in the hands of the studio. The homework assignments would not go the way the studio wanted them to go. Today, Todd would find the courage to tell Skipper that he was leaving the show.

And that's a wrap, Todd briefly smiled to himself in the mirror. The stressful years working on the show did a number on him. Todd was barely eating lately, he seemed to constantly have bags under his eyes, and his once thick brown hair was now either falling out or turning grey. To make matters worse, he woke up with a large zit right in the middle of his forehead. In an attempt to pop it, he only made the area around the zit much more red and harder to gaze upon. Today was not his day... he barely even recognized the man who looked back at him in the mirror.

He threw on his now oversized camouflage jacket and made for the door. Before leaving the bedroom, Todd looked back at his wife. He stared right at her cheek which at one point constantly called for his lips. They were not calling for them today, however, and Todd left without saying goodbye. There was a time when he would have said goodbye. During that time he would have woken her up by tickling her just so they could spend a little time lying next to each other, staring into each other's eyes before he left. But that time was long gone. Instead, he quietly closed the door to ensure she did not wake up and make his mood worse.

Todd walked past both his kids' rooms and down the stairs. He bought this house before the TV show, but because of his income from the show they added an extension onto it. It may appear to be an average bungalow from the front yard, but it was actually quite large.

Marissa loved interior design, so much so that Todd often thought she should be the one with her own show. But he would never say that to her. If he did it would probably happen, then she would become a completely different person. Getting even a tiny bit of fame completely changes people. In fact, they would most likely be divorced within a year. She would go off and marry some rich studio executive in LA, and he would live a lonely life in the middle of nowhere.

He walked past the many useless pieces of decoration that Marissa had accumulated over the years, out the front door, and into that nowhere.

Todd already packed up everything they needed for their hunting trip and left it in the shed. He opened the large doors of his colossal shed, also thanks to his income from the show. Inside sat a matte black pickup truck, a matching ATV, and a golf cart, surrounded by a myriad of guns and knives hanging from the walls. He picked up his hunting bag and threw it in the back of the ATV before drifting out of the shed, sending some mud flying into the tall trees of The West Woods.

He started driving down the dirt pathway behind his house. The pathway was surrounded by a dense forest. The West Woods span over two million acres across Northern California. According to stories passed down from generations of people who lived in the small town of Westwood, no one has ever been to certain areas deep in the forest. Some claim that there are places in The West Woods used for dark magic. Todd obviously thought these were all just stories to scare children. He grew up just outside of Westwood and had adventured very deep into the forest many times himself, never encountering any dark elves or evil witches.

He continued driving down the dirt path through the enchanted West Woods. Partly because he was deep in thought about the day ahead of him, it seemed like no time had passed before he saw Skip's house.

Seeing the house in front of him made him sigh. If anyone else had owned this monstrosity of a home, Todd would respect them for having a house so large. But Skipper should not have a house as big as this. They made a decent chunk of change from their show, but not the kind of green to be able to afford mansions. Skipper had spent almost all his life's savings on building this house. The money he didn't put towards the house, he used to fly out to LA and party. Todd did not know how Skipper still had money left over. He was likely in debt, but was retaining his image so people thought he was living the best life imaginable.

"What's up, Brotha?!" Skipper screamed from his front porch in a ludicrous tone.

It drove Todd crazy when Skipper called him brother, or in his words, "brotha". He agreed to act like brothers for the camera but has made it clear to Skipper that they are not brothers in real life.

Skipper used to be a scrawny guy, but over the years he had put on more weight. This was most likely due to his alcohol-filled nights alone here in Westwood and surrounded by tons of fame-seeking models in LA. He had bright red hair and a matching beard that he tended to spend way too much time grooming. As he walked down his porch Skipper almost fell.

"Are you drunk?" Todd frowned.

"Is that how you start a conversation with your brotha? C'mon, Todd, loosen up for once," Skipper replied while swaying his head and arms back and forth.

"Wanna know what, let's just cancel this trip, go back to bed," Todd said this partly because he didn't want to hunt with a drunk Skipper, but also because he wanted to put off the conversation he had to have with him.

"You can't command me, Brotha, the studio commands me!" He stood up straight and saluted. "Sir yes sir!" Skipper said with a ridiculous smile on his face.

Todd sighed once again. "Fine, let's get going then." This conversation was inevitable.

Skipper got onto his ATV, which was parked in front of Todd's. His ATV was beyond ugly, it was bright red with flames on it. "Try to keep up!" Skipper said as he started his engine.

"Try not to fall into a ditch," Todd snarked back at him.

Skipper shouted and raised his arms in the air as he drove away. "WOO!!" It was such an obnoxious shout.

Skipper drove faster than Todd felt comfortable going. But Todd did not rush to keep up with him, he knew where they were going. They had always started their hunts by a cave just outside of Westwood. Once they made their way past the cave, there was a good mixture of small open fields and forests, always filled with lots of deer.

As they drove to their destination Todd thought about the magical stories he heard about The West Woods as a kid. They had always claimed that no one had ever seen all of The West Woods. Today was the first day Todd had ever considered maybe that was true.

Todd admitted that he had never ventured into the cave that they were heading to. He had gone in the entrance, but it was obvious that there was a lot more to explore. People had claimed that this was one of the largest cave networks in the world. His grandma had once even told him that this cave covered all of California, but The West Woods was its only entrance.

As Todd approached the cave, it seemed to loom over him. He got sucked out of his body and pushed towards the mouth of the cave.

Darkness. Darkness surrounded him. He looked around but could not see a thing. He started to panic, it was as if he was floating in a dark void and could not move. He looked to his left, darkness. He looked to his right, darkness. Then he turned around.

Red. Red was all he saw, it blinded him. He tried to look away but he couldn't. He was meant to be looking at this. As he kept looking his eyes adjusted. He was no longer looking at a flash of red, but just two red dots in the distance.

The red dots began to move. The longer Todd looked the closer they got, and he realized they weren't just dots. They were eyes. Something was moving towards him... or someone.

He tried to scream but was silenced. He tried to run but was frozen in place. The figure with the red eyes sprinted towards him. As it approached, Todd felt his whole body begin to shake uncontrollably. Then the figure leapt towards him.

The blaring of Skipper's horn snapped Todd back to reality. He quickly pressed on his brakes, sending mud flying in all directions and only missing Skipper's ATV by a mere inch.

"What are you doing, Bro?!" Skipper yelled, almost out of breath.

Todd looked around. There was no more darkness. It was almost 5am, the sun was rising over the trees. No red eyes, no mysterious figure. But the cave was still there, looming over him.

"Sorry, I must've got distracted," he said.

"Don't be doing that again. You break it, you buy it," Skipper said, pointing down at his ATV.

After readjusting his parking position, Todd got off his ATV and took his gun out of its bag. Holding his gun made him feel like he had at least some control in his life. It gave him joy even in situations where he had no control. Even though he was one of the stars of the show, there were always people barking orders at him. Because of that, this feeling of control had been false for the last four years, but today that was not true. Today, he was in charge.

Skipper was impatiently waiting for him by the cave. "I didn't realize I'd have to tie you up and drag you around in order to move a little faster," he said.

I wish I could just throw you down that cave, into the darkness, Todd thought. But instead he gave him a slight smirk while walking past him.

Past the cave there was a path that led downwards. This area was often a hot spot for deer, but even if they did not find anything in this area, there was a small, open field not too far ahead.

As he walked along the path, Todd debated when he should talk to Skipper about his decision to leave the show. He was hoping a deer would pop out soon, or something else exciting would happen. Anything to give him an excuse not to have this talk with Skipper. He waited and waited and waited as they walked in awkward silence, but nothing happened.

They got to the third open field and still had not seen a deer. This never happened. It was just after 8am, and they were still empty handed. This would not be an odd occurrence in any other forest, but The West Woods were always filled with many animals. No matter how many deer they killed, there were always hundreds more available to them. Out of those hundreds of deer, apparently none of them were around to say hi today.

After surveying the field, they decided to wait a little longer to see if anything came out of the forest. Todd dreaded this. They had already been hunting in silence for hours, and it could not go on any longer. This was the moment he had to talk with Skipper.

No matter what Skip says, I'm leaving the show, he said to himself over and over again before he finally opened his mouth to speak.

This was the moment his life would change forever.

"What the hell?!" Skipper yelled after hearing the news. He said this countless more times as Todd tried to explain himself.

Todd had to explain this life-altering decision over and over again. Explaining it to Skipper was like giving a philosophy lesson to a three-year-old. No matter how many times he explained it, Skipper would not understand. He felt as though he was trapped at the bottom of the sea. He was drowning on his words and no matter what he said he could not escape. Skipper's objections were like tiny piranhas who swam by and chewed on him as he slowly lost his breath.

"Calm down!" Todd said a little more aggressively than

he intended to. Skipper's voice had slowly been getting louder as their conversation went on. Even though they were in the middle of an empty forest, he felt like they were in a crowded mall. This gave Todd anxiety, he did not like being watched. As Skipper continued to yell at him, he looked around to see if anybody was watching. He knew nobody was but he still felt the need to check.

"We've worked all our lives for this show!" This was Skip's first argument. Todd did not really know what he meant by this, as they never once talked about having their own show. He thought that maybe Skipper was saying he continuously went to parties in LA in hopes that he would become famous. That was the only scenario where this argument would make sense, and therefore, it would only apply to Skipper, proving that Todd could indeed leave the show.

Skip would not listen to logic though, and these thoughts continued to circulate in Todd's head as he was being screamed at. Todd wanted to keep this conversation as peaceful as he could. He knew a civil discussion with Skipper would not be possible, but he would still try his best.

"You need this show to support your family!" Skipper's second argument was better than his first, but still not true. Unlike Skip, Todd had actually saved most of the money he made from the show, and could therefore leave the show and take all the time in the world looking for a new job before having to worry about money. Boom, another lesson in logic.

When Skipper presented this argument, he patted Todd on the shoulder. To Todd, this was a way to exert his dominance. He didn't put it past Skipper to threaten him with violence. When he was drunk, Skipper became a very aggressive person. There were even nights where he would walk over to Todd's house and start yelling obscenities on his front porch. Todd thought it was sad to see Skipper do this. The first few times it happened Todd would go out and try to take him home, but Todd inevitably gave up. Eventually, Skipper would pass out on his front porch. At that point, depending on the mood Todd was in, he would either take him home or just leave him there.

Todd only hoped Skipper's buzz wasn't still strong enough to incline him to make his next argument a quick punch to the gut.

Skipper's third argument was the most convincing, and very unexpected.

"You have to do this for me," Skipper said, crying. "I'm nothing without this show."

Todd surprisingly felt bad for Skipper in that moment. It had been years, even before the show, since he had shown any affection towards Skipper. In fact, he had not even seen Skipper cry in years. It was as if the show turned Skipper into someone else, and now that their journey was over, he was going back to the person he used to be.

"I'm sorry, Skip," Todd lowered his head. "This is just the way it has to be. I haven't been happy doing the show in a long time. Yeah, the money's good, but I can make ends meet without it. This all seemed like a good idea a few years ago, but I'm a different person now. I need to spend more time with Marissa and the kids. To be honest with you, if I don't leave the show, I think I might lose them." Todd had never said this out loud to anyone before. He never used to let their problems bother him, but that changed recently. He realized that without Marissa he had nobody. She kept their family together. If she left him, he would not be able to take care of the kids on his own.

This was a hard thing for Todd to admit. He was a bad father and a worse husband. Even though he had a successful show and a nice house, deep down he was still a loser. The fact of the matter is that he and Skip are both small town boys, they have no place in the world outside of their town. While Skipper was trying to reject that idea, Todd had come to terms with it.

For the first time in years, he felt like he was talking to Skipper like an actual human. He really thought this would work. Skipper would realize what Todd was going through and understand his decision.

Skipper had his head down for a few moments. When he finally looked up, he glared at Todd intensely for a few seconds before speaking up.

"I can't believe you're doing this to me," Skipper said under his breath.

Skipper's face grew more red as Todd watched him. He was breathing heavily, as if he was suffocating deep in a cave, away from any air, fighting for his breath. He put his head down again and kept it down for another moment. Todd saw the blue veins popping out of his forehead, it looked like his head was about to explode. When Skipper looked up again, Todd did not see his old friend, he saw a monster. His eyes were what scared Todd the most. They were bloodshot, with a few tears dripping out of them.

"Skip, you look horrible, get off your feet and take a seat, it's gonna be okay," Todd said while grabbing Skipper by the arm.

Skipper pushed him away. "I can't believe you're doing this to me!" He said again, much louder than the first time. Skipper's booming voice scared Todd, it was filled with so much anger and sadness at the same time.

"Just calm down, take a seat," Todd said, trying to move closer to Skipper.

Skipper let out a loud scream and charged at Todd. Skipper wasn't exactly moving with a lot of grace, so Todd managed to sidestep him.

"Skipper, calm down!" Todd now screamed back at him. He didn't like the idea of being stuck in this forest with Skipper, who resorted to acting like a wild animal.

"I'm not gonna calm down, you're ruining my life!" Skipper screamed. The combination of all the saliva in his mouth and him being out of breath made him hard to understand.

Skipper charged at him once again so Todd moved out of the way. Although, Skipper's arms were flying recklessly all over the place and one of them was able to catch Todd on the lip. Todd moved his fingers across his lips and saw blood on them.

"Stop it!" He said, but knew it would not work.

Skipper came running at him again but tripped over a branch and fell.

Todd did not want to be here anymore, he knew this was a mistake from the beginning. He knew the type of person Skipper was and shouldn't have had any hope that he would behave professionally. He looked down at Skipper, who was still lying on the ground. He decided to run while he still had a chance at a head start, hoping to make it to his ATV before Skipper caught up with him.

He ran up a small hill. Once he got to the top, he looked back down and saw that Skipper was now coming after him. The chase was on. He hoped Skipper was still hungover enough from last night so that he would stumble a few more times while running.

Although Skipper did not have the best form, he was surprisingly fast. He caught up to Todd and tackled him to the ground, knocking his gun out of his hands. They landed on the muddy forest floor and started to wrestle.

Todd was surprised that Skipper was still trying to throw punches at him when he got on top. While he expected Skipper to get aggressive, he did not expect this to turn into an actual fist fight.

After rolling around a few more times, Skipper gained control of the fight. He was on top of Todd, throwing some rough punches. None of these actually hurt Todd, however, because half of the punches he threw missed and hit the ground. Todd could actually see Skipper's knuckles getting bloodier every time he brought them up to throw another punch.

Skipper's saliva came down and landed on Todd's face. Todd spat back at him and while Skipper wiped his face, he threw his first punch which knocked Skip off of him. He did not want to do this but knew he had to get out from under him.

Skipper looked up at Todd, who was now standing over him. He looked shocked, as if even after he threw all those punches at Todd, he did not expect him to actually throw a punch back.

"Don't follow me!" Todd yelled at him as he sprinted away.

Todd ran down another hill. He looked back and did not see Skipper. He was relieved, maybe Skipper finally listened to him and realized he had to stop.

Suddenly, he heard a loud noise and felt a sharp pain in his shoulder. A gunshot. He immediately grabbed his shoulder and felt a pool of blood rush out of him. He turned around and saw Skipper standing at the top of the hill, holding his rifle.

Todd felt paralyzed but knew he had to make himself move. Through his now-blurry vision, he saw Skipper reloading the rifle. He couldn't believe it. Skipper truly believed everything good in his life was being taken away by Todd, and he was going to kill him for it.

He turned around and started running away. He was running as fast as he could but now stumbled in every direction. He heard another shot and waited for the blow. Would it hit one of his legs, his other shoulder? Would it go through his stomach, or even his head? He waited to see whether the shot would be lethal or not, but soon realized he had been waiting for too long. Skipper had missed. Todd's frantic stumbling from side to side had paid off.

He looked back again and saw Skipper running down the hill. While Skipper was a good shot, it turned out he wasn't confident enough to hit Todd from that far away.

Todd was scared. Skipper had already caught up to him once and now that Todd was injured, he would surely catch up to him again. That would be the end of Todd, that would be the end of his worthless life. Of all the ways Todd could die, being shot by Skipper was probably the most humiliating.

He looked back again and saw a figure running after him. While he could no longer clearly make out Skipper's face, he knew it was him. He turned his head and continued to run, it was all he could do at this point.

He turned back again, Skipper was still coming after him. A few seconds went by and he looked again, Skipper was still there. He knew that turning back was likely slowing him down but he could not stop himself from doing it. He looked back again, the blurry figure was still charging towards him.

Todd was out of breath, he did not think he could keep going. He ran for his life, but that run was almost over. He decided to turn around one more time, this would be the last time before he stopped running. He only hoped he would see clearly again before he died, just so he could look Skipper in the eye as he shot him down. He wanted to see him. He would not think of his old best friend, but of the monster he had become. Skipper would kill him today, but he would deal with the consequences for the rest of his life. Skipper was not smart enough to cover up a murder. The police would probably figure out it was him by tomorrow, then he would spend the rest of his life behind bars. That gave Todd some joy. He let out a quiet laugh, knowing that Skipper would never be able to party in LA again.

He looked back for the final time. He saw two figures. He thought he was hallucinating. But once he stopped running his vision became clearer.

He saw Skipper, who was being held up by a much taller man.

"Todd!!!" Skipper screamed. Todd's vision temporarily came back to him as he profusely rubbed his eyes and could see the terror in Skipper's gaze.

The tall man now looked over at Todd as well and he quickly realized that this was no man at all. A monster dressed all in black was holding up Skipper. There was one feature that Todd noticed before anything else, however, and it terrified him. He saw it right when the figure looked over at him. His eyes. They were red.

The figure continued to look at Todd, his red eyes staring deep into his soul.

"Skip!!!" Todd screamed as he began to cry.

The figure looked back at Skipper, and Todd watched as he lifted him higher off the ground. With no effort at all the monster ripped Skipper in half. Todd saw his intestines fall to the ground at the monster's feet.

Skipper's gun also fell to the ground. Todd could try to run and grab it but there was no hope. He once again felt the pain in his shoulder, he had forgotten about it for a moment, but now it was more excruciating than ever. His vision started to fade, he felt like he was about to pass out at any moment. But he still saw the monster, who now turned towards him. He thought Skipper was going to kill him today but he was wrong. He never could have imagined this happening, but he did. He had imagined himself deep in the cave, he had seen those red eyes before. They were chasing him in his daydream, and now they were about to chase him in the dreamscape that was The West Woods.

Todd's vision became fuzzier with each passing moment. He could no longer see the world around him, but he still saw those red eyes.

The red eyes began to move towards him, they leapt up in the air and just before they got to him everything went black.

Darkness. Darkness surrounded him.

CHAPTER ONE

"You are trespassing!" Sam heard this faintly as he was on the verge of falling asleep. He resisted the urge to turn over and look at the light shining in his backyard. His mom had purchased this light just in case anyone tried to break in. If there was movement in the backyard it would turn on and the very intimidating robotic voice would call out to the trespasser.

"You are trespassing!" Sam saw the glow of the light but still did not turn around. Outside, the light still shone on the house that Sam barely recognized anymore. This house had never really felt like a home to Sam, especially now that his father wasn't around. His mom was on the brink of losing it after his father died, but his stepfather, Jason, helped them with the payments and they were able to keep it. His mom had never been good with money so he thought it was a good thing she met Jason.

Even though Jason was always nice to him, he always had a

feeling that he did not want him around. It was as though Jason wanted his mom all to himself, and Sam was in the way. He tried to tell himself that this feeling was just in his head, but it was hard not to think about. He thought about moving out after high school. He always liked the idea of living in residence at the university. Maybe then he would make some more friends and could move into a house with them, but neither he nor his mom had enough money to pay for that. They barely got by paying for his classes, so anything else was out of the question.

Although Sam felt like he was always intruding, he did enjoy having the basement to himself. He had his own bedroom, washroom, and a small kitchen down there, so it worked out quite well.

"You are trespassing!" Sam finally turned around and saw the light illuminating the top of the grass through his window. Soon the light turned off and his window was shrouded by darkness once again. Sam did not think much of the light coming on, the sensor was often triggered even when there was nothing there. It was either that, or a squirrel or rabbit had run by. Sam turned away from the window and closed his eyes, ready to get some sleep.

"You are trespassing!" Once again Sam thought nothing of it. Although the light shining in his room annoyed him, he knew it would turn off soon, and it did.

Then it came back on.

"You are trespassing!" Sam turned around and looked out his window once again. He then looked up at the ceiling, hoping to hear footsteps. He expected Jason to get up any second to go outside and check things out. Worst case scenario, he would have to go himself to look. He knew there was nothing out there, so that was not a big deal, but it was a slight inconvenience.

He continued to look at the ceiling. No footsteps.

The light had turned off by this point. It had been off for about a minute so Sam hoped it would not come on again. If it didn't he would forget about it and act like nothing ever happened.

The light came on once again.

"You are trespassing!" It was now Sam's job to walk upstairs and check the backyard. He let out a sigh before forcing himself out of his warm bed.

Sam felt quite sore as he got out of bed. Although, he had no reason to be sore as he never went out of his way to exercise. As he slowly walked up his stairs, he felt pieces of hair shifting on his head. He never bothered to do his hair in any fancy styles, so there were often pieces of his dark brown hair out of place. "The messy look," his mom would call it.

Sam went straight to the back door and looked out. Just as he got there the light turned off again. He went to the cupboard beside his fridge to grab a flashlight. He shined that out the window but saw nothing but his own reflection being lit up, like he was an angel.

For the few moments he had been standing at the door, the light had not come on again. But he still decided he should go out and check.

He slowly opened the door while making sure to shine the flashlight in front of him at all times, he didn't want to be attacked by a skunk or raccoon out of nowhere. Sam now stood at the wide-open door, moving the flashlight from one side of his backyard to the other, as if he was in charge of a spotlight in a prison yard, trying to catch any escapees.

He saw nothing, just darkness. He decided that there was no one out there and the light must be broken. He was stepping back inside when he heard his fence rattle. He quickly turned around and flashed the light towards the fence. Nothing was there.

Even though he saw nothing through the bright beam of the flashlight, something told him he needed to go see. Sam sauntered past their firepit, which had not been used in years, and neared the fence. He leaned over the short chain-linked fence and shone the light to his right, then to his left. Nothing. He flashed it back to his right, then to his left. Still nothing. It gleamed to his right, then to his left. Something.

A being leapt over the fence and tackled him to the ground. Sam felt his head pound against the firm dirt and thought he was about to black out. He tried to scream, but there was so much weight on top of him that he couldn't. The being forcefully pinned Sam down and hissed at him.

"You are trespassing!" Sam heard the speaker say. The light was shining on them like it was the spotlight on two main actors in a play. While Sam was holding back the head of his attacker, he kept looking at the back door.

"You are trespassing!" He heard again. He was hoping he would see Jason or his mom run out and save him from this nightmare.

"You are trespassing!" He could've sworn the speaker was screaming at this point, but still no one came out. The being covered Sam's mouth.

"You are trespassing!" He frantically tried to remove the hand but the being only pushed down harder. He had just about lost hope. He knew he could not win this battle. The trespasser was going to kill him.

"You are trespassing!" The being looked away from him for the first time and turned its head towards the speaker. It let out a piercing hiss.

The being looked back down at Sam. It was no longer putting as much pressure on his chest. As Sam caught his breath he looked up at the being in awe. What he was feeling was a mix of shock and terror. The being jumped up and stood over him. Sam slowly crawled away from it before finally gaining the courage to stand up and face it. He could not believe what he was seeing. The being was about Sam's height, but to him it still seemed like he was looking up at it. It had black hair and pale skin. Although Sam did not focus too much on those features, he focused more on its eyes.

Red.

The being looked back at Sam with its flaming red eyes, as if it was also studying him. Suddenly, the being hissed and Sam noticed its fangs. He could not believe he hadn't noticed them before, he must have been too focused on the pounding on his chest. The being had a regular set of teeth, but two long, sharp fangs on each side of his mouth.

They revealed to Sam what the being was. A vampire.

"Beat him," the vampire said as he stared deeply into Sam's soul.

"You are trespassing!" This was the last thing Sam heard before he passed out at the sight of the vampire's fangs.

"You are trespassing!" The vampire now stood over Sam, continuing to study him.

"You are trespassing!" The vampire leapt over the fence and fled.

"You are trespassing!" Sam remained, unconscious and alone, in his backyard.

The vampire ran into The West Woods, its red eyes disappearing into darkness.

CHAPTER TWO

Sam's alarm went off louder than ever. It was like a police car driving through the entire town, with its siren blaring over and over again, notifying everyone that they were on an emergency lockdown. Notifying everyone that there was a monster on the loose. Was there a monster though? Sam's encounter with the vampire seemed so vivid to him, but he awoke safely in his bed. Sam rubbed the sleep out of his eyes and squinted towards the sunbeam shining through his window. It was light out now, the darkness was gone. It was now clear to him that he only encountered the vampire in a nightmare.

Sam turned off his alarm and got out of bed. He put on shorts and looked at himself in the mirror. No marks on his chest, no visible cuts. It was a nightmare indeed. One thing irritated him though. A zit had formed on his forehead. This immediately put him in a bad mood. He threw on a baggy t-shirt and kept his eyes fixed on the floor as he walked upstairs.

His mom, Monica, and Jason were already up, drinking their morning coffee at the kitchen table. They were always up early. Jason was a mechanic and owned his own garage, so he had to be up early to open that. His mom owned her own bridal shop. She needed to look good herself so all the brides would want to buy from her, so she woke up with Jason to give her as much time as possible to pamper herself in order to impress them.

Sam always thought of his mom as a very pretty lady. She was nearing fifty but still looked young for her age. She had blonde hair that draped down to her shoulders and bright blue eyes to accentuate her hair. From what Sam had seen in old photos, looks had never been a problem in her life. Although, even she admitted that she had always been naïve. Over the years, Sam heard numerous stories about her getting into trouble with boys when she was younger. They did not treat her well, but she never wanted to admit that.

Her luck with boys changed when she met his dad. Sam did not know too much about his dad, his mom never liked to talk about him and Sam respected her wishes. But Sam did know that his dad played a big role in turning her life around. He was her rock and was not afraid to deal with her problems, including her many ex-boyfriends.

Jason picked up where Sam's dad left off and helped his mom through the hardest time in her life. While he was a little rough around the edges, Sam was grateful his mom met Jason when she did, and not someone else who would take advantage of a grieving widow. Jason had black hair, perhaps the darkest hair Sam had ever seen on someone. He also had dark eyes and relatively pale skin. Jason was skinny, but very tall. Sam remembered the first time he had ever seen Jason, it felt like the man was towering over him. Sam knew that Jason had to be at least six foot five. He was also nearing fifty but still had a youthful look in Sam's opinion.

His mom was still in her robe while Jason was in blue jeans and a black shirt, ready for work.

"Hey, honey," his mom said while sipping her coffee.

"Good morning," Sam replied bluntly.

"How ya doing, bud?" Jason asked.

"Uhm, pretty good, I guess," Sam mumbled before throwing his lunch into his bag and quickly walking out of the kitchen. While he appreciated his mom and Jason for everything they did, it seemed odd that he never knew what to say around the two people he was supposed to be closest with.

Before heading out he went downstairs to change. He put on black jogger pants, all black low-rise converse, and the first t-shirt he could find. None of these items mattered to him, however. He went into his closet and carefully pulled out his sherpa-lined blue jean jacket. He put it on, then fixed the collar so that the fur was visible. His mom did not talk about his father a lot, but she had once mentioned to him that he would wear a jean jacket everywhere they went. From the first time he saw an old picture of his father wearing the jacket, he wanted one that looked identical.

Sam began his morning commute. He was forced to ride his bike since neither he nor his mom could afford to buy him a car. He didn't mind though, he found riding his bike very peaceful. He rode through Westwood, as he did every morning. He was always riding before the town woke up. Sheriff Pines had not started patrolling the streets, Mr. Ferguson had not yet opened his variety store. Sam enjoyed being up before the rest of the town. In such a small town everybody knows each other, so Sam often thought he was being watched everywhere he went. But that's not the case at the crack of dawn.

Once he reached Jason's garage, which was still locked up, he was at the edge of town. From there he rode down a long, straight stretch of road into The West Woods. He could exit on the west side of the town and ride past a few farms, but he preferred the solitude of the woods. Not many people knew about the path through The West Woods that led to Finnegan Welles University. The West Woods are so large that there are a plethora of trails hidden deep in the forest, and it's easy to lose your way.

On this particular trail Sam had to ride up a steep hill, but this was well worth it because the next ten minutes of the ride was all downhill. He rode through clearings that had small ponds filled with tiny fish. During his ride, he saw two deer drinking water from one of those ponds. They looked majestic as the sun rose over them. Sam reached another small hill that had a waterfall leading to a small creek. He loved the sound of the water trickling around him as he rode by. He cleared that hill and reached the next one. To him, this hill was the most interesting place he had discovered in The West Woods. The rock formations on this hill were so different from all the others. Some rocks had pointed tops while others were perfectly rounded. Several of the boulders had holes in them, as if they had mini cave systems that ran through them. Sam thought that was fitting, since the top of the hill featured the entrance to an actual cave.

Sam had heard that there are many caves that ran under The West Woods, but this was the only cave entrance he had found. As he rode by, Sam peaked at the entrance to the cave. There were several sharp-edged rocks that formed around the entrance, as if they were telling people to stay away. Sam always listened to their warning and rode extra fast past that part of the trail. Even though he was fascinated by the hill and the cave entrance, he would not risk hanging around there for too long. He had been avoiding it ever since he was a young boy and didn't feel like breaking tradition.

A few minutes away from the ominous cave entrance, Woods Drive crosses through The West Woods. Sam rarely looked both ways, as he knew barely anybody would be out driving this early in the morning. Although, he did spend a little more time looking eastward down the road, knowing that led to Sarah's house.

After crossing the road, something unusual caught his eye. Among the normal shades of green and brown that inhabit the forest, Sam spotted something red. He slowed down a little and saw something bright red hidden behind a series of bushes. He rode up the next hill to get a better vantage point and realized he was looking at an ATV. It appeared to him that this ATV was abandoned by someone, which confused him. It looked almost brand new, and whoever owned it cared enough about it to get it wrapped. Sam thought the flames on it were an eye sore, but everyone has their own taste.

Sam debated going closer to investigate but decided not to. There was not a trail leading closer and he did not want to risk touching a mysterious plant that could give him some kind of rash.

Sam finally emerged from the forest and rode down a long, curving road leading towards Finnegan Welles University. The university was not a big school compared to some others, as there were about twelve thousand students. But, to the residents of Westwood, it was massive. When they announced the university six years ago everyone was very excited about it. Before, if someone from Westwood wanted to pursue post-secondary education, they would be forced to move away. But after they opened Finnegan Welles, that was no longer a problem.

The university opening was bittersweet for Sam. While he often dreamed about moving away and going to school somewhere else, he did not have enough money to do that. So, Finnegan Welles was his only chance at an education.

Sam studied business at school. He did not know exactly what he wanted to do in life, but he believed taking business courses would lead him down the right path. Sarah was studying business as well, so it was a great excuse to spend time with her.

Sam rode in between two cars lined up to get into the parking lot, and got on the pathway. He rode to the bike racks in front of the student centre and got off his bike. Out of the corner of his eye he saw an older man sitting on the bench, about twenty yards away from him. The old man stared at him from behind his dark set of sunglasses.

Sam quickly glanced over and saw the man was wearing a Westwood Demons baseball hat. He could not see his eyes but knew he was the target of the man's gaze. The man's ominous presence sent shivers down his spine and reminded him of the vampire.

It was just a dream, he reminded himself.

Sam turned to lock his bike and when he looked back the man was gone. He looked all around him to see where the man had gone, but he couldn't spot him anywhere.

"Hey you!" Sam's feet left the ground and he almost let out a scream. "Woah, sorry jumpy!" Sarah punched Sam playfully on the arm.

Sam felt blood rush to his head. He was nervous, even though he had spent so much time with Sarah this year, he still got nervous every time he saw her. He just hoped that it was not noticeable. Sarah would have a lot of questions if she saw butterflies coming out of his stomach.

Sam and Sarah were childhood friends. Their fathers had also grown up together. Sarah's dad, Colton Connelly, was one half of Connelly and Bond Studio's, which produced many television shows set in Northern California. Their most popular show in recent years was *The Wilson Brothers*. Everyone in Westwood knew Todd and Skip were not actually brothers, but that did not stop them from watching it.

Colton and Sam's dad grew apart after he started the studio. But after his dad died, Colton seemingly felt some remorse and would often invite Sam to their huge estate within The West Woods.

Sam had had a huge crush on Sarah ever since he was a kid, but they stopped talking to each other in high school. After all, rule number one of high school states that the pretty popular girl and the shy guy cannot be friends. But now they are both studying business and their schedules lined up, so they were back on a more even playing field. Although they were on friendlier terms now, Sam only saw her at school. As bad as Sam wanted them to, things had not gone back to the way they were before high school.

Something felt different today, however. Sam was speechless right after Sarah snuck up on him, but the more he looked at her the more comfortable he felt. He completely forgot about the man on the bench and focused on Sarah. He looked at her beautiful blonde hair, her bright green eyes, and her slightly tanned skin and felt hopeful.

"Hey," Sam said with confidence. "Sorry, I didn't see you coming up behind me."

They both laughed. "It's all good!" Sarah said with a smile on her face. There was no doubt in Sam's mind that she was the prettiest girl in the world. "Ready to walk to class?" She asked.

"Yeah, let's go!" Sam replied.

As they walked side-by-side down the path, Sam couldn't get his mind off how much he adored Sarah. However, he never planned on doing anything about this little crush of his. After re-uniting with her this year, Sam realized how much he missed out on in high school. He wished more than anything that he could go back and spend all four of those years with her too, but he could not. He was just grateful that he was spending all this time with her now, and he would not do anything to mess that up. Even if making a move meant they could possibly start dating, then one day get married and be happy forever. As great as that sounded, the other alternative to asking her out seemed far more likely. In this outcome of his risky move Sarah would deny him, never want to be near him again, and he would go on living his lonely life. Maybe he'd buy a few cats to keep him company. Since he thought the happy outcome was too unrealistic and the sad outcome far too realistic, he decided to do nothing and be satisfied with the moments he had with her now.

"So how did your paper turn out?" Sarah asked as they were walking through a garden of red, white, and blue roses, an effort for the university to show its patriotism.

Sam stopped in his tracks. "Shit! I forgot to finish it."

"What?! You were so close to being done though," Sarah said.

"I know… I was just doing other stuff last night so decided to leave it till this morning since I only had a few sentences left but then the va-"

Sam stopped talking suddenly. Why did he almost bring up the vampire to her? *It was just a dream.*

"But then what?" Sarah asked, confused.

"I just forgot about it," Sam replied.

Sam panicked, this paper was worth thirty percent of their mark. How could he forget about it? He asked himself this question even though he knew the answer. The vampire still clouded his thoughts this morning and he forgot to finish the paper. *It was just a dream. It was just a dream. It was just a dream.* But was that entirely true? If it was just a dream, why did it feel so real?

Sam could tell from the look on her face that Sarah was worried for him, and that brought him a little bit of joy.

"It's no big deal," Sam said, now trying to comfort Sarah, instead of vice versa.

Sarah looked at him, confused. "Sorry to say, but it kinda is a big deal."

"Don't worry about it, I'll be fine."

Sarah grabbed Sam by the arms and shook him, immediately causing goosebumps to form. "Is this the same Sam that almost had a heart attack when he forgot about our quiz last week?!" She exclaimed.

Sam laughed, still trying to comfort a panicked Sarah. "Don't worry about it, I'll talk to Doctor Allen and ask for an extension. He likes me! It won't be a problem."

Sarah let go of his arms, seeming to agree with him. "You're lucky that Doctor Allen has a crush on you. You probably don't even have to hand in the paper."

This was true, Sam did not know why but Doctor Allen had taken a liking to him almost immediately. After only the second class he went up to Sam and introduced himself. Doctor Allen claimed that he just liked to get to know his students, but it did not seem like he cared about checking in on anyone else. He had talked to Sarah a few times since they started sitting together, but still not nearly as much as Sam. As much as this confused him, he was not going to complain about it. It doesn't hurt to have a professor who likes you.

Sam and Sarah walked down a ramp and into the large lecture hall. There were two sections of seats that sat about seventy-five people each, with staircases going up on either side and in the middle. Doctor Allen was already standing at the front desk watching the students walk in from the doorway at the top of the stairs. He quickly turned his head when Sam and Sarah walked in, however, as if he sensed them the moment they stepped into his class.

Doctor Allen was a very intimidating man, which explained why Sarah was still secretly worried for Sam. He had a large, muscular build, so much so that his biceps were pushing his dress shirt to the limit. Although he was very muscular, and likely very fun for people to look at, his face was not symmetrical at all. His left lazy eye was too far apart from his right eye, and his lips were noticeably small.

As they walked past him, he smiled and nodded his head. If his lips were big enough Sam was sure he would have smiled from ear to ear every time he saw him. Sam always forgot how tall Doctor Allen was until he walked past him. Sam figured he was easily six foot six, if not taller.

As they were walking by Sam almost told him about the paper but decided to wait until after class. Doctor Allen's towering body scared Sam momentarily, but it passed quickly. Once they were seated in the fourth row from the bottom, Doctor Allen seemed much smaller than he was. Sam decided he would take the hour-long class to figure out what he was going to say and be prepared to talk to him after.

Sam approached Doctor Allen once class was finally finished, "Hey, Doctor All-"

"You didn't finish your paper, did you?" Doctor Allen quickly cut Sam off. Sam had planned out exactly what he was going to say, but now he didn't have the chance. Doctor Allen was taking control of the conversation.

Doctor Allen patted Sam on the shoulder. "I could sense you were a little nervous from the moment you walked in." He kept his hand on Sam's shoulder for an uncomfortable amount of time before taking it off.

"I… uh," Sam muttered. He was not nervous coming into this conversation, but now he was.

Doctor Allen laughed. "Don't worry about it, Sam! Shit happens, sometimes we can't get our work done on time, there's nothing wrong with that."

Sam was still speechless, but relieved.

"Don't be nervous around me, Sam," Doctor Allen said while raising his hands in the air. "You can talk to me like a friend."

"Yeah… okay, thanks, I appreciate that!" Sam finally got some words out.

"I've read all your papers, I know you're a good student, and you've gotten every other paper in on time. So I have no reason to be worried, right?"

This question caught Sam off guard. Every other professor he had did not care about any of their students, it was not their problem if they succeeded or failed. They simply showed up, turned on their powerpoint presentations, and collected their massive paychecks. Doctor Allen, on the other hand, showed a lot of interest in Sam. Sam did not know if that was weird or if he was just a better professor than the others.

"Uhm, no, of course not, I'll have the paper ready by next class," Sam said.

"That sounds good to me, I look forward to reading it!" Doctor Allen said with his widest smile, which was still quite small compared to most.

They both walked out of the now-vacant lecture hall together. Sarah was waiting at the top of the ramp for Sam. "You like her, don't you?"

Another question which caught him off guard. Sam looked over at Doctor Allen in shock. That was not a question a professor should ever ask a student. But, as Sam has already realized time and time again, Doctor Allen was not your average professor.

"Uhm, I don't know," Sam muttered quietly, they were getting closer and closer to Sarah and he did not want her to hear anything.

Doctor Allen laughed. "I can tell you do. Let me give you some advice," he put his hand on Sam's back. "Go for it, you'll regret it if you don't," he patted Sam on the back and sped up, he clearly had no interest in being Sam and Sarah's third wheel. "Have a good night, guys," he said as he walked away.

Sarah waited until Doctor Allen was out of earshot. "How'd the date go?" She asked.

"Good," Sam chuckled, still dismayed by the advice Doctor Allen gave him. Then he looked up at Sarah, deep into her green eyes, and everything seemed so clear.

Sam had always heard of successful people having mentors, someone who would guide you through life. Having a mentor was always an idea that was appealing to Sam, but he did not have enough connections with people to get one. Sam realized that Doctor Allen could be a type of mentor for him. After all, Doctor Allen was very successful and was clearly interested not only in Sam's academic life, but also in his personal life, so it seemed like the perfect match.

Sam then realized that Doctor Allen gave him his first piece of advice today.

Go for it, Sam thought to himself. Sam had never had a serious girlfriend. In fact, he never really wanted one, that was until he started spending time with Sarah this year.

Go for it. All throughout high school he never met the right girl, but everything felt so right with Sarah.

Go for it. For the first time ever Sam was not afraid of the sad outcome, because he believed in himself. Doctor Allen was meant to give Sam that advice, and Sam was meant to follow through and go for it. Sam felt as though the universe was guiding him on his path, this was his destiny.

Sam and Sarah were walking back through the patriotic garden when Sam suddenly stopped. "Sarah," he said.

"Yeah!" Sarah said as she jumped up in front of him. Her feet actually left the ground, like a cute little bunny.

"Can I ask you something real quick?"

"Of course! But only as long as it's really quick," Sarah winked at him.

He took in the entire atmosphere around them: the red, white, and blue flowers, the sound of the water from the fountain in the distance, the birds chirping from the trees. Everything was so perfect.

```
EXT. THE UNIVERSITY GARDENS - DAY


                    Sam

          Wanna go out with me?


Sarah's mouth opens wide as Sam waits for a re-
sponse. They stand in silence for a few moments as
the camera circles around them.


CUT TO BLACK.
```

Sam panicked. *Oh no… she doesn't wanna date me. Why would she ever wanna date me? My life is over.*

He snapped out of his romantic comedy infused imagination and started saying whatever he could think of to make the situation better. "Look, I know we're friends and I value our friendship so much. Just forget I ever asked you anyth-"

"Yes!"

"What?" Sam asked, he felt all his blood rushing up to his face.

```
FADE IN:
EXT. THE UNIVERSITY GARDENS - DAY


                    Sarah
          I said yes! Of course I wanna
           go out with you! I've been
          waiting for you to ask me for
               so long, dummy!


The boy got the girl and all was right in the world.


FADE OUT.
```

"Really?" Sam was shocked. Had she really been waiting for him to ask her out? He could not believe it.

"Obviously! I've only given you about a thousand hints."

A smile burst from Sam's mouth and he could not control it. All he wanted to do was smile, he never wanted to lose this feeling. "I had no clue," he said, laughing.

Sarah was also laughing. "So where are you taking me?"

"I didn't think that far ahead…"

"Well… how 'bout the fair that the university is having? Tomorrow night!" Sarah suggested.

"Yeah! That sounds great!" Sam said in his state of euphoria.

"Good! I didn't wanna wait any longer than that." Not only had Sarah said yes to the date, she wanted it to happen as soon as possible. Sam realized that she truly had been waiting all year for him to ask her out.

"Me neither!" Sam replied.

"So I'll see you around eight tomorrow night?" Sarah asked.

"Yeah, that sounds great!" He said, joyfully.

Sam left his last class of the day feeling like he just found the cure for cancer. He felt like he had a successful day at school simply because Sarah said yes to a date. He unlocked his bike and passed the bench, forgetting all about the mysterious man. He once again rode past the ATV but didn't acknowledge it. He parked his bike in his backyard and didn't even think of the fight he had with the vampire in his nightmare. And best of all… he completely forgot about the zit on his forehead.

CHAPTER THREE

"Oh wow! Look at my handsome boy!" Monica said.

Sam blushed. "Stop it, Mom," he said, but hearing her say that made him smile.

"Let me take a picture!"

"Why would you take a picture?" Sam laughed.

"So we can remember this day!"

"Mom, it's not like it's a special occasion or anything," Sam replied, trying his hardest to avoid the picture. But there was no stopping her. Monica already had her camera app open with a huge smile on her face, as if she was the one having her picture taken. That pulled at Sam's heartstrings. To make his mom happy, Sam stood awkwardly at the front door as she snapped a photo. It made it even more awkward that Jason was standing right behind her, watching him through her phone. Sam continued to smile as Monica fiddled with her phone.

"How annoying," she muttered to herself, clearly struggling to rotate the camera.

"Swipe up, what about that button?" Jason tried to help her but also failed.

Sam sighed, "Mom, just swipe up from the bottom and turn off the rotation lock."

"I did swipe from the bottom, that button's just not there."

"It's definitely there," Sam said.

"Oh! I got it! Okay, keep smiling, sweetie," his mom said as she pointed her phone at him once more.

Sam was suddenly blinded by an unexpected flash. "Perfect!" His mom said, "Now one with both of us!"

"Why do we need so many pictures?" Sam was getting more impatient with each passing second.

"Because I want pictures with you," she replied, still smiling.

Jason took about a hundred and fifty pictures of him and his mom, then offered to be in a few pictures as well, making Sam even more snappy.

Jason handed the phone to Monica and stepped beside Sam before either of them could respond. As awkward as Sam felt taking pictures with his mom, he felt even more uncomfortable with Jason. Jason put his arm around him, Sam quickly looked up and was surprised to see him grinning from ear to ear. While this was awkward for Sam, he admired Jason for trying to be a father figure, even though he had never thought of him like that.

"Now you are free to leave!" His mom proclaimed, before giving him a five-minute speech on safe driving. By the end of it Sam was halfway down their front steps.

"Okay, yes, don't worry," these are the three things Sam

continuously said throughout their conversation, whenever he could get a word in. Now he said all of them at once, signalling the end of his mom's lecture.

His mom got more words in as he was getting in the car and reversing down the driveway, but Sam barely registered them as he knew he was finally free.

Sam drove on his usual biking route but instead of getting off the main road to cut through The West Woods, he stayed on it. He continued to follow Woods Drive, with the forest on either side of him. Getting to Sarah's house was very simple, as it was just off of Woods Drive. He drove for nearly ten minutes until he noticed the gated driveway on the left. He turned and stopped right in front of the gate. He noticed a keypad with numbers, what appeared to be a fingerprint scanner, and a button with a speaker beside it. Above all these things was a camera, it made Sam uneasy to know that they could be watching him right now. He tried not to gaze directly into the lens while he pressed the button beside the speaker. Immediately a buzzer went off and the gate opened. As he drove down their long driveway, he was reminded of just how large Sarah's house was.

The Connelly Estate had been around for almost a hundred years. It was owned by another wealthy family before Colton Connelly bought it in the 90's. Since then he had overseen many renovations, but for the most part he had kept the basic architectural design intact. Sam drove down the driveway lined with fully bloomed pink Japanese crabapple trees until he reached the roundabout, which featured a monstrous fountain in the centre. The centrepiece of the fountain was a statue of what looked like a Spartan warrior who stood guard as water shot up around it.

Sam drove to the top of the roundabout but then decided to move up a little more so he was not parked right in front of the porch. He didn't want to risk seeming rude. Once he got out of his mom's car, a well-dressed man in a sleek black tuxedo walked up to him. His grey and black hair was slicked back and he had a thin mustache. This man was born to be a butler.

"Hello, sir," the man said.

"Uhm, hello," Sam replied.

"My name is Vincent, the Connelly's butler, it is a pleasure to meet you," Vincent extended his hand.

Sam extended his hand as well, preparing to shake hands, but was surprised when Vincent lightly kissed the back of his hand.

"I'm S- Sam," he stuttered, taken aback. "It's a pleasure to meet you as well."

"If you don't mind, Sam, I can park your car in the parking lot," Vincent said.

Parking lot? They have their own parking lot?

"Uhm," Sam did not know what to say, as he was still shocked by the surprise kiss and the fact that the Connelly's had their own parking lot. Then he saw Sarah walk out onto the porch. She wore a beautiful loose black shirt that was tied at her stomach and white shorts.

"Yeah, go ahead," he said to Vincent, handing him the keys. After seeing Sarah, Sam felt a little less nervous.

As Vincent got in the car, Sam walked up to Sarah and anxiously gave her a hug.

"Sam Sparks! It's great to see you!" Sam looked over and saw Sarah's dad, Colton Connelly, master of The Connelly Estate, standing at the door.

Colton had dark brown hair that was combed over and a full beard. He wore round glasses with tortoise shell frames. He was wearing black jeans and a white dress shirt with the sleeves rolled up.

"It's great to see you too!" Sam replied. Colton seemed like he was happy to see him again, and that made Sam a little more confident. Sam walked up the stairs and gave him a tight handshake. Sam looked into Colton's eyes and noticed that he looked impressed by his grip.

Colton was smiling. "Come into my home," he said, moving away from the door to let Sam and Sarah through.

They walked in and Sam was greeted by Sarah's mom and little brother, who were standing at the bottom of the stairs. Sam was surprised that the whole family was there to welcome him, it made him feel like they had been awaiting his arrival.

"Hello," Sam said to them.

"Hi, Sam," Sarah's mom walked over and gave him a hug.

Margaret Connelly was wearing a bright blue sun dress. She had bright blonde hair and green eyes, just like Sarah.

"It's great to see you again!" Sam said to all of them.

"You too!" Margaret replied.

Sam was the most surprised to see Harry, Sarah's little brother. He was thirteen years old, six years younger than Sarah. Last time Sam had seen Harry he was just eight, so he was almost unrecognizable now.

"Wow, look at you, all grown up!" Sam said to him, then realized Harry probably thought that was very weird. Sam laughed, "You probably don't remember me, but I've known you since you were a little kid."

Harry glared at him, saying nothing in response, forcing

Sam to look back at the smiling members of the family.

"Nice!" Sam felt the need to fill the awkward silence before Colton's booming voice announced the tour was about to begin. The master of the house was taking charge.

Sam looked around in awe as Colton led the way through the house. He had forgotten how big it was. He walked lightly on his feet in fear of dirtying the shiny marble floor beneath him.

Colton ran his hands across the red cloth of their pool table as he led them into the billiards room. There were large paintings hung on either side of the room. The painting on the right wall was of three men bowing down to who Colton claimed to be Ares, the god of war.

"Do you play any pool?" Colton asked.

"No, I've never really gotten into it," Sam replied.

"Really? That's a shame, your dad and I used to go out and play pool all the time," Colton said.

Sam was well aware that his dad and Colton used to be friends, but he was not prepared for him to bring that up. He hoped this conversation would not go on for much longer.

"Really?" Sam asked.

"Yeah!" Colton replied. "We would go to Fireside Pub for drinks every weekend…" he paused. "Those were good times."

Sam did not know what to say, thankfully Colton moved on to the next room and saved him from having to say anything.

"This is the living room," Colton said, with his arms spread.

They were now at the back of the house. Sam was just about to look out the window to see their backyard, but got distracted once he looked to his left. In between the living room and the kitchen was an indoor pond.

"Wow," Sam said, causing Sarah to giggle beside him.

"That's usually the reaction we get," Colton also laughed.

The pond was circular, and there were even circle platforms across the middle so that people could walk over it. As he crossed it Sam felt like he was walking through an actual pond. There were even two lily pads floating in the water and Sam could see the fish swimming around. The pond was also lit up, so he could see plants and rocks under the water.

"Do you want anything to drink?" Sam turned around and saw Colton standing behind the bar on the other side of the pond.

"I'm okay, thanks though," Sam replied.

"I assume you're okay, but you'll be even better after having some of this whisky," Colton winked at Sam whilst pouring a glass.

"He's driving, Dad," Sarah told her father.

"One drink won't kill him!" Colton said, handing the glass to Sam. Sam glanced over at Sarah, but knew he didn't have a choice. He took his first sip as she sighed. He held back a cough as Colton laughed at him. "You'll get used to it!" He patted Sam on the back and led them into the kitchen, where Margaret was preparing a meal that almost made Sam want to stay for dinner. He took another drink of the whisky, which was an unpleasant experience, but being able to smell the meal afterwards helped him deal with the aftertaste.

Colton then grabbed the bottle of whisky before leading them into the backyard. While Colton's back was turned, Sam gulped down the rest of his whisky. He nearly threw up all over their deck. Luckily, he managed not to and shot Colton a big smile as they stood at the end of the deck.

"Wow! You're already done!" Colton patted him on the shoulder. "Do you want a little more?" He almost looked like a pirate, proudly holding up the bottle of whisky while the sun set behind him.

"No, thank you," Sam replied, laughing. Sarah was a little less impressed, however, and pointed out that he's driving once again.

"He's fine, Sarah. Aren't ya, Sam?" Sam had no choice but to nod. "And plus, it's your first date! I'm sure you're a little nervous so this is just a bit of liquid courage!" Colton forcefully grabbed the glass out of Sam's hand and poured the rest of the whisky into it, which thankfully was not that much. They clanged their glasses together before finishing them off. Sam was glad there was no more whisky in that bottle as he forced the last sip down his throat.

Sam handed over his glass as Colton and Margaret walked them out the door. Harry, of course, found an opening to slip away and escape to his room.

"You guys have fun tonight!" Margaret said with a huge smile on her face.

"And Sam," Colton's loud voice made Sam stop in his tracks and turn back to lock eyes with him. "Take care of my girl," he not-so-jokingly commanded, which sent shivers down Sam's spine. Sam smiled and nodded as he walked towards the side of the house with Sarah.

This side of the house featured a large garden surrounding a wooden shed. Although it was just their shed, it was about the size of Sam's house. They walked through the garden on the stone path and entered the shed. It was packed with all the necessary gardening and landscaping equipment needed to maintain an estate. Although, it wasn't the messy work shed that most would imagine. Everything seemed to have its own spot and nothing was out of place. It was so carefully put together that Sam thought touching one thing would mess up the whole flow of the room. Sarah was standing on the left side of the shed, in front of four weed whackers hanging on the wall.

"Come stand with me!" She said.

Sam walked up to Sarah and stood beside her.

"You ready?" She asked as she scanned her fingerprint on a screen on the wall.

Suddenly the floor began to drop, throwing Sam into a panic. "What's happening?" He asked.

Sarah wrapped both her arms around his left arm. "Don't worry," she said. The floor continued to drop as they sunk beneath the shed. It was not dirt surrounding them, it was metallic walls. Sam realized that they were in an elevator.

"Wow, now this is cool," Sam said, laughing now that he was no longer scared.

After travelling about thirty feet underground, the metallic door parted in the middle and they walked into the Connelly's underground garage. As Sam looked around, he thought there must have been at least fifteen cars parked down there. Sam noticed a red Ferrari beside a matte black Lamborghini, then at the end of the row was Sam's mom's car. Her run-down silver car looked outrageously out of place in the garage.

Sarah skipped across the garage towards the car. As Sam followed, he spotted Vincent, who sat still on a folding chair at the other end of the garage. Vincent blew a kiss towards him. Sam caught it and tucked it into his front pocket. He was beginning to feel the effects of the alcohol.

Sam caught up to Sarah just in time to open her door. He then hopped into the driver's seat and started pulling out of the parking spot. As he backed up, he realized there was no garage door. He saw a ramp ahead of him but it led to nothing.

"Wait, where am I going?" He asked.

"Just keep driving straight," Sarah looked over at him and smiled.

Sam drove slowly towards the ramp and suddenly the ground above them began to move. "It's fake grass," Sarah said. "It's almost impossible to tell from outside."

"Wow," Sam did not know what else to say.

He drove up the ramp which connected to the driveway and watched the garage door close behind him in his rear-view mirror. They left The Connelly Estate and headed towards the university.

The university was lit up. All the lights, with the sun almost set in the background, was a beautiful sight. Sam looked over at Sarah and could see the reflection of the lights in her eyes. He did not feel like he was approaching the university, it had transformed. Finnegan Welles was a place where he would stress about classes, where he was now was a place where he would have an unforgettable night with an amazing girl.

He noticed a ferris wheel looming over the nursing building. It was one of those raggedy old ferris wheels that you know you should not trust, but you do anyways. As they got closer to the school, he noticed other rides and games surrounding the ferris wheel, with crowds of people around them.

He parked the car and they started walking towards the lights. He wanted to hold her hand so badly but was too nervous to ask. He continued to inch closer to her, desperately hoping that she might initiate things. They were walking on a pathway in between the nursing building and the engineering building when Sam finally decided to reach his hand out. He endured a strong gust of wind as he took his hand out of his pocket, adding to the goosebumps he already had. Just as he was about to grab her hand, he heard whistling behind them. They both looked back at the same time and saw the three boys approaching.

"Hey, Sarah! What's up?" One of them called out. Sam knew all three of them. He had known them for years. However, all their eyes were locked on Sarah.

"How bout you ditch him and come hang with us?" Another one said. Sarah didn't respond and Sam only caught a relieving glimpse of her rolling eyes. The three boys walked past them, laughing. In that whole encounter not one of them even batted an eye towards Sam. It was as if they had not been stuck working on a group project in tenth grade science class. Sam watched their matching white Air Force 1's shine in the darkness as they walked away.

"Just ignore them," Sarah said. As they were about to go underneath an arch leading to the centre field, where the fair was being held, she stopped. Sam kept walking for a second but then looked back, puzzled.

"Oh, you actually wanted to go to the fair?" Sarah said.

"What do you mean?" Sam replied.

"I mean, if you wanna go to the fair we can go to the fair."

"I thought that's what we were here for," Sam chuckled as Sarah walked closer to him and grabbed both his hands. Her palms felt warm in the cool evening breeze.

"Follow me," she pulled him and he went with her.

She tugged on the side door of the engineering building, it

was unlocked. They both walked in and let the door shut behind them. The lights were still on in the hallway, but Sam could tell that all the lights in the classrooms were turned off. Sarah raced down the hall, then jumped in the air and turned around, towards Sam.

"C'mon!" She yelled.

"What are we doing?" Sam asked sheepishly, scared of someone hearing them.

"We could go to the fair… or we could explore the empty school," Sam could see Sarah's bright smile from down the hallway.

Sam looked around and admired the intricate architecture. This was not an ordinary, boring hallway. The ceiling was curved and had hexagonal mirrors hanging from it, all pointing in different directions. He saw Sarah through one of the mirrors, still standing there, smiling at him.

"Okay, let's explore the school then!" Sam said as he followed her down the hallway.

She went through the tall doors which led to a spiral staircase. He was being a bit more cautious than her, as he was afraid of being kicked out, so he was about twenty steps behind her. Although, he enjoyed being behind because he could watch her joyfully running around in circles as he also climbed the stairs.

Where did all this confidence come from? He asked himself. Sarah was always a confident person, and she had every reason to be, but she often worried about getting in trouble. The Sarah he was with today seemed completely different from the girl he asked out yesterday. He thought that maybe she was confident because she felt comfortable around him. At least that's what he hoped it was.

He was almost at the top of the stairs when he heard the door above him open and shut. When he arrived at the door, he did not see Sarah. Where could she have gone? He looked down the hallway, which was a little dimmer than the one downstairs, and did not see any open doors. Sam walked up to the closest door on his left and turned the knob, but it was locked.

"Sarah!" He yelled down the hallway. He no longer cared about being caught, he only cared about finding Sarah.

He tried opening two more doors but they were also locked. Sam jogged down the hallway while looking through the small windows on the doors, praying that a light would be on in one of the rooms.

"Boo!" A door swung open and a vampire jumped out. Not just a vampire… the vampire.

Sam saw its red eyes and let out a loud yelp. He stumbled all the way back to the wall on the opposite side of the hallway.

The vampire quickly ran over to him, put one arm around his waist and covered his mouth with its other hand. The hands were so soft, as if the vampire had just moisturized. As Sam's heart stopped beating so fast, he realized that he was not being held by a vampire, but by Sarah.

Sarah was laughing as her smooth, lavender scented hands moved away from Sam's mouth. She kept her other arm around his waist. Their bodies were pressed up against each other. Sam was now looking into her bright green eyes, not the terrifying red eyes of the vampire he had just imagined.

They continued gazing into each other's eyes. It was clear to Sam that Sarah wanted him to kiss her, but he was overthinking everything.

Should I put my arms around her? What if she thinks I'm a bad kisser? I forgot to use a mint…

Sam's mind was overflowing with thoughts. He wanted to kiss her more than anything but was far too nervous.

"I can't believe you did that!" Sam said as he took a step back.

Sam could hear the disappointment in her tone, which was elevated by the time she took to respond. "I thought it was funny," she said while giving him a slight smile.

Sam now felt regret. It was clear that she really wanted him to kiss her. *I should've just done it,* he chewed himself out.

"It was funny… uhm, sorry, I just wasn't expecting it, that's all."

Go for it. Sam thought about what Doctor Allen said to him. *Go for it. Go for it. Go for it.*

Sam looked into the open classroom. "So this door was un-locked?"

"Yeah! I was trying them all on the way down, I got lucky with this one," Sarah replied.

"Wanna go in then? It looks like a nice view," Sam could see the lights from the fair shining through the windows of the classroom.

"Yeah!" Sarah said as she walked towards the room.

As Sam walked in behind her he got a better look at the view from the window. The ferris wheel was in the centre, sur-rounded by other lit up rides spinning around in circles. Christ-mas lights were also hung between the light poles. Sam closed the door of the classroom, hoping nothing else would be sur-pring him this evening.

Sarah walked to the window to admire the view. She looked so beautiful as the fair lights illuminated her from behind. The more Sam thought about what Doctor Allen said to him, the more confident he became. He grabbed two chairs on his way to the window and placed them down. They both sat and Sam continued to stare at her angelic face as she looked out the window. He then noticed her fidgeting hands.

Sam was the one who was nervous at the beginning of the date, but now the tables were turned. She comforted Sam just by being herself, and now it was Sam's turn to do the same.

Go for it. Go for it. Go for it. While it was not like Sam to be outgoing, he wanted to change who he was for her. He had already begun to feel like he was a different person.

She finally looked over at him, probably wondering why he had been staring at her for so long. She smiled and looked back out the window.

"Hey," Sam said in his calmest voice.

She looked back over and he leaned in to kiss her. His lips met hers. After about five seconds their lips parted. They stared into each other's eyes and smiled. Sam tried to think of something to say, but his mind went blank. Just before the awkward silence kicked in, she grabbed his face and kissed him again. This time he finally built up the courage to grab her waist. It was a little awkward to do since they were both sitting, but once his arms were in a comfortable position he kept them there as they continued to kiss.

He had never felt this feeling before and he wanted to savour every second of it. He did not know why he had seen a vampire jump out at him instead of her, but immediately after their kiss he decided to forget about that. He never wanted to think about that nightmare and those red eyes again. All he wanted to do for the rest of his life was stare into Sarah's beautiful green eyes.

That's exactly what he did for the rest of the night. Eventually, they left the classroom and enjoyed the fair. Time flew by, and before he knew it, it seemed like they were the only students left. They walked back out to the almost empty parking lot and got into his mom's car. The night was silent, the road was silent, and they were silent. It wasn't a bad silence, however. They looked into each other's eyes and smiled. This turned out to be the perfect night that Sam wanted so badly.

He looked back onto the road and noticed a flash of light ahead of them. Suddenly, the street wires above them exploded and something fell onto the road. Their silence was broken. Their peace was broken.

"OH MY GOD!" Sarah screamed.

The flash of light blinded Sam. He saw something in the middle of his lane and tried to swerve out of the way to avoid it. It almost looked like a body. The wires above them continued to explode and created more bright flashes of light. Sam felt himself run something over on Sarah's side so he tried to swerve even more. All of a sudden, he lost control of the car and it flipped over into a ditch at the side of the road.

Sam and Sarah sat unconscious in the overturned car.

CHAPTER FOUR

Darkness. Darkness surrounded him.

Sam's eyes shot open and all he could see was red. Blood. Blood everywhere. He looked down and his arms were stained. The blood had been on him for so long that it dried up and became crusty. He was sitting in the field between Finnegan Welles and The West Woods. He could still see the lights shining at the university but he was far enough away that nobody could see him. He couldn't gain his footing as his vision continued to make everything around him blurry. He reached around, wiping his blood-soaked hands on the grass until he felt something that wasn't grass. He felt somebody. His vision blurred more and the last thing he saw were a pair of bright white sneakers.

White encompassed his vision until he finally opened his eyes.

"Sam!" His mom screamed as she and Jason charged into

the room, followed by a nurse. Sam studied the terrified expression on her face before he finally noticed the blood squirting out of his arm. He looked at the gash on his right arm, a dark red line that ran from his elbow to his wrist, and quickly covered it up with his other hand. Blood continued to shoot out through the cracks between his fingers and the nurse rushed over with bandages to cover up his wound. As she did that Sam looked for anymore damage and was horrified by the sight of his blood-stained hospital gown.

"What happened?!" His mom yelled. "He was fine before."

"His cuts have opened back up," the nurse said while swiftly wrapping a bandage around his arm. Apparently his mom could not handle the visuals anymore, as she buried her face in Jason's chest.

Ten minutes later, the blood-soaked nurse finished wrapping the bandage around his arm and re-covering the puncture wound in his stomach. His mom was now sitting in a chair in front of the window. Sam wondered if she even had the strength to stand up. As Sam stretched his legs, he felt like he didn't have any strength left either. He was lying on a bed with his arm hooked up to a machine to his right. The machine's repetitive beeping became irritating very quickly.

Jason stood at his bedside. "Do you remember anything?" Jason asked, but Sam did not respond. "You were in an accident, buddy."

It all came back to him at once. The flash of light, the wires exploding, the body on the street.

"Sarah!" Sam jumped up so quickly that it made him dizzy.

His mom found her strength and jumped out of her seat to grab him right away. "Sarah's okay, honey, she's in the next room," she pointed towards the wall ahead of him while slowly guiding him back down to his bed.

By the time he was lying down again he was no longer dizzy. "You can see her soon, pal," Jason said. "The doctors said we should explain the situation to you, so I guess I'll do that," Jason smiled at Monica. "I guess when you were on your way back to Sarah's house some wires above Woods Drive exploded. The police don't know how that happened, they think they most likely just overheated. Anyways, I guess this distracted you and you swerved into the ditch. Does that sound right to you?"

"Uhm, yeah, they exploded, but-" Sam thought he saw what looked like a body fly into the wires. The more he thought about it the surer he was.

Jason interrupted him before he could explain himself more. "There was one more thing… the doctors did some tests," Jason paused again. "They found alcohol in your system. Why would you drive after drinking?" Jason raised the volume of his voice.

"What?" Sam couldn't believe what he just heard. "I wasn't drunk, I was fine, I barely had anything to drink." *This can't be blamed on a drink and a half.* The beeping beside him seemed to grow louder.

"Why would you drink anything then think it was a good idea to drive your mom's car?" Jason's mood had completely shifted. His face contorted with rage as veins popped out of his forehead.

"Jason, stop," his mom tried to mumble out more words but could not as she held back tears.

"No!" Jason looked directly at her with the same look on his face. "Do you know how much damage was done to the car?

You have no idea what kind of money that's gonna cost. Is that coming out of your pocket?" He turned back towards Sam. "I can't believe you were so irresponsible with your mo-"

"I wasn't drunk, Jason!" Sam cut Jason off. Judging by the look on his face it looked like Jason was ready to hit him across the head.

Sam took a moment to calm down, he didn't notice but he had been breathing very heavily while Jason was yelling at him. "I wasn't drunk," he repeated, staring him down. "I had one drink with Sarah's dad, I wasn't even close to being drunk. As I was saying, I didn't just get distracted by the exploding wires and I doubt they just overheated. I saw something fly into those wires... I think it was a body."

Jason smirked. "A body? How would a body fly into those wires?"

"I don't know, I'm just telling you what I saw."

Jason looked over at Monica. "It just doesn't make sense," he let out a brief laugh.

Monica took a deep breath and looked at Sam, who was clearly irritated by Jason. "We're gonna take you home later today, okay? Then Sheriff Pines is gonna come by and he can get your statement, you can tell him everything you remember about last night."

Sam and Jason exchanged glares. Clearly Jason didn't believe him but Sam hoped other people would. Did his mom believe him? She seemed to stray away from the subject every time it came up. He looked at her, trying to gauge what was going through her head, but couldn't find any answers in her worried expression. The room remained silent so Monica spoke up again. "Okay, I think we should give Sam some space. You should get some rest," Sam's mom kissed him on the cheek before leading Jason out of the room.

Sam took a deep breath as they left. He removed the band aid that was on his arm and then pulled out the small tube that attached him to the machine. He slowly leaned forward this time, learning his lesson from before, but was still quite dizzy. Once his vision cleared, he hopped down from the bed. He looked out the window and noticed that the sun was beginning to rise. It was only hours after the crash. A few hours ago he was having the best night of his life but that quickly turned into a nightmare. He felt silly wearing only his hospital gown as he made for the door but knew he had no other options. He didn't even have any shoes on, making the hospital floor as cold as ice on his bare feet. He entered the beige hospital hallway and began walking towards Sarah's room. He approached her door but hesitated before opening it. He stopped and glanced down the hallway, at one of the many benches that lined the walls.

On the bench he spotted a man, a man wearing a Westwood Demons baseball hat. Sam knew he was looking at the same man he saw two days ago, sitting on the bench outside of the library.

Sam started walking towards the man in the baseball hat, who wore dark jeans and a black jacket, which made his beige and red hat stand out even more. Just as he began his pursuit, the man on the bench got up and started for the exit.

"Hey!" Sam exclaimed, now far enough from Sarah's room for him to speak loudly and not draw any attention.

Sam sped up more when the man walked through the door with the bright, illuminating letters reading "EXIT" over it. Sam followed him through the door. There was a staircase to his right but he decided to go left, towards the door leading to the parking lot.

Sam burst through the door and looked around the parking lot.

"Hey!" He screamed, knowing he was in a more appropriate setting to yell. There was no answer. The man he saw before, whoever he was, was gone.

"You can't handle your alcohol, can you?"

Sam turned around and locked eyes with Sarah's dad. "O-oh, hi, Mr. Connelly."

"You only had a little bit of whisky but you still managed to crash your car," he said in a soft, almost sinister voice, before taking a puff of his thick Cuban cigar.

"I wasn't drunk," Sam said, struggling to maintain eye contact. "Something fell from the wire. A body."

"Now bodies are falling from the sky?" Colton took a step towards Sam, blowing a cloud of smoke in his face.

"I saw what I saw," blood was rushing to Sam's head.

"My daughter didn't say she saw a body though."

"Wait, what?" Sam was shocked. Sarah was sitting right beside him in the car, how did she not see the body? *It was there*, he told himself.

"Sarah didn't see a body," Colton said again. "The police are searching the area now and they haven't found a body either…"

Sam didn't know what to say. *It was there*, he told himself again, although this time he was a little less sure. How did the police not find the body yet?

When Sam didn't say anything, Colton continued speaking. "I told you to keep my girl safe… and this happened."

"It wasn't my fault. I-" Sam barely knew how to defend himself anymore.

Colton gripped Sam's shoulder. "I'll give you the benefit of the doubt this time. People make mistakes," he said, tightening his grip. "But if anything bad happens to her… I don't want to think about what would happen to you."

"Dad!" Sam had not even noticed Sarah standing at the doorway, but once he saw her tears began to form in his eyes. "Dad, stop!" Sarah continued. Sam was horrified at the sight of the cut which ran from her jawline all the way up to her forehead, stopping only at her eye, which was as red as the glowing eyes from his nightmare. He did that, that cut was all his fault.

"Don't worry, honey," Colton said. "I'm just making sure Sam and I are on the same page."

"Sarah," Sam immediately called out to her. "I'm so sorry," he said, only paying attention to her scarred face.

She didn't say anything in response and Sam completely understood, although Colton still had more to say. "You see what you did to my daughter?"

"I said stop!" Sarah approached her dad and grabbed him by the arm.

"I'm coming!" Colton yelled, abandoning his sinister whisper. "I just need him to know the effects of his actions. After all, his family has a bad history with car accidents."

Sam's heart dropped.

"Dad!!" Sarah snapped, tugging on his arm harder even though she did not need to. Colton freed his arm from her grasp and walked in on his own, Cuban still in hand. Sarah decided to still guide him from behind though, only sending an uneasy glance Sam's way before they re-entered the hospital, leaving Sam alone in the parking lot.

CHAPTER FIVE

"Todd!"

Todd had already been awake for a few minutes before Marissa called his name. He didn't have to look at the clock to know it was just past 11am. While he used to automatically wake up at four in the morning every day, that had changed recently. Todd was lying in bed, already smiling when Marissa came charging through the door. Todd immediately noticed her auburn hair and the smile on her face as she jumped on top of him. Everything she had to do in the morning was already done. She woke up at 6:30am to make sure the kids were awake and ready for school. Taking care of the kids before school could be a hassle, you have to get everything ready for their day while listening to them whine about not wanting to go. Todd was appreciative that Marissa had always taken on those responsibilities. Since she was done her job and he was now awake, it was time for them to have some fun with no distractions.

Marissa was lying on top of Todd as he caressed her body, moving his fingers up and down, from her thighs to her neck. She was most ticklish on her neck, so every time his fingers would make it up there she would giggle until he moved them back down. As they looked into each other's eyes, Todd wondered what Marissa was thinking. It was obvious she was overjoyed lately. The fire that had been lost in their relationship had recently been rekindled. For years they had barely shown each other any affection, but lately they could not keep their hands off one another. Todd knew this was the cause of Marissa's remarkably good mood, but he wondered if she ever questioned why their marriage suddenly worked again.

One month and three days ago, Todd thought. *One month and three days ago their marriage had changed.*

He was on top of her, he had all the control. He could feel the power coursing through his veins, he loved that feeling.

Twenty minutes later Todd and Marissa laid naked in bed together. She was still catching her breath when she rolled over.

"Remember, you gotta go see the sheriff at twelve-thirty," she said while moving her fingers through his chest hair.

Todd sighed, while it amused him to play games with Sheriff Pines, this would be the fourth time they met since Skipper's death. It was becoming inconvenient for Todd to continue attending these interrogations, but he could not deny the sheriff or else he would become the number one suspect. Todd laughed at this thought, simply because he knew he was already the number one suspect.

No one will ever know how Skipper was killed, Todd told himself.

"I don't know why he keeps insisting on meeting with you. There's no evidence that points to you. For Christ's sakes, they don't even know if he's dead. I just don't get it," Marissa commented.

"The fact is, as far as they know, I was the last person to see Skip alive. As annoying as it is, it's understandable that he keeps asking to meet with me," Todd replied. It had impressed him to see how loyal Marissa had been to him. People in Westwood had no clue if Skipper died or just disappeared, but everyone had been looking to Todd for answers. Todd knew that most of them thought he was the killer, it was quite obvious judging from the looks they gave him around town. But ever since the incident, Marissa had been adamant that Todd did nothing wrong. Despite all that Todd had been hiding from her, they had made a good team over the last month.

She could be useful, Todd thought to himself while watching her get dressed.

Todd arrived at the police station at 12:38pm. He knew he was late, but he was not concerned in the slightest. Sheriff Pines walked out of his office as soon as Todd came in, as if he was staring at the door and watching the clock for the last eight minutes. Ben Pines wore his sheriff's uniform, as always. Even when he was off duty he was always seen around town in his uniform. This amused Todd, especially recently. He assumed wearing the uniform made Ben feel like he had more power than he actually did.

You don't know what true power feels like, Todd snickered to himself.

The sheriff walked up to Todd in his cream-coloured button up that perfectly matched his pants and shook his hand.

"How you doing today, Todd?" He asked.

"I'd be a lot better if I didn't have to be here," this response made Ben laugh.

"You know we have to get to the bottom of this, I-" Ben stopped himself, realizing anything said would be off the record. "Wanna know what, how 'bout we head into the room and talk some more?"

Todd didn't feel the need to respond, as he knew Ben would take him into the interrogation room anyways. He stared sternly before Ben finally made the first move and led the way. Todd felt so much power as he walked behind his interrogator. Although, Ben never seemed intimidated by him despite the fact that Todd was four inches taller.

He should be intimidated, Todd thought. *He should be terrified.*

Ben opened the door of the interrogation room and let Todd in, although he did not follow him in. After meeting with Ben so much lately, Todd knew this routine all too well. He knew that Ben would watch him for about five minutes through the one-sided glass. Ben was hoping to determine if Todd was scared or not but he would never know. For those five minutes, Todd sat emotionless in the interrogation room that had just one table and two chairs in it.

Exactly four minutes and forty-two seconds later, Ben came in and sat across from Todd. "How have you been lately?"

"You mean how have I been since we talked last week?"

"I mean in general, how have you been feeling lately? Since everything happened with Skip."

Ben knew that Todd always called Skipper "Skip". He was trying to get some sort of emotional reaction out of Todd, but Todd would remain impenetrable.

"As I've told you before, we were close. It's been tough, but I'm trying to move on," Todd replied.

"You're trying to move on by leaving the show?" Ben questioned further.

"The show was called *The Wilson Brothers*, we couldn't continue the show any longer without one of the brothers."

"The studio wanted to though, didn't they?"

Todd hated talking about the show. After wanting it out of his life for so long, it was finally gone. He wanted to forget about it once and for all, but he knew he had to talk about it with Ben. "Yeah, they wanted to continue the show, but I didn't think it was right," Todd replied.

"Tell me again, how did they wanna continue the show without Skip?" Ben asked.

"They thought it would be pretty easy to find someone else to take his place. Someone who was a big fan of the show and Skip. Their idea was that I would film a new season with this new person and it would serve as a sort of memorial to Skip."

"And you didn't wanna do that?"

"No," Todd answered bluntly but then decided to elaborate. "Like I said, the show was called *The Wilson Brothers*, I didn't wanna continue it without Skip."

"You didn't wanna continue it with Skip either though, did you?" It was time for Ben to try and get a confession out of Todd.

"I don't know where you get that from, we were actually preparing for the next season when-" Todd paused. "You know what I think, Ben? I think you've been spending too much time looking into me and not enough time actually looking for Skip. You seem to think he's dead but you never found his body. As I've been saying for weeks, there's a very good possibility he could just be partying in LA," Todd lied.

"We've checked his LA condo, no one's been in there since he died," Ben said.

"If Skip died… but we don't know that," Todd would not be tricked into saying something again.

"You know he died," Ben stood up and leaned over the table, his face only about six inches away from Todd's. "I know you do."

I could rip you in half right now, Todd resisted the temptation.

"I have no clue what happened to Skip," Todd said, hoping Ben would sit back down before he could not control himself anymore.

Luckily for both of them, he did indeed sit down. "You knew Skip well, what do you think happened to him?" Ben asked.

"Skip did a lot of partying in LA, I wouldn't put it past him to get mixed in with the wrong people. He probably got himself in some trouble… I'll admit, he could be dead, or he could just be gone."

"What do you mean gone?"

"I mean gone, disappeared. If he didn't want people to find him, he wouldn't go back to his house, or his LA condo. He could be hiding in a hotel, staying off the radar."

"What made you think of this theory?"

Todd could not help but laugh at that question. "You asked me what I think happened to Skip… I told you. And like you said, it's just a theory."

"Okay, fair enough," Ben smiled. "Earlier you said you didn't wanna leave the show, you said you were actually preparing to film a new season. But last week I talked to some people from the studio… and they said there was some tension between the two of you. They actually forced you guys to go hunting to mend your differences, is that correct?"

"Yeah," Todd realized that Ben was not running a sprint, he was running a marathon. Todd expected he would eventually talk to the studio, but he had no clue that he already did. Unfortunately for Todd, today was the day of the blindside.

"So, why have you been telling me that your relationship with Skip was good, but the studio told me it wasn't?"

Todd would have to be very careful with what he said next. "Our relationship was good. It's true that the studio wanted us to fix any problems we were having, but we did that quickly. The day Skip disappeared, everything was great between us."

"So no argument took place in the forest that morning?" Ben asked.

"No," Todd said. "Look, Skip and I grew up together, then we worked very closely with each other for years. When you're that close with someone there's bound to be fights, but we always resolved our issues."

"Okay," Ben said, Todd could see a little disappointment in his face. Ben had thought he trapped Todd in a hole but Todd had escaped. It was clear that Ben wouldn't give up though. "I know I've asked you this many times, but I'm gonna have to ask you to recount what happened the morning of Skip's disappearance." Todd noticed that Ben used the word "disappearance" instead of "death", as if he was trying to agree with Todd.

Todd began telling his account of what happened, he had

told this story so many times that it was almost scripted. He remembered the night before he met with Ben for the first time. He stood in front of his mirror for an hour telling this same story. He made sure he got everything perfect, from the wording he used to his facial expressions. Since then his story had not changed at all, Todd had thought about every detail to remain consistent.

"It was just over a month ago now, September 20th. I woke up at about four that morning 'cause me and Skip were going hunting. I probably left my house around four-thirty and rode my ATV over to Skip's house."

"Skip had a bigger house than you, didn't he?" Ben interrupted.

"Yeah… he has a bigger house than me," Todd replied.

"Were you jealous of Skip?"

Todd laughed at this. Every time they met Ben would add something else to his long list of accusations against Todd.

"Me and Skip made the same amount of money, if I wanted a house that big, I could have one."

"So you don't want a house that big?"

"No," Todd quickly responded.

"Okay," Ben paused. "So is it safe to say that you and Skip lived different lifestyles?"

Todd took a moment to think before responding. "I have a family, I spend my free time with them. Skip was never interested in having a family… so yeah, you could say we live different lifestyles."

"Did you ever disagree with the decisions he made for himself?" Todd knew Ben was grasping at straws.

"Ben, let me ask you a question. Do you agree with every

decision your wife makes?" Todd waited for a response but it was clear Ben chose not to answer this question.

Todd laughed. "I definitely don't agree with every decision my wife makes. I don't agree with every decision anyone makes. It's completely natural to have our own opinions on things. While Skip and I live different types of lives, I still love him… and I support him with everything he does," a tear began to form in Todd's eye. Todd loved thinking that Ben was infuriated by his answers. He wanted to give himself a pat on the back for the performance he was putting on. Todd had been on TV for many years, even though he starred on a reality show there was still acting required. Even if he tried, he could not count the number of days they were filming where he had to act happy in front of the camera, when in reality he wanted nothing to do with the show or Skip.

Ben continued to remain silent, still hoping Todd would let something slip, but Todd would not give him the satisfaction. "It seems like you don't wanna talk anymore, Ben, should I just leave?" Todd smirked.

"Not just yet… sorry, I interrupted you, continue your story. Tell me what happened the morning of Skip's death," Ben committed to saying "death" instead of "disappearance".

"Me and Skip rode our ATV's deep into The West Woods. We were there for hours but we didn't get lucky. I'd say it was probably around seven-thirty when I started feeling sick, I don't know what it was from but I decided to fight through it. Although around eight it got worse so I told Skip we should head back. As you know though, Skip loved hunting. He didn't wanna go back empty-handed. So I left and he stayed. I got home just after nine and went to bed."

"And you never saw Skip again?" Ben asked.

"No… unfortunately not."

Ben decided it was time to change the subject. "As you know, we brought your wife in for questioning a few weeks ago. She let it slip that you've been in a remarkably better mood lately. Why's that?"

Todd laughed once again, knowing it annoyed Ben when he was amused by his questions. "First of all, she didn't let anything slip. She told the truth… isn't that what you're supposed to do here?"

Ben responded right away, he didn't want to give Todd any time to think. "I just think it's weird that your mood improved after your best friend, someone who you thought of as a brother, died."

"I don't know what happened to Skip, but I was deeply affected by it. I wish he would walk into this room right now and everything would go back to normal. That could happen eventually, but there's no way of me knowing that. You have a family, Ben, I think I'd be correct in assuming when something goes wrong in your life, you have to act strong. That's your duty as a father," Todd forced a few more tears out. "I didn't show my pain to my family, I didn't want to do that to them. But more importantly, Skip's disappearance made me realize something. It made me realize that things can change in an instant. The people you love most can leave your life out of nowhere," Todd paused to let out more tears. "My marriage wasn't in the best place, but after losing Skip I knew I couldn't lose Marissa… I knew I couldn't lose my kids. Over the past month I've tried my best to become a better husband and a better father. So yeah, I have been in a better mood, because I have used all my energy to be positive around my family. Positivity is what we need in times like these."

And the Oscar goes to... Todd wanted to smile but had to stay in character.

"Okay, I think we're done for today. I'll be seeing you again soon," Ben said.

Mission accomplished, Todd thought. While Ben was an obstacle he had to overcome, for the last month he had been doing just that. Ben would soon not be a problem for him anymore. He was confident that an ordinary, by the books sheriff like Ben Pines wouldn't solve this case.

How could Ben figure out that Skip was killed by a vampire? Todd amused himself on the way out of the police station. *How could Ben figure out that his world was about to be taken over by an army of vampires? He couldn't.*

Ben followed Todd closely from the interrogation room all the way to the street, as he always did. He liked to watch Todd walk away, just to see if anything strange would happen.

Todd started walking down the street but decided to turn around, "Hey, Ben."

"What?"

"I hope you listened to what I said in there... about how the people you love can leave out of nowhere. Spend time with your family, Ben. You never know what could happen to them," Todd examined the horror in Ben's face before turning around and continuing his walk down the street. Todd knew he had taken things too far. After hearing that, Ben would surely work even harder to catch Todd. Could you blame Todd though? He had to have his fun.

Todd woke up at exactly 2am, as he had every night since he turned. Marissa's arm was draped across his chest and her leg was wrapped around his. He slid out of bed as discreetly as a ghost moving through a house. An amazing thing about his newfound powers was how quietly he could move. Every night he needed to, he would leave his house and return later without anyone knowing he was ever gone.

Todd snuck into his closet and put on black pants and a long sleeve black shirt. He walked out of his bedroom and into the hallway. It was as if he was in the military on a stealth mission but all the pressure of being caught was gone. He successfully reached his front door, put on his black boots, and walked outside.

Now time for the fun part, he thought.

Darkness. Darkness surrounded him. But then he blinked and saw red. Todd stood at the bottom of his porch with his real eyes. His red eyes.

Todd had been turning for over a month but the feeling never got old. He felt the power rushing through his body as his red eyes looked up at the night sky. The cool glow of the moon created some light, but he knew it was still dark enough for the others to successfully sneak out of their homes. The feeling began at his feet and slowly moved up his legs and into his torso. It flowed up his chest and down his arms. It reached his hands and he felt his fingernails grow. He looked down at his claws, they were sharp enough to pierce through someone's skin. It continued to flow until it finally reached his head. He felt his fangs pierce through his gums. The first few times he had felt this he screamed in agony. Todd remembered the feeling, lying on the ground near Skip's dead body. He felt like he was going to die as well and join Skip in Hell. He screamed and cried and it felt as though the pain would never end, but then it stopped.

All his pain went away, even his gunshot wound from Skip disappeared quickly. When he rose, he felt all the power that was in his blood for the first time. Over a month after his first time turning, Todd was used to the transition.

Todd burst into a sprint and leapt into the forest. He jumped thirty feet into the air and landed on top of a tree. He looked across the sprawling West Woods. The cave was calling him, and he would go. He jumped from tree to tree, hearing the rustling of leaves behind him. He landed back on the ground and continued to sprint through the forest. Before turning, Todd was never much of a runner, now he ran faster than any human ever could. He soared from pond to pond, watching the bewildered wildlife run in the opposite direction. He could catch them all if he wanted to, but they were not his target. Humans were.

Ben, he thought. But he would have to control himself.

A plan was in place and any wrong move could ruin it. He needed to obey his master. He was not the only one with these powers, not by a long shot. There are those who have lived their whole lives, hundreds of years, with these powers and are much stronger than Todd could ever hope to be. He needed to tread carefully and stay the course. If he did, he could live up to four hundred years... if he was lucky.

Once the vampires take over this world, we will all live in harmony.

Todd continued to soar through the sky and sprint through The West Woods until he reached the cave. It was the same cave that he got sucked into when he almost crashed his ATV into Skip's. He remembered the vision he had that day, the figure with the red eyes running towards him. That vision came to life when he witnessed Skip's red-eyed killer leap towards him. Skip's killer and Todd's saviour jumped towards him and bit him on the neck. The bite mark went away almost instantly, but the effects that bite had on Todd would hopefully last forever.

Todd saw torches lit in the cave and walked towards them. He joined the crowd at an opening in the cave. The vampires formed a circle along the walls of the opening, leaving a wide, open space in the middle for their master. Todd looked around the circle and saw many familiar faces, citizens of Westwood who had also been turned and promised an enhanced, extended life. He did not recognize other faces and knew they were from The Ash.

We are fighting for their world now, Todd thought.

After Todd, many others joined the circle and he knew it was almost complete. As he looked around he realized there were about a hundred vampires in the dimly lit cavern. It was an overwhelming number, but he knew there were thousands more waiting in The Ash, at least that's what he was told.

A whole army of vampires, ready to take over this world.

The circle was now complete, it was time for their master to show himself. The opposite side of the circle parted and their master walked out, followed by two other vampires: his sister, Freya, and Batraz. From the stories Todd had heard, Batraz was the largest vampire, standing at almost eight feet. The only vampire who was close to his height was his master's father, Israfil, although he rarely left his fortress anymore.

Batraz was holding a much smaller vampire by his neck.

Before getting a better look at this vampire, Todd had to kneel on one knee and put his head down, as did all the others in the circle.

"ALL HAIL PRINCESS FREYA," the circle said in unison. "ALL HAIL PRINCE JAREK," the name of their master, although he also had another name. He was one of the only vampires who had been born in The Ash but lived in their world. Over the past fourteen years he had successfully assimilated himself into the town of Westwood. He had spent his time learning about humans so that the vampires could destroy them all. He was the one who convinced his father, king of all vampires, that they must take over this world. They must do it so the vampires can survive…

"ALL HAIL THE ROYAL FAMILY," they all said before rising.

After everyone had risen, Batraz threw the smaller vampire to the ground. Todd did not recognize this vampire. He could see the fear in his red eyes, as if the vampire was looking at the Devil.

He is looking at the Devil, Todd thought as he watched Jarek look down at the now fragile vampire.

"What do you say to us?" Jarek questioned the vampire while motioning towards Freya.

The vampire seemed as though he had to think about the question for a second but then clumsily knelt and bowed his head. "A- All hail Princess Freya," he stuttered.

"Continue," Jarek commanded.

The powerless vampire looked up at him but then quickly bowed his head once again. "All hail The Royal Family."

He did not acknowledge Jarek. Todd knew it took all this

vampire's courage to do that, especially right in front of Jarek.

The revolt, Todd realized. He had heard rumours of a group of vampires starting an uprising against Jarek, this vampire must be involved. Todd knew there were always doubts about Jarek. Many have said he has taken too long to get to this point, they believe they should already have control over this world. But true believers know that they only have one shot at this. Jarek cares about his people, so he has been a careful leader. That's why he has spent so many years interacting with and becoming one of the humans he so desperately wants to destroy.

Jarek took a step towards the vampire, whose whole body began to tremble.

This is your fault, Todd wanted to tell him. *You disobeyed our master, and you will pay.*

Jarek bent down and grabbed the vampire by his neck. "Who else shares your beliefs?" Jarek asked him.

"I w- wo- won't tell," the vampire managed to get the words out.

"Yes, you will," Jarek began to squeeze his neck harder. The vampire's face quickly turned from white to red to purple. Just as his eyes began to shut Jarek lifted him higher then slammed him into the ground. The force of his throw created a crack in the stone.

Jarek bent down and picked him up again. He looked into the poor vampire's eyes for a few moments then threw him back down. This time the vampire broke through the floor of the cave. Jarek followed him into the depths. Todd could see larger openings in the cave through the hole.

One of the largest cave networks in the world, Todd thought. It was so large that the vampires were able to enter their world through it and no one noticed. Todd could hear water crash down on the rocks deep below. He had not seen the entirety of the cave system, no one had, but he had seen enough to know how deep it went. There were several corridors and he had seen at least ten waterfalls, all varying in size on his way down. The flow of the water was interrupted by screams. A moment later Jarek flew back up through the hole he created, once again holding the vampire above his head.

"You have one more chance. Unless you want to be rid of your long life and powers, you must tell me. Who shares your beliefs?"

Todd knew the vampire was going to break. No being from The Ash or Earth would be able to withstand Jarek in a moment like this.

"B- Bassam, Iapetus, Erekle, a- and Aldara. Th- That's all of us," the vampire said.

"Good," Jarek said, staring into the weak vampire's eyes. He launched him over the heads of the vampires. All of them, Todd included, ducked down. Todd scurried alongside his fellow vampires to make room for Jarek to walk out of the cave. Several vampires picked up torches and walked behind him, so Todd followed.

Todd exited the cave as the vampire crawled towards a tree, trying to escape Jarek, but that was not possible.

Jarek approached him. "You went to my house," Jarek grabbed the vampire's neck. "You tried to sabotage my plan," he lifted him up. "I will never let anyone live for that." The vampire began to scream as Jarek ripped him in half. His screams turned to whimpers. Todd watched his intestines fall to the ground, just as he had watched Skip's. Jarek was still holding the top half of his body and Todd could sense his rage. Jarek stuck his claws into the vampire's skull, putting him out of his misery. Suddenly Jarek wound up and threw him across The West Woods, he must have flown at least three hundred yards. He then grabbed the bottom half of the body and looked at his captive audience before he launched it in the same direction.

"Don't sabotage my plans," he said in a calmer tone.

There was a flash in the distance, as if something had exploded. All the vampires turned their attention to it.

"What was that?" Freya asked.

Jarek did not answer. It was clear that everyone was scared of what Jarek would do next.

That vampire went to his house.

"It probably hit a wire," Todd decided to speak up. Jarek looked directly at him and Todd felt himself begin to sweat. He didn't know why he decided to answer the question, something in him just told him he had to.

"You," Jarek pointed at Todd. "Come with me. You two," he pointed at the two vampires beside Todd. "Come with us."

The four of them sprinted and leapt through The West Woods until they got to Woods Drive. Todd was right, the body did hit a wire above the street. He glanced to the left side of the road and saw a car flipped over in a ditch. Jarek approached the car and studied it for a few moments. He then walked around to the driver's side and bent over. Todd followed him, but made a conscious effort to keep his distance. He stood further back but could clearly see that there were two people in the car, a boy and a girl. They both looked young, probably only twenty. They both wore jean jackets, Todd assumed they were on a date. As tragic as this was, he did not feel sorry for them, their lives were meaningless anyways. Todd watched as Jarek focused specifically on the boy.

We have to either kill them or turn them. What if they saw something? But Jarek stood up and began to walk away.

"What should we do with them?" Todd asked.

"Leave them."

Todd realized that Jarek knew the boy.

"Leave the car and the kids, I'll take care of the body," Jarek said before picking up the bottom half of the body, mangled and burnt, and disappearing into The West Woods.

CHAPTER SIX

Abe approached the sirens in the distance. He didn't want to get too close, so he ducked behind a bush and watched an officer get out of his police car and enter the forest. Abe was quite far away but could recognize the officer. Barry Pickett, the newest addition to the Westwood police department. Barry walked through The West Woods looking for something. Abe didn't know what, but knew it must be connected to the accident that took place last night.

There were two police cars parked on Woods Drive and the road was temporarily blocked off. Not too long after Barry started his search, Sheriff Pines and Liam Freburg got out of the other car.

Not this way, Abe thought as he continued watching the two officers from behind his bush. He could handle Barry but didn't want to deal with Ben Pines too.

Abe watched anxiously as Ben paced from side to side, but was relieved when he and Liam chose to search the northern stretch of the woods. Abe set his sights solely on Barry.

Barry strutted in his beige uniform, with his back towards Abe. He continued to scan the ground and did not look behind him once, which made it a very easy job for Abe, who was just twenty feet away from him. Abe crept behind a large tree stump and slowly bent down to pick up a rock that fit perfectly in his hand. He threw it to the right of Barry, which startled the rookie cop. Barry quickly regained his composure and pointed his gun towards the source of the sound.

He slowly walked towards the bush. He didn't know what he expected to find, it could just be an innocent squirrel or worse, a skunk. The last thing Barry expected was to feel a crow-bar smash him across the back of his head. Barry slowly turned to face his attacker but didn't make it all the way before he plummeted to the ground.

Abe quickly dragged Barry's body behind a larger bush and began undressing. He knew he looked foolish, a sixty-seven-year-old man in tighty-whities in the middle of The West Woods, but soon enough he looked like a proper officer of the law. Before walking away he realized he forgot to take off one thing. Abe removed his Westwood Demons baseball cap and placed it under a pile of large leaves with the rest of his clothes.

"Have you ever seen that show, *Your Friend Frederick?*" Luke asked as Dishon drove down Woods Drive.

"The kids show?"

"Yeah, that one."

"Why would I ever watch that?" Dishon snarled.

"C'mon, man. I'm just asking," Luke stuck his arm out the window and began to make waves in the air. "Anyways," Luke continued. "My kids were watching that show the other day and that little kid, Frederick, found a dead bird and was so sad about it that he cut it in half and taped it onto one of his action figures."

Dishon didn't say anything in response so Luke continued his story. "That Frederick kid is pretty messed up if you ask me. I don't even know if I want my kids watching that anymore. That little creep literally pretended the bird was alive the whole episode. He's just delusional, man."

"Don't let your kids watch it then."

"Easier said than done, partner. My kids love that little weirdo," Luke brought his hand back into the car and rolled his window up as they approached the site of the crash.

Ben stood thirty yards into the forest as they pulled up. "So we're looking for a body?!" Dishon called out to him.

"Yeah, Barry went that way," Ben pointed across the street. "You two follow him."

"So the kid says he saw a body before he crashed?" Luke asked Dishon. "He's delusional too."

"That family has some bad luck," Dishon said as they split up.

As he walked further into The West Woods, Dishon noticed another beige-suited officer searching the area but did not recognize him. From a distance he looked like an old man and his eyes were proven correct as he got closer.

"Hey!" Dishon called out to the old man. No answer. "Hey!"

Still no answer. Dishon lightly jogged towards the old man and grabbed his shoulder. The man finally turned around.

"Who are you?" Dishon asked.

"I'm sorry, Son. My hearing isn't as good as it used to be."

"Alright, alright. Now who are you?"

"The name's Edgar, I'm from the town over, Quarryview. We heard about everything that's been happening here, so my boss wanted me to check it out."

"You know this is our crime scene though, right?"

The man named Edgar started laughing and patted Dishon on the shoulder. "Look at me, I'm almost seventy. I'm retiring next year," he continued to laugh. "I'm not here to step on your toes. My boss sent me here so I came, I don't wanna hear him complain about this all week. Don't worry, Son, I'll be out of your hair in no time."

"Fair enough," Dishon did not feel the need to question Edgar anymore and walked away.

Abe watched Dishon leave. He knew who Dishon was but was confident his own identity remained a secret. After all, he had been living off the grid for a few years. Abe walked in the opposite direction of Dishon. He continued further into The West Woods, past a pond and over a hill, until he saw something out of place. A little pile of loose dirt. Whoever buried this body had done a good job tamping the dirt down, but not good enough.

Abe pulled his work gloves out of Barry's back pocket and began to dig. Scooping up dirt by hand wasn't the most efficient method but he couldn't have had any of the officers asking him why he had a shovel. This was the only way to do it, he was grateful that the hill blocked him from the officers' view while he continued to dig.

His hands were about four feet into the ground when he felt something. It was slippery. He continued to shove dirt out of the way to get a better look. Guts, he was feeling the inside of someone's body, touching their intestines. He began to rapidly move more dirt away, the last thing he needed was for Dishon or another officer to come peek over the hill.

The dirt was not close to being cleared away but Abe mustered all his strength to pull the mangled body out of the ground. He had a hold of the neck and hauled it like he was ten years old again, in an impassioned match of tug of war. After one roaring grunt, the body came loose from the ground and knocked him over. Abe quickly rubbed the dirt from his eyes and was immediately disappointed by what he saw. He had just pulled a dog from its grave.

"Shit!" He said as he looked at the once white and grey husky, which had been stained by the coarse dirt it was stuck in. "Sorry, buddy," he said remorsefully.

"Who you calling buddy, buddy?"

Abe leapt back at the sound of the voice. He looked to his left and saw Dishon standing on top of the hill.

"What do you got down there?"`

"I'm sorry, officer. It appears I have a false alarm," Abe nervously chuckled. "I thought I saw the body poking out of the ground but it's just a dog," he plugged his nose as he looked down at the husky and shuddered at its rotten corpse, which he hoped sold his dismay to Dishon.

Dishon stared at the dog then back up to Abe. At the dog. Back to Abe. "Alright," he finally said. "If you find anything else suspicious, let me know. I'm gonna go talk to the sheriff."

"Sounds good, friend," Abe responded, and held his breath before taking a sigh of relief once Dishon was out of sight again.

Even though he was relieved, he unfortunately had to abandon his mission. Dishon was going to find Sheriff Pines and Abe was sure the old man from Quarryview would be a topic of conversation. Abe shook his head at the husky before turning around and walking away from Westwood's finest and the crime scene. Not only had he not found the body, he revealed himself to another officer. Today was an unmitigated failure. Abe walked through The West Woods with his head down. He felt the cool breeze pick up and wished he had time to retrieve his hat to cover his bald head. Thankfully he had a dozen more baseball caps at home. Further down the path, he even felt a drop of rain and thought a downpour on this unsuccessful day would be fitting. But he didn't feel another drop after that. Finally, he looked around him. It wasn't raining at all. He wiped his hand across the surface of his bald head and what he saw on his fingertips brought a broad smile to his face. Blood.

He turned around and began walking back down the path, this time with his head up. After only twenty steps, he hit the jackpot. He jumped out of the way as another drop of blood fell from the body caught in the tree. As he studied the halved corpse above him, he gazed upon its intestines, wrapped around the branches, before adjusting his gaze to its face, specifically the eyes. He saw exactly what he expected to see as he locked eyes with it. Red.

Bingo.

It had been almost an hour since they started searching The West Woods and none of them found squat. Dishon approached the cars, where the other four officers were already engaged in a meeting.

"Anything?" Ben asked.

"Nah," Dishon said as he still scanned the forest around him.

"Okay," Ben said. "I doubt a body fell onto the road last night, but the boy thinks he saw one so we have to check. Just a little while longer then we can call it a day. Where's Pickett?"

"I didn't see him out there," Luke said.

"What?" Ben replied. "He was on your side."

"All I saw was that old man. I didn't get a good look at him. Who was he, Dishon? I saw you talking to him," Luke motioned to Dishon.

Shit, Dishon wasn't planning on saying anything about the man named Edgar.

"What old man?" Ben asked, looking directly at Dishon.

"This old cop, I asked him who he was and he said he was from Quarryview."

"What did he look like?"

"He had long grey hair and a full beard, that's all I can remember about him," Dishon lied about his appearance, he did not want Ben to look further into the mysterious man.

They'll find out, Dishon thought. *And they'll deal with him.*

"I know the officers in Quarryview, none of them look like that," Ben said.

"I'm just telling what I saw and what he said, boss."

After asking more questions about the old man, Ben sent

them back out to their side of the forest. "I wonder who that old man is, probably some pervert with a thing for dead bodies," Luke laughed.

"Who knows?" Dishon replied bluntly.

He's not someone with a thing for dead bodies. He's someone who's getting involved in something he shouldn't be.

He looked forward to telling his master about the old man.

Only a couple minutes later, they stumbled upon Barry, who was only now regaining consciousness. Dishon smirked as they watched him, wearing only his underwear, struggle to his feet. They led Barry to the cars when they heard their names called out.

"We found something! Get over here! NOW!" Ben yelled. They followed his voice into the woods.

What Dishon saw was unexpected.

This was not planned. He looked forward to telling his master about this as well.

All hail Jarek. All hail The Royal Family.

CHAPTER SEVEN

Jason woke up at exactly 2am. There was no need for him to be quiet, as far as Sam knew he was going to visit his family in Seattle, as he did a few times a year. He slept on the side of the bed closest to the door. As he got up, he glanced at Monica, who had her back to him, although Jason doubted she was actually sleeping.

"You up?" He asked.

No response.

"I'm gonna leave soon," Jason said. "I understand if you don't wanna talk to me right now," he continued after a few moments. "You do a good job, for a long time you've done a good job. Soon you'll be rewarded for that."

"I don't want to be one of you," Monica said. "I'd rather die than be like you."

Jason smiled. "We made a deal. You help me and I keep

your family safe. You may not believe this but I want you to be happy. Why do you think I haven't already turned you? But you have to understand, our time is coming. We're gonna take over this world. Very soon you're gonna have to make a choice. You either let me turn you or you die, there's no alternative."

"I- I just want to be with my children," Monica's voice quivered.

"Letting me turn you and Sam is the only way that can happen."

"I don't want that life for him."

"It's the only life he'll have."

"You don't know that," Monica said under her breath.

"What did you just say?"

"Nothing."

"Don't lie to me," Jason raised his voice. "What did you say?"

Monica did not respond so Jason stomped over to her side of the bed. "Answer me when I ask you a question," but she still didn't respond, even with Jason standing over her. He grabbed her by the neck and picked her up while she squirmed. He held her up over their bed. "I am Jarek, Prince of The Ash, and you will answer me," he tossed her back down on the bed.

She curled up in a ball, hiding her face from him. "I said you don't know that. You don't know turning Sam is the only life for him."

"Your world is gonna be taken over by u-"

Monica interrupted him, a bold move. "And what if it's not? What if you lose?"

"We won't lose."

"You don't know that," she said. "When you try to take

over this world you'll have to fight our military. Not just our military, every country's military. What if they drop a bomb on that little cave of yours? I know you think you know what you're going up against but you don't," Jason slapped her across her face with the back of his hand. He made sure not to leave a mark.

"You don't understand our power," he said before opening his mouth and revealing his fangs. "If you did, you wouldn't be talking to me like this. I've been good to you… but if you don't want to become one of us, I'll respect your wishes," he began walking towards the door but stopped before leaving. "But maybe your son will want something else."

"Don't say that. Don't you dare say that," Monica continued to cry.

"I look forward to seeing what he decides. Either way, whether I turn him or kill him, I'll enjoy myself."

Monica curled back into her ball, now sobbing. Jason walked back over to the bed, and as much as she resisted and tried to swat him away, he leaned over and kissed her on the cheek. "I hope you feel better soon. Have a good few days, honey," he said before leaving.

Jason held his head high as he walked out their front door. He got in his car and drove through the silent town of Westwood. As he drove past the dark houses full of people peacefully sleeping, he thought about their naïve happiness, and that brought a smile to his face. He loved to see people go about their pathetic lives, not knowing what was coming.

He left the town he would soon destroy and drove down Woods Drive. The section of the road where Sam flipped the car was no longer blocked off. He drove by it and remembered seeing Sam and Sarah the night before, upside down and unconscious. When he first saw Sam, he wanted to save him but immediately stopped himself. If he saved Sam he would have to explain why he was on the road, without a car, at that time of night. He would not risk the survival of his people to save the boy.

He drove past the site of the accident and further down the road, past The Connelly Estate, to the dump which was situated within a large opening in The West Woods. Two spotlights were shining on Jason as he pulled up to the front gate of the dump, as if the clouds parted and God shone his light onto him. But Jason knew there was no God.

God's come from The Ash, not the sky.

The gates opened and Jason drove through. In his headlights he saw Garry coming out of his office, waving at him. He remembered turning Garry very early on, about thirteen and a half years ago. Back then Garry was only fifty-two and just found out his wife had been cheating on him for some time. Jason was at Fireside Pub one night when he overheard Garry going on a drunken rant about his soon-to-be ex-wife. Everyone in the bar had been listening to Garry's spiel for about half an hour before people started getting annoyed. Another Fireside Pub regular, Jack Kent, who slaved away for The Westwood Star and wrote pointless stories about his dying town, got so irritated that he picked a fight with Garry.

"Shut up about it!" Jack hollered from the other side of the bar.

"What did you just say?!" Garry was slurring his words and stumbled as he jumped down off the stool.

"I said shut up! We're tired of listening to you," Jack said as Garry neared him.

"I don't hear anyone else saying anything!"

"Because they don't wanna talk to your drunk ass."

"Who you calling a donkey?" A few too many beers led Garry to come up with this offbeat reply, which in turn made Jack laugh out loud along with many others in the bar.

Jason began to laugh with them. He had been sitting in the corner of the bar for the majority of the night. He was not there to get drunk, he was there to observe the citizens of Westwood. While it was clear the bar had turned on Garry, Jason was fascinated by him. He could hear the pain in his voice. It was clear that Garry was heartbroken and was now wondering what to do with the rest of his life. That made him the perfect victim.

As Garry neared Jack he began to laugh as well in an attempt to mock him. He stopped right in front of Jack, leaned over so their faces were almost touching, and made a farting noise with his mouth. Jack shoved Garry backwards with a forceful push. Garry, who was made up of two hundred and fifty pounds of fat, only moved a foot or two. Garry then forced himself back towards Jack, most likely planning to hit him, but instead did something much worse. Jason watched Garry grab his stomach and hesitate as he reached Jack, before vomiting all over his lap. All of the beer Garry had poured into his gullet that night poured back out of him and drenched Jack.

"What the hell!!" Jack yelped, silencing all the laughter in the bar. He stood up and allowed the puke to drip off him.

"You think this is funny?!" Jack marched towards Garry but stopped when the bar doors swung open. Everyone in the bar stopped what they were doing and looked towards the door. Someone even turned off the jukebox, cutting off the chorus of "Sunglasses at Night". No one walked in at first, keeping everyone in suspense. It could have just been an ordinary person, taking a break from their family, but for whatever reason it seemed like everyone knew who was about to saunter through those doors.

Richard Bannerman stepped into the bar. The man who Garry's wife cheated on him with.

Garry's smile left him as he looked over at Richard, "Hey, Dick."

"Hey, Garry," Richard replied, staring him dead in the eye. The tension in the bar heightened as the two men stared each other down. Garry didn't even break eye contact to wipe the puke off his mouth. Even Jack, who only a minute ago was ready to knock Garry's teeth out, sat back down and completely forgot about his vomit-soaked pants. Jason was enjoying the show, throughout the night he had become more and more interested in Garry and now wanted to see what the man was capable of.

"What are you doing here?" Garry finally asked after a long moment of silence.

"Just getting a drink."

"I think you should go somewhere else."

"Nah," Richard walked past Garry and took a seat at the bar. "I like it here."

"I think you should go somewhere else… Dick," Garry repeated himself. That one must have stung.

Richard took a breath before responding. "Wanna know what, if you want me to leave, I'll leave," he started walking back towards the door but stopped right beside Garry. "And you know where I'll go… your wife's house." Garry turned his head to look directly at Richard. Jason could tell he was fuming and loved seeing that kind of anger. "Or should I say… your ex-wife."

Garry leaned over, grabbed a beer bottle off the counter, and smashed it over Richard's head. For a big guy, Jason was impressed at how quickly Garry moved. Richard let out a yelp and covered his blood-ridden face with his hands. Garry grabbed him by the back of his neck and walked him over to the bar. Richard's blood dripped from his face, creating puddles on the floor. Garry swept aside some loose peanuts from the counter before smashing Richard's face against it.

"Hey!!!" Malcolm, the bartender, yelled in his booming voice.

Garry was able to bash Richard's face against the hard wood three times before people started pulling him off. They shouldn't have let him do it once, but people were so shocked that it took them a while to react. It took four guys to pull Garry away and even then he fell backwards onto them. They stumbled and landed at the foot of the pool table. Luckily, three more guys ran over, including Jack, and blocked Garry from getting his hands back on Richard.

The men prepared to use all their strength to stop Garry, like they were playing red rover, but he decided to give up and dropped to the ground. He sat with his back against the leg of the pool table while Richard laid in his own blood. Malcolm and some bar patrons leaned over him, trying to stop the blood from shooting out of his face.

When the dust settled, Jason decided the party was over. He locked eyes with Garry on his way out the door, who was all alone against the pool table. Jason closed his eyes and when he opened them again, they were red. He watched Garry's mouth open wide as he maintained eye contact. Jason then looked away and walked out of the bar. He knew Garry was still in awe as he walked through the empty streets of Westwood, and that brought a sinister smile to his face.

Richard decided not to press charges, most likely because the cause of the conflict, Sadie, convinced him not to. Garry didn't face any consequences for his actions and still had no idea what to do with the rest of his life. For him, the only logical course of action was to continue going to Fireside Pub and pass out in his own vomit every night.

One night, Jason decided to go back to the pub as well. As soon as he walked in he saw Garry sitting in the spot where Jack sat just a week ago. Hopefully Malcolm did a good job cleaning the vomit off that stool. Garry also saw Jason right away. Jason knew Garry's eyes followed him as he moved across the bar, back to his spot in the corner. Jason sat down in the booth and waited only two minutes before Garry came and sat across from him.

"Hello, Garry."

"Who are you?"

"My name's Jason."

"You new in town?" Garry puffed up his chest.

"I've been living here for about half a year."

"Really… I haven't seen you around since just last week."

"I used to live in Seattle, I've been slowly moving my stuff here but I've been there a lot too."

"Seattle's a big city! What made you wanna move to the middle of nowhere?"

Jason had been looking at Garry before, but now he really dialed in on him. His stare was death and destruction. He did not sense Garry's fear but wanted to change that. "Love!" He laughed.

"Love?"

Jason stopped laughing, "Yeah, love… you used to be married so you know what I'm talking about, right?"

"Go to Hell, man," Garry started to stand up.

"There's no such thing as Hell," Jason replied, immediately halting Garry. "Sit down," Garry obeyed.

"Who are you?" Garry began to shake.

"No, Garry, who are you?" Jason's eyes were now red and staring deep into Garry's soul. "You're a loser. No wife, no kids, a miserable job. You're going nowhere in life," Jason started laughing at him. "Don't you just hate thinking about that? Your life is pointless, and why? Because of Richard Bannerman? Is that why? Or because of your ex-wife? Is it her fault? Answer me Garry, why?"

Garry was shaking so much he struggled to get the words out of his mouth. "B- be- becau- because of b- both of them."

"Because of Richard and your ex-wife? Is that why your life is pointless?"

"Y- yes."

"Wrong. Look around, Garry, look at everyone in this bar." Garry obeyed Jason and turned to survey the bar, looking at all his fellow Westwood citizens. "Their lives are pointless… not yours," Jason reached across the table, grabbed Garry's chin, and tilted his head back towards him. "Did you hear me? Your life is not pointless, not anymore."

"W- what do you mean?"

"I'm your saviour, Garry," Jason smiled widely.

"Why? Who are you?"

"You told me to go to Hell. Well, I come from a place far more terrifying than any Hell you've ever imagined. I've encountered monsters beyond your wildest imagination, Garry… and

I rule over them. Your people talk about a huge red figure with horns on his head and call him the Devil. They couldn't be more wrong," Jason extended his arm across the table to shake Garry's hand. "Nice to meet you, Garry. I'm the Devil."

Jason's grip tightened as he laughed. "You asked me where I'm from, definitely not Seattle. I'm from The Ash. You asked me what brought me here and I said love… while you could argue that, it's also not true. I'm here because this is where I'm meant to be. I told you your life is worth something, and I meant that," it was now Jason's turn to look around the bar. "Everyone in this worthless town will be dead soon, Garry. Everyone in the world will be dead soon, consumed by The Ash. But congratulations! You are one of the lucky few who can join us!"

"J- join you?"

"Yes, Garry. You want revenge on Richard and your ex-wife… I can give you that revenge," Garry's eyes opened wide and Jason knew he was ready. "Do you like the sound of that?"

"Y- yes."

"Perfect, follow me," Jason got up and walked out of the bar with Garry following closely behind him. They walked deep into the alley at the side of the bar until Jason thought it was a safe place to stop. The alley was dimly lit, there was only one flickering light on the side of the building. Water was dripping from the pipes and if you focused on it it kind of sounded like a clock. Tik tok. Tik tok. Garry's time as a human was almost at an end, and the clock was counting down.

Jason turned around to face Garry. "Kneel before me," Garry knelt on the wet pavement. "Repeat these words: All hail Prince Jarek."

Garry looked up at him but then quickly put his head back down. "A- all hail Prince Jarek."

"Now rise," Garry rose. "I am your leader. I am your prince. I am your God. Will you serve me?"

"Yes," Garry said with a newfound confidence.

Jason leaned over and bit Garry's neck, tasting his blood.

It didn't take Garry long to get used to his powers. Only a week after becoming a vampire he wanted to go after Richard and his ex-wife but Jason convinced him not to. If they both were killed then Garry would be the only suspect. Jason continuously told him to remain patient and he obeyed. He continued running the dump, which became a great place for Jason to hide his car when he went into The Ash, pretending he was just taking another one of his road trips to Seattle.

Jason remembered waking up just about a year after he turned Garry and read about two Westwood residents being brutally murdered while on their honeymoon in Mexico. After only a glance he knew who the two people were. The murderer was never caught.

Jason got out of his car and was greeted by Garry, who was on one knee with a bowed head, just as he was in the alley all those years ago.

"All hail Prince Jarek," Garry said.

"You may rise," Garry no longer had the beer belly that he once had. In fact, he was quite muscular, especially for a man of his age. Once he rose Jason shook his hand, both of their grips were equally tight. "It's good to see you again, friend."

Garry smiled and nodded, "You can head out, I'll hide the car in the garage."

"Your service will not be forgotten," Jason said before turning around and leaving the racoon infested dump.

He leapt into The West Woods and headed towards the

cave. He would arrive later than all the other vampires for their gathering, but they always waited for him. The light from the torches only became visible once he took a few steps into the cave. Jason could feel their heat on him as he approached the other vampires. Once he entered, they all got down on one knee.

"ALL HAIL PRINCESS FREYA," Jason looked over and saw Freya standing at the natural doorway leading deeper into the cave.

"ALL HAIL PRINCE JAREK," they said as Jason reached the middle of the circle.

"ALL HAIL THE ROYAL FAMILY," they concluded.

Jason glanced over at Batraz, who was standing beside Freya and beckoning him over.

"This one has something to tell you," the eight-foot vampire said once he walked over. He pointed at Dishon, a police officer who they turned.

"Hello, Dishon," Jason said.

"It's a pleasure, my prince."

"What news do you have?"

"We were searching for the body that the boy, S- Sam, claims he saw," Dishon paused for a moment. "None of us found it." Jason grunted. "I even went back after my shift and the top half of the body was nowhere to be seen. But there was someone else searching with us."

"Who was it?" Jason moved closer to Dishon.

"I don't know… an old man. He said he was an officer from Quarryview. Luke told Ben, but apparently there's no old man that works in Quarryview."

"Thanks for telling me about this," he began walking towards the circle before Dishon called him back.

"My prince, there's something else you must know…"

Jason was deep in thought as he took his place in the middle of the circle. "You have all served me well for a long time. And we are so close to taking over this world," they started to cheer. "For years vampires have been moving across the world, continuing to learn about our enemies. We are almost ready, but we all knew this would not be easy. We knew there would be people who would try and stop us… and that has already begun. As you all witnessed last night, I dealt with a vampire who turned against me… but he was not acting alone. Aldara, Iapetus, Bassam and Erekle were part of this revolt. We have discovered that they have fled back into The Ash, and I'm going after them. I will hunt them down and they will pay for the choices they made. We are the strongest army this world has ever seen!" They continued to cheer. "We are the strongest army The Ash has ever seen!" They cheered even louder. "And we will not be stopped. Batraz, Cassander, Saija… and Todd," Jason glanced at the new vampire. "You proved yourself last night, so you will go on this mission. Dishon has discovered that someone in Westwood may know about us. I am tasking the four of you, with the help of Dishon, to find this person."

Batraz, Cassander, and Saija all knelt down on one knee, "We will not let you down, Prince Jarek."

Jason looked at Todd, it was time to see if he was truly loyal to him or not. "Can you do this?"

Todd moved a few steps forward and took a knee, "I will not let you down, Prince Jarek."

"Good," Jason said before turning his attention back to the crowd. "I will be back in a few days. You are my people, and I will not let you down. Soon we will take over this world, and enjoy our lives in the new world we build!" Their cheers erupted as Jason walked deeper into the cave.

"Brother!" Freya called after him.

He turned around to face her. "You want me to come with you?" She asked.

"No, Sister," he put his hand on her shoulder. "I need you to stay here and make sure everything goes well while I'm gone."

Freya nodded. "Give Father my regards."

Israfil was the last person Jason wanted to see, but he knew he could not go into The Ash without reporting to him. "I will," he said to his sister before walking off.

Jason followed the torchlights further into the cave. He walked down the spiraling path which led into the depths, towards the portal. He passed three waterfalls on the way down, each larger than the last, which all poured into their own underground ponds. Through the third waterfall Jason saw the glow of the portal. Red. It glowed so vibrantly it made the water appear red as well. He walked further down the path and faced the portal, which stood across a small pond. The portal mirrored the ovular shape of the cave and was surrounded by black, unbreakable rock. The red in the middle of the portal matched his eyes. As he approached it, he could feel its slight vibration and hear its constant hum. No one knew where the portal came from but it was as if it was a living being.

Jason, the Devil himself, walked through the portal and entered The Ash.

CHAPTER EIGHT

Sam could hear the phone ring from the basement. His mom picked it up and he knew exactly who she was talking to.

"Did you find anything?" He heard her ask as he slowly walked up the stairs.

Sheriff Pines came by yesterday morning, about an hour after they got home from the hospital. They talked for about fifteen minutes and the sheriff assured him he had all the information he needed. The plan was for him and his officers to search the area of the crash to see if they could find the body. Sam walked into the kitchen and gazed upon his mother, knowing she didn't expect much from the call. She looked at him like a pessimistic mother whose child just told her they wanted to pursue the great career of acting. Sam sensed an aura of disappointment in her gaze, which seemed to stab into him. As he stood in the doorway, Sam began to doubt himself. After hearing what Jason and Colton thought about the situation, he expected the worst. Although, Sam's somber expression changed right after his mother's mouth grew wide.

"Really?!" Monica said to Sheriff Pines.

As guilty as it made Sam feel, knowing the police did indeed find a dead body, it brought him great relief to know he did not imagine the whole thing. He smiled but immediately wiped it off his face as his mom continued to stare at him.

"Wait," she said. "Who?" She reverted to her previous pessimistic expression.

Sam's expression changed with hers. He wanted to grab the phone from her hand and hear everything the sheriff was saying but elected to wait until his mother was done. He continually tapped the wall to ease his nerves until the conversation finally ended.

"What?" He asked as his mom hung up the phone.

"They found the body," she said in a somber tone. "It was Wyatt Jessings."

Sam sat alone in Doctor Allen's class. His mom told him to stay home from school but he decided to go. He needed something to take his mind off of Wyatt Jessings. Unfortunately for him, Doctor Allen's lecture wasn't working as a distraction. He was lost in his own thoughts, thinking about the newscast him and his mom watched just after speaking with Sheriff Pines.

"Just two nights ago, three university students disappeared at the university's fall fair," Sam and his mom sat close together as the reporter spoke. "Wyatt Jessings, Parker Smith, and Lucas Armstrong went missing. The Westwood sheriff and his team have tried their best to solve this mystery, but it has remained unclear what happened to the boys. However, last night they may have found an answer. Whilst searching the scene of a car accident on Woods Drive, our police found the body of local teen heartthrob and amateur male model Wyatt Jessings in The West Woods."

Sam stared at his mom's trembling fingers as the reporter continued. "There was one notable feature on his body. His eyes were bright red."

No, Sam thought. *That can't be true.* Sam was still only focused on that detail of the story in class, as his eyes were locked on the glowing red power button at the bottom of the smart board. That red glow seemed to pull him in. He tightened his grip on the arm rests of his chair as the walls began to close in on him.

Sam's hands began to sweat. It seemed as though the air around him increased to a scorching temperature. His hands slipped off the armrest. He was now vulnerable, powerless, any second he would be pulled into the light.

"Wanna know what, let's end class there today," Sam heard sighs of relief behind him as Doctor Allen dismissed the class. That brought him out of his trance. He looked away from the red light as he took a deep breath of relief just as his other classmates had.

His feeling of ease quickly dissipated as the reporter's words echoed in his head. "These are trying times for the citizens of Westwood. Just over a month ago, Skipper Wilson, host of the popular hunting show *The Wilson Brothers*, was reported missing. While many speculate that he was murdered, no body has been found. Todd Wilson, his brother and co-host of their show, informed police that he hasn't seen Skipper since the morning of his disappearance, when they were out on a hunting trip. With two murders in a month's time and two boys still missing, Westwood is in turmoil."

The look his mom gave him after hearing the newscast remained in his mind. He knew that people in Westwood had been scared over the past month, after Skipper's disappearance, but he had no clue it was affecting his mom so deeply. It hurt him even more since he knew what the likely cause of Wyatt's death was.

Red eyes. Sam could not get that thought out of his head. It was all the confirmation he needed but didn't want. His encounter with the vampire was not a mere nightmare. He knew what Wyatt looked like, so he knew that Wyatt was not the vampire he saw. That means that there was more than one vampire haunting Westwood. Sam had never even considered that as a possibility.

How many are there? He asked himself. If Wyatt was a vampire, does that mean that Parker and Lucas are vampires too? If there were more vampires out there, then some of them could be dangerous. For the first time Sam realized that Westwood could be in grave danger.

"Hey, Sam," Doctor Allen said, causing Sam to notice that everyone else had already left the room.

"Hi," Sam replied, still trying to shake himself out of his dazed and confused state.

"I heard about the accident… I'm so sorry that happened."

"Uh, thanks."

"How are you feeling?" Doctor Allen patted him on the shoulder.

"It's been a hard few days but I'm doing okay."

"And Sarah was in the car too, right?"

"Yeah."

"That's horrible, how is she doing?"

"She's…" Sam paused, picturing the scar etched into Sarah's face. "She's okay."

"Well I just wanted you to know that you have people around you who care about you. I know we don't know each other well, but I'm here for you too." When Sam didn't say anything, Doctor Allen continued. "Have you talked to Sarah today?"

"No, things didn't really go over well with her father after the accident."

"I'm gonna tell you something and I hope you listen to me, kiddo," Doctor Allen leaned in closer to him. "Only you and Sarah were in that accident. You two went through that together. Her dad may want to have an opinion about it but you shouldn't have to listen to him. That girl loves you, Sam. I can tell by the way she looks at you. Send her a text and see how she's doing, I guarantee she'll be happy to hear from you."

Sam couldn't help but smile. *Go for it,* Sam thought about the words Doctor Allen had said to him before. He listened to him then and knew he should listen to him now. "Thanks," he said. "I actually really appreciate that."

Sam unlocked his bike from the bike rack. He rode down the winding road leading into The West Woods. As he entered the forest he looked back and noticed a run-down, blue pickup truck that seemed to be driving slowly. While it looked like there were two people in the truck, he could not make out their faces.

He rode through the forest for about twenty minutes, longer than usual since he was in no rush to get home and see the disappointed face of his mother, until he reached Woods Drive.

Exiting The West Woods, he did not bother to look both ways, but a car was speeding down the road. He heard the squeak of its brakes as it missed him by an inch and he fell off his bike.

Not again. He looked up from the pavement and saw a truck. A run-down blue truck.

Sam instantly panicked. Did this truck hit him on purpose? As he slowly lifted himself off the ground, he thought this was more and more likely.

"Are you okay?!" The driver yelled out. Sam was so focused on the truck that he did not even look at who was getting out of the car. He lifted his hands and rubbed his eyes as he tried to focus on the driver. Sam watched as the man wearing a Westwood Demons baseball hat approached him.

Not you.

"Hey… are you okay?" The man asked again. Sam finally got a good look at him and saw that the man was older than he originally thought.

"Uhm," Sam did not know what to say. Was this man trying to hit Sam or was it an accident? Had he seen this man before or was it all in his head? Given the things he had seen recently, the latter seemed more than possible.

"Is he okay, grandpa?" This was unexpected. Sam watched a girl who could not have been more than ten years old walk out from the passenger's side of the truck. With eyes and hair as dark as the night sky, the girl's blue flannel blew in the wind. Sam noticed her flurry of freckles before looking back over at her apparent grandfather.

"Well, are ya?" He asked.

"Uhm, yeah, I am. Don't worry… you didn't hit me or anything," Sam replied.

"I know I didn't hit ya," the man laughed. "I didn't do anything wrong, I was driving the speed limit when ya came flying out of nowhere. Did ya even look for any cars?"

Sam didn't feel the need to answer that question, as the answer was obvious to all of them. "Sorry about that… I'm just gonna go," Sam took a few steps backwards and picked up his bike.

"Are ya sure you're okay to ride?" The man asked. "Ya fell pretty hard."

"Yeah, don't worry about me, I'm fine," Sam said.

"Look at his arm, grandpa," the little girl said as Sam walked his bike across the road. Sam did not even notice but looked down and saw blood dripping from his forearm.

"Aw man," her grandpa said. "We can't let ya leave like that. I have some bandages in my truck, let me clean that up, will ya?"

"Uhm, no. I mean, thanks anyways, I appreciate it, but I live close by," he continued walking towards the forest but knew something was wrong. He had a feeling the man was following him.

"I think you should stay," the man said, causing Sam to turn around.

"Like I said, I appreciate it, but I'm gonna go."

"Sam," the man's facial expression immediately changed. He turned from someone who was just trying to be a friendly neighbour to someone who was facing their ex-wife in court, fighting over the custody of their children.

"How do you know my name?"

"Sam… we have something to talk about," the man said with a stern face.

"Who's we?" Sam looked over at the girl but her grandpa continued to do the talking.

"I'm Abe, this is my granddaughter, Chelsea. It's nice to finally meet ya."

Finally? Sam knew for a fact that this had to be the man he kept seeing. *He's been haunting me.*

"Stop following me, just leave me alone," Sam said whilst getting on his bike.

"Don't ride into that forest!" But Sam disobeyed. "We'll come after ya!" He heard as he disappeared into The West Woods. His heart raced as he rode down the path. He continuously peeked over his shoulder to see if they were following him… they were not. But he saw the blue truck drive away and knew that they were not giving up yet. Good thing he knew The West Woods so well because he was riding faster than he ever had before, successfully avoiding the rocks and roots that could cause him to fall. He rode up the hill and past the cave that he would normally try to study more.

It's nice to finally meet ya, Sam heard Abe say in his head. He wondered how much Abe knew about him. Did he know where he lived? Because that was where Sam was heading to now, he didn't know where else to go. He considered going to Sarah's instead but couldn't find the courage to face Colton again. Sam had been asking himself if he could keep Sarah safe throughout the day, but he no longer knew the answer.

Sam raced down the steep hill that led out of The West Woods and towards town.

The blue truck was there. It was parked at the side of the road and Abe and Chelsea stood near the entrance of the forest.

Sam hastily squeezed his brakes.

"We just want to talk, Sam," Abe said.

"Just leave me alone," Sam turned around, ready to ride

back into the forest, when he saw a long stick fly right past him. He looked at the tree to his left. It was an arrow.

Who is this guy? He thought, but when he looked back he saw Chelsea holding the bow.

"Try to leave again and maybe this will go through your skull," her ominous tone contrasted her sarcastic smile. Sam couldn't tell if she was joking or not.

That stopped Sam. Even if he wanted to leave, he was too shocked to move. He couldn't even fully turn his body to face Abe and Chelsea.

"Get your bike and throw it in the truck," Abe said. "Let's go for a drive." Even though Sam didn't want to, he knew he had no choice but to go with them. Once he finally gained the courage to move he grabbed his bike and walked past them. Chelsea lowered her bow but she still had the same smirk on her face.

He threw his bike in the cargo bed. Abe held the door to the back seat for him, smiling. Abe closed the door behind him, harder than Sam thought was necessary, and got in the driver's seat.

"Where are we going?" Sam asked once Abe started driving.

"To talk," Abe replied.

Chelsea turned around in her seat and faced Sam, "I like your jacket!"

"Uhm, thanks," Sam responded.

"Hey, uh, sorry for almost killing you earlier," she winked at him.

"It's okay I guess," Sam said as Chelsea turned around. She laughed out loud and he noticed Abe chuckle to himself through the rear-view mirror.

"Grandpa, you really need to get an aux cord in here."

"You don't even have a phone," Abe turned towards Chelsea.

"Yeah, but if you get an aux cord then I have a reason to get a phone!"

"You don't have enough money for a phone."

"You can get me one for Christmas," Chelsea turned to her grandfather and smiled ear to ear. "I just wanna play some Hannah Montana, that's all."

"I think I've done us all a favour by not getting you a phone."

Chelsea, wearing a shocked expression, turned to Sam, "Do you like Hannah Montana?"

"Uh, yeah, she's okay I guess."

"Okay?" Her shocked expression remained. "Hannah Montana is more than okay, she rocks harder than anyone alive."

Abe turned onto Woods Drive and followed the road for a few minutes as Chelsea hummed what Sam assumed to be a Hannah Montana song. Abe turned left, taking the dirt road.

"So we're going to The Cliff?" Sam asked.

They drove up the winding road which led to The Cliff, a small, overgrown parking lot with the best view of Westwood. The Cliff was a common place for teenagers to hang out, but at that moment there was no one else there. Abe and Chelsea got out and started towards the edge of The Cliff. Sam waited a moment longer before joining them at the railing.

"Ya see that?" Abe pointed off to the distance.

Sam squinted as the sun was shining bright in the sky. "What?" He asked.

"Westwood."

Sam could not help but chuckle, "Yeah, I see Westwood." He looked at Abe, who was not laughing with him.

"There's a very good chance everyone in that town will soon be dead."

"What?" Sam said, his smile now wiped from his face.

"I'm gonna talk, and you're gonna listen," Abe declared.

Sam looked down at Chelsea who had the same stern expression as her grandfather. He decided not to say anything else and let Abe speak. "Vampires live in Westwood. I know that might sound crazy, but it's true. I've done my research, I've even seen some things myself. What happens around Westwood doesn't happen anywhere else in the world. Yeah, there's brutal murders everywhere, but not like here. In just the past month multiple people from Westwood have died or gone missing. You could say there's a serial killer on the loose but I don't buy that. You said you saw a body fall from the sky before your accident. No one else seems to believe ya, but I do. In fact, I know you're right… 'cause I found the body."

"What?" Sam interrupted him in disbelief of what he just heard. "The police found the body. It was Wyatt Jessings."

"I don't know exactly what happened to Wyatt Jessings but it wasn't his body that fell onto the road. I searched the forest and found someone else. And there's one thing that ties both bodies together. They both had red eyes. Now I don't know about you, but I've never heard of people having red eyes. That leads me to one conclusion: they were vampires. And I'm sure Wyatt's two friends are vampires too."

"I saw one," Sam spoke before he had enough time to decide if he actually wanted to reveal this key piece of information. It was too late now, however.

"What?" Chelsea took a step forward but Abe blocked her with his arm.

"I- I saw one."

"You saw one? One that was still alive?" Abe questioned him.

"Yeah. A few nights ago, I heard something in my backyard so I went to go check it out. That's when I saw it."

"What happened next?" Abe kept his arm across Chelsea's body.

"That's the thing… nothing happened. It jumped on me and I fell to the ground. I thought I was gonna die… but I didn't. Eventually it got off me and just ran away into the forest."

Abe removed his arm from Chelsea and took a step forward. "Sam, listen to me, there've been signs of vampires in Westwood for the past fourteen years. I can't fill ya in on all the details yet, but eventually I will. Their activity in the past month has increased drastically. I- I just have a feeling something bad is coming. And we need to stop it."

"Who? You two?" If Sam was not so shocked, he would have laughed as he looked at Abe and Chelsea. An old man and a little girl, not exactly who you would picture as vampire hunters.

"And you!" Chelsea sounded excited by the idea.

No, Sam had been trying to forget about the vampire and he was not about to go against them all with these two strangers. "Do you know how crazy you two sound?"

"I know it sounds insane," Abe said. "But you more than anyone else should know how real this threat is, you saw one yourself."

"I know I saw one. But it didn't kill me, did it? I must not be a threat to them or whatever. This isn't my problem, it's not my fight."

"Sam," Abe grabbed him by the shoulders. "This is your

fight, this could be the whole world's fight. For all we know we're facing the most dangerous threat mankind has ever faced."

"So tell the authorities, tell someone who can actually do something about it," Sam said.

"You think they would believe us? I'm just an old man and she's a little girl," it was as if Abe had read Sam's mind.

"Yeah, exactly, and you two can't fight vampires," he remembered Chelsea's skill with a bow and doubted himself, but then his common sense kicked in and he knew he was right. "And look at me, do I look like someone who can fight vampires? No," he answered his own question. "Look, guys, this isn't my fight. And it shouldn't be yours either," Sam walked back to the truck and grabbed his bike.

"Then whose fight is it?" Chelsea asked but Sam did not have an answer for her. "Exactly," she continued. "No one will fight them if we don't."

"Then fight them if you feel like you have to, just count me out," Sam could see the pain in Chelsea's eyes but began to ride away.

"Wait, Sam," Abe stopped him.

"Just let me leave," Sam said.

"I will, I just wanna ask you one question. How'd your dad die?"

Sam let his bike fall to the ground. "What did you just say?"

"He killed himself, didn't he? He jumped off a cliff. But what if that's not what actually happened?"

Sam's world flipped upside down.

"You can leave," Abe continued, now Sam could see the pain in his eyes as well. "But think about that," Sam thought he saw a tear running down Abe's cheek.

"I don't know if I can do this right now." As Sam talked to Sarah near the outskirts of Westwood, his mind was still running from his conversation with Abe and Chelsea. He listened to Doctor Allen and texted Sarah after all, although this was probably not the conversation Doctor Allen intended them to have.

"What are you talking about?" Sarah asked, confused.

Can I keep her safe? Sam remembered Colton interrogating him in the hospital parking lot. After listening to everything Abe just told him, he knew his focus needed to be on his father. He needed to know the truth, and right now Sarah was in the way of him finding that truth.

"There's just so much going on in my life right now. I need some time to figure everything out," he looked deeply into her disappointed eyes.

"Sam," Sarah grabbed hold of his hand. "I'm so sorry for what my dad said to you. He didn't mean any of it, you have to believe me."

"He still said it though," Sam quickly responded. "After what happened, your dad will never trust me again."

"Don't say that."

"It's true and you know it," Sam paused for a moment. Sarah gripped his hand tighter but he pulled away.

"I just need time to figure everything out," Sam began to walk away from her.

"You owe me more than that!" She called out to him.

He couldn't bear to face her. It broke his heart to leave her, but he knew it was the right thing to do. He hoped he would have more answers for her soon. For now, he was only prepared to face one thing… the truth.

CHAPTER NINE

"You are trespassing!"

Sam had been in and out of sleep all night so he was not surprised when he woke up to this. He turned away from his window without even bothering to check outside. He knew it was nothing.

But what if it's something? He tried to get that question out of his mind. He closed his eyes in an attempt to fall back asleep.

"You are trespassing!"

Don't turn around, he told himself.

"You are trespassing!" He couldn't resist anymore. He flipped over in his bed and looked out the window. The light was shining on nothing.

Probably just a squirrel or something. He had thought the same thing the night he encountered the vampire.

"You are trespassing!" It continued to announce a trespasser even though no one was there.

"You are trespassing!"

"There's nothing there!" Sam said aloud.

Then he saw it. A boot, then another boot. Sam froze, he tried to move but he couldn't. All he could do was watch as the light shone on someone in his backyard.

"You are trespassing!" The person began to bend over. As they bent down further and further, Sam saw that the person had on a jean jacket, just like his. The person stopped moving just before revealing their face.

Please go away.

But then their face came into view. Red eyes. Their glow was all Sam could focus on. His muscles tensed up and he still couldn't move. He continued watching as the vampire reached out and put its hand on his window. He removed it and waved at Sam, all whilst smiling. Suddenly the vampire started punching Sam's window repeatedly. Sam began to panic more and more as he watched the glass shatter.

"You are trespassing!"

He tried to scream but couldn't. Why was his mom not waking up? She was never there to save him. Before he knew it the vampire had completely broken his window.

"You are trespassing!" Sam knew that would be the last time he heard the robotic voice.

It poked its head through the window. The red eyes were surveying Sam's room then stopped and stared at him. It smiled while continuing to crawl through the window. Sam was trapped in his bed, completely powerless, while he looked up at the vampire looming over him.

But it was not a vampire anymore. Sam was no longer scared. He looked past the red eyes. He saw a man with short brown hair and a little stubble, just like Sam remembered. And then it all clicked, Sam saw the fur on his jean jacket.

"Dad?"

Sam could finally move. He leaned over and turned his lamp on. He now knew for a fact that he was looking at his dad, whose smile was now warm and welcoming. Sam jumped up and wrapped his arms around his fallen father.

"Dad, it's really you."

But the man was cold as ice. Sam backed away slowly. His father's smile faltered as he continued to stare at Sam, emotionless and motionless.

"Dad?"

"Join me," his dad said. Sam now noticed the red eyes again as his dad began to breathe heavier and heavier.

"Join me."

Sam closed his eyes as his dad leapt at him.

And he jumped up, opening them again. It had been a nightmare. For a moment, when Sam believed he was face to face with his dad again, it was the best dream ever. But that moment didn't last long.

The next three hours flew by, even though Sam had just been lying in bed the whole time. After his nightmare he knew he would not fall back asleep. At one point he even had to turn his lamp on, just as he had done in the nightmare, because he kept imagining shapes moving among the darkness. It was now 6:06am and Sam heard his mom get up and start getting ready. He hoped she would not come down to see if he was awake. He had decided hours ago that he was not going to school and didn't want to talk about it. He waited, lying completely still in his bed, for another two hours until she finally left.

How'd your dad die? Sam thought about what Abe asked him. This motivated him to get up and granted him the courage to walk upstairs. He paced around his living room for half an hour before finally walking into his mom's room, kitchen chair in hand.

He went into her closet, thinking it was shared between her and Jason, but discovered he was wrong. Only three of Jason's shirts were squished against the right side. The rest of the closet was occupied by dresses his mom was still workshopping. He stood on the chair and pulled the latch that opened the door to the attic. He used just about all his upper body strength to pull himself up, but finally made it and was surrounded by a cluster of boxes.

He thought their dusty, insect infested attic was an appropriate setting for what he was doing. It was a place in their house that nobody talked about, perfect to learn more about somebody no one talked about.

The first box he went through was filled with old photo albums, before the days of Jason. This was not what he was searching for but he couldn't help but take a look. He spent the next hour looking through the photos. There was one photo that stood out to Sam. He removed it from its sleeve and held it in his hands. It was a picture of him and his dad in their backyard. The sun was setting and their firepit was lit behind them. Sam didn't remember that day but apparently they had carved pumpkins. Sam's dad, wearing his jean jacket, was lifting him into the air. Sam's dad was looking directly at the camera but Sam seemed like he was more focused on his small, carved pumpkin. It was clear that he carved the pumpkin, as it was not the most impressive craftsmanship. However, Sam could make out what he was going for. The two eyes were triangles, both pointing upwards, but the pumpkin's grin was what really caught Sam's attention. It had fangs. He made his pumpkin into a vampire.

A happy vampire? Sam thought as he folded the picture in half and put it in his pocket.

Sam shoved that box to the side and opened another box, which contained what he was looking for. Newspaper articles.

A picture of Sam's dad was displayed on the front page of The Westwood Star. Even though this article was announcing his death, they chose to use a photo of him smiling. In the picture Sam's dad was standing in a field, wearing a suit. He must have been at a wedding, Sam guessed that his mom was the one behind the camera. The title of the article read: *Lifetime Westwood Citizen Couldn't Bear the Pain of His Daughter's Tragic Death.*

Jerk, whoever wrote this article clearly did not care about offending his mother. He looked for the name of the author. Jack Kent.

He began reading the article. *Born and raised in Westwood, Ben Sparks was found dead by police last night. He was reported missing by his loving wife Monica on Sunday, October 16th. According to reports, she made the call just after 4pm. Based on this information and the state of the body when they found it, police presume he had been dead for at least 48 hours. While they are still in the beginning stages of their investigation, the apparent cause of death is a fall from a large cliff deep in The West Woods. His body was found at the bottom of the cliff, and while his face was almost unrecognizable, they found ID in his pocket. As stated above, it is thought that Ben committed suicide by jumping off the cliff sometime on Sunday. Ben leaves behind a wonderful wife and a four-year-old son. This comes just three weeks after they lost their daughter, Mia Sparks. She passed away in a tragic accident on September 26th. While the citizens of Westwood have been giving the Spark's family their condolences, Ben obviously could not escape his pain.*

"Shut up," Sam said out loud, the more he read Jack's writing the more he disliked him. But he was almost at the end of the article so he decided to bear it.

The Westwood Star will continue to follow this story as more information is revealed to us. Although, there was one detail about his body that stood out to police and will most likely be a key point in the investigation moving forward. I would like to now warn all of you of the graphic details which will follow. When Ben jumped from the cliff, his face appeared to have hit a large rock upon impact. The result of this was the deformed face that the police found. His eye actually popped out of its socket. While the police could no longer examine his right eye, they did get a good look at his left one. While Ben Sparks had blue eyes his whole life, this eye was red.

Sam stopped. He didn't want to read on but knew he had to. He absolutely despised Jack Kent's trashy writing but now his eyes were glued to the page like he was reading a Stephen King novel.

The police are most likely going to write it off as a bloodshot eye, but I was on the scene myself. This wasn't your average bloodshot eye, this sucker was as red as Mama Kent's sweet cherry pie. Therefore, I believe there's more to this story. So why was his eye red? No one can answer that for us right now but we will continue to ask the hard questions in the coming weeks. We would like to send our condolences to Ben's family, and we would like them to know that the entire town of Westwood is here for them.

Sam was speechless. He thought about the nightmare he

had last night. He knew it was just a bad dream, but was it trying to tell him something?

Red eyes.

Was his dad a vampire? Maybe his nightmare answered that question for him.

Red eyes. Sam put that article down and read countless other ones. In the following weeks Jack Kent continued to ask why his dad had a red eye, but he never got his answer. Now red eyes were becoming a topic of conversation again, but the name Ben Sparks was nowhere to be found. Had the town forgotten about him?

Sam jumped down from the attic and made his way to the kitchen. He was happy to see a stack of newspapers still on the counter. He began searching through them, hoping to find a recent article written about Wyatt Jessings and his red eyes.

Bingo, Sam said to himself, removing one of the newspapers from the pile. He found an article about the three boys who were kidnapped and looked for the author's name, expecting to see Jack Kent. The credited author was Holly Gold. *Why wouldn't Jack write this article, especially considering his fascination with red eyes?*

He pulled out his phone and typed in: westwood jack kent. He did not think Jack's name deserved capitalization. He was expecting he might see an article titled "Jack Kent Fired from The Westwood Star" but was shocked by the one he did find. It was the first result, "Jack Kent Found Dead After a Night of Drinking."

Sam learned that Jack Kent died not even a year after his father. On the night of July 16th, 2006, Jack drove home after a night of drinking at Fireside Pub, except he never made it home.

The next morning his car was found flipped over near a farm just outside of Westwood. Jack was dead in the driver's seat. Reading this sent shivers down Sam's spine. As much as he had come to hate Jack Kent over the last hour, he felt sorry for him. The way he died was all too familiar.

He thought of his mom. He thought of her crash. He thought of everything he lost on that day so long ago. That led to his dad's death, found dead at the bottom of a cliff… with red eyes. What if that resulted in Jack's death? Sam began to think of every possibility and kept going back to one. What if Jack was killed by a vampire because he was suspicious of the red eyes? What if these deaths were all a chain reaction?

What if this chain reaction is starting again? He finally asked himself. *Who will die?*

His mom.

Jason.

Sarah…

But if anything bad happens to her… I don't want to think about what would happen to you, Sam heard Colton saying to him.

He began to look around his kitchen. He looked at the three chairs at the table, perfect for his family. He looked at the newspapers. The only paper dedicated to the people of Westwood, he was part of a community. He looked at the fridge. There were two new pictures put up, the ones he took with his mom and Jason on the night of his date. He remembered being in a rush and feeling awkward standing next to Jason. He didn't feel awkward anymore, he just felt joy.

This town. His family. He had taken it all for granted for so long.

What if it's all gone soon? He saw the vampire, he remembered how alienating it was to be the only one who knew. But he wasn't. Abe knew, Chelsea knew. They would stand with him.

As he stood in his kitchen, looking at photos of his family, Sam decided to join Abe and Chelsea.

Half an hour later he was packed and ready to walk out the door. He didn't expect vampire hunting to be an easy job. He wouldn't be working nine to five then coming home to eat dinner with his mom and Jason. He knew if he was going to commit to this he would have to stay somewhere else, most likely with Abe and Chelsea. He peeked through the blinds of the front window, looking for a blue truck. He expected to see one, maybe a few houses down, but was surprised when he did not. He wasn't worried though, he planned on walking through town. Abe would be around soon enough.

He had his hand on the doorknob, ready to leave his life behind, but then remembered he forgot to close the attic door. He walked back to his mother's closet but hesitated before shutting the door. He felt the need to go up into the attic again, it was like something was calling him. Sam climbed up and his eyes immediately locked onto a box in the dark corner of the attic. He swatted at cobwebs as he crawled through the tight space. He put one hand over his mouth as he opened the box, in disbelief of what he was looking at. Sam picked up his dad's jean jacket and held it out in front of him.

"What happened to you?" He asked the jacket. Sam was now determined to discover what really happened to his father. He went downstairs and grabbed his own jean jacket, the blood on the collar was now dry but still stood out. He took it, placed it in the box, and tucked it back into the corner as if no one had ever touched it. He would take a piece of his dad with him on this journey. He knew that's what he had to do.

Sam was ready to leave. He left the attic, picked up his bag, and made for the door. Just then the door opened, his mom was home.

"Oh, hey! Are you not at school today?" She was wearing a beige coat overtop a floral dress.

"Uhm, no I'm not," Sam replied.

"Well it's always good to have a day o-" she stopped talking when she saw his bag. "Where are you going?"

Sam didn't know what to say. He wasn't planning on having this conversation. He was just going to leave and send her a text. "Why are you home?" He asked.

"I forgot my lunch here, I just came back quickly to get it," she was no longer speaking in her normal cheery voice.

"Oh, okay."

"What's going on?"

Sam did not reply.

"Honey?"

"I gotta go away for a bit, Mom."

She took a deep breath, "Let's go sit outside."

Sam followed her onto the porch and sat beside her on the bench.

"So you have to leave?" She asked.

"Yeah."

She took a long pause. Sam felt the need to fill the silence, but didn't know what to say.

"Okay," she finally responded.

"Mom, I-" she put her hand on his leg, stopping him.

"It's okay," she said. Sam was confused. She was not asking any questions. She was barely even reacting. He thought she would definitely be yelling at him by now.

Maybe listening to her yell would be better than what I'm getting myself into.

"It's okay, honey. You're not a boy anymore, you don't have to tell me anything," she put her head down but her hand remained on his leg. "Wherever you're going though, just be safe. And don't forget about me," she looked back up at him.

"I would never forget about you, Mom."

She smiled at that. "I'd hope not. I've been far from perfect, but I've tried my best. I want you to know that. I love you more than anything, Sam."

"I love you too, Mom," he leaned over and hugged her. Her grip was strong, she did not let him go for at least a minute.

She stood up right away after letting go. "Well, I think it's about time I head back. Good luck, Son," she began walking down the steps but then turned around. "That jacket looks great on you," she smiled once more.

"Thanks," Sam replied, trying his best to hold back tears.

His mom got in her car and drove away.

Bye, Mom.

Sam made sure to lock the front door before leaving. He walked down his street and further into town. He sat at the bus stop across the street from town hall. He looked down at his phone and saw a text from Sarah.

"Can we please talk again. You need to tell me what's going on…"

As he read her message, he knew he couldn't respond. He needed to be alone. He needed to figure things out. After putting his phone away, he noticed a blue truck driving towards him. He stood up and the truck pulled over in front of him.

"I had a feeling you'd be around," Sam said to Abe as he threw his bag into the cargo bed.

Sam and Abe drove off into the sunset, although they both knew there was a good chance this was not going to have a happy ending.

CHAPTER TEN

First her husband. Now her son.

"Mom, I-" Monica put her hand on her son's leg. She didn't need an explanation.

"It's okay," she said to Sam. It was not okay but she wouldn't tell him that… not yet. "It's okay, honey. You're not a boy anymore, you don't have to tell me anything," if she knew, he would only be in more danger. "Wherever you're going though, just be safe. And don't forget about me."

Please be safe, she thought.

"I would never forget about you, Mom," his words were comforting but she still felt empty inside. She had felt that way for fourteen years and knew it would not go away anytime soon.

She reluctantly smiled, "I'd hope not. I've been far from perfect, but I've tried my best. I want you to know that. I love you more than anything, Sam." She truly had tried her best. It had been hard to live with herself… but she had done it for so long.

I'm doing it for them, she told herself.

"I love you too, Mom," he hugged her, she hoped this hug would last forever but knew it could not.

She finally ended their hug and stood up. "Well, I think it's about time I head back. Good luck, Son," she walked away but couldn't help turning around one last time. "That jacket looks great on you," she was heartbroken but still forced herself to smile. As long as he thought she was okay, she was doing her job… she was playing her role.

"Thanks," Sam said. Once she was by her car, she realized she never got her lunch from the fridge. She didn't have an appetite anymore though. She sat down in her car and almost screamed. But she couldn't do that, Sam was still sitting on the porch, waiting for her to drive away. She felt like a prisoner whose parole was declined, she had to keep serving her life sentence.

It will never end, she thought.

She backed out of her driveway and drove far, far away from her son. She approached her bridal shop but did not stop, she just kept going. As she drove through Westwood she watched its citizens and asked herself if she really knew them. She always wondered who else snuck away in the middle of the night. As she drove she remained composed, she knew she could not let herself break down yet.

She drove out of Westwood until she was far away from society and pulled over to the side of the road. She looked around and all she saw were cornfields. No one in sight. She adjusted her rear-view mirror and looked at herself. Her composure transformed into terror, anger, but most of all sadness.

She was looking at a monster. She knew it… but there was nothing she could do about it.

Monica let out a scream. An ugly scream that felt like it lasted forever. She hoped all of her problems would vanish when she finished screaming her lungs out, but knew that would not happen. It never happened.

She stopped screaming and started bawling. She looked at herself as makeup oozed down her face and told herself she deserved to feel this way.

No I don't, she considered. *Yes I do,* she knew.

Fourteen years ago her husband learned about the threat of the vampires. It consumed him, he dedicated his life to stopping them. She told him he couldn't but he would not listen. That led to his death.

She didn't have to ask Sam to know that he was going down the same path. Her worst nightmare had come to life.

First her husband. Now her son.

She screamed again, so loud her throat started to ache. She hit the steering wheel repeatedly, using all her strength to cause what little destruction she could. She jumped when her car horn went off. That put an end to her meltdown.

After calming down Monica continued to sit still, emotionless once again. She felt like she was in shock, like her muscles stopped working and would never work again. All she could do was think. She thought about Sam and prayed for his safety, but knew there was no God. She was a prisoner who was now being led to the electric chair. Only instead of dying and escaping this cruel world, she had to face an even worse punishment. She had to watch her son die.

Her husband had not known the power of the vampires, and it got him killed. Sam was just as clueless and would likely meet the same fate.

You don't know what Jason is capable of, she wanted to find Sam and tell him but could not. *All hail Prince Jarek.*

CHAPTER ELEVEN

"All hail Prince Jarek," Erekle knelt before Jason atop the Collapsing Hills. Not as tall as its surrounding mountains, these hills still sprung high into the sky. Within these hills were a labyrinth of caves, all of which had entrances at various points. Just a few hours ago Jason was walking through the dying grass of the Venwood Plains when he spotted a light shining from one of the caves. As he neared the cave the light died out and he knew Erekle had spotted him. He chased Erekle upwards to the peak of the hills, hurdling over the large rocks which populated the land.

He arrived at the peak but didn't see Erekle, although he sensed him. Just as he approached a boulder Erekle leapt into the air. Jason did not know whether he was once again trying to flee or attack him, but either way his plan would not work. Jason took hold of his neck before he could get too high and held him in the air.

"You thought you could get away from me?" Jason let out a laugh before cracking his skull against the boulder. Erekle, with blood dripping down his face, tried to crawl away but would not get far. Jason stepped on his ankle, stopping him. Erekle reached frantically for a nearby rock but Jason crushed his hand with his other foot. He felt every bone in the traitor's hand crack and watched it shrivel as he lifted his foot. He grabbed Erekle by the neck once more and smashed his face against the rock two more times before throwing him into another boulder. Erekle's spine cracked and he curled into a ball as Jason stood over him.

"All h-" Erekle spit out some blood before trying again. "All hail Prince Jarek," he was drowning in his own blood but fought to get the words out. "All hail Prince Jarek," Erekle said again when Jason did not respond. He knew he had been beaten, he had no other choice but to submit. "I said the words," Erekle continued. "Master… I made a terrible mistake, you have to understand that. I should've never betrayed you."

"But you did," Jason immediately replied.

"I'm sorry, forgive me and I will serve you loyally for the rest of my days."

"Look at you," the sun had almost set and the incoming darkness made Jason's beaming stare all the more sinister. "You had all the power in the world but you tried to use it against me. You are a disgrace to our people," Jason picked Erekle up by the neck.

"P- please no," Erekle begged.

"Look behind me," Jason said. "You see that fire that was lit just a few moments ago? Bassam, Iapetus, and Aldara. The three other traitors. I wish I could bring you with me and show you what I'm going to do to them, but you'd just be a burden," Jason threw Erekle to the ground and he immediately fell to his knees. "Say the words again."

Erekle was still regaining his breath, "A- a- all hail Prince Jarek."

"Those are appropriate last words," Jason snapped his neck and brought his boot down on him when he fell to the ground, turning his face to pulp.

Two down, three to go. Jason looked past the narrow portion of the Venwood River ahead of him and at the faint fire in the distance. He began to walk downhill, past the large boulders which were known to come loose from the ground and roll down the hillside. These boulders have caused countless cave-ins. When Jason was just a boy, he was told stories about explorers who dared to venture into the caves of The Collapsing Hills, never to be seen again. He reached the bottom and kept walking. He jumped from rock to rock to cross the Venwood River, which ran all the way from Venwood Forest to the Ash Mountains. Crossing the river marked his exit from the Venwood Region and his entrance into the Ydahm Region.

Home, he thought.

He walked through the swarms of Yudis, little black bugs which came from their hives in the Southern Ydahm Woods and have since taken over the Hissing Plains. It was as though Jason was blind walking through those plains on that starless night. For a while he was using the firelight in the distance as a waypoint but that was eventually put out, as he anticipated. If they were the traitors, as he suspected, they were smart not to leave a fire going for long. *Smarter than Erekle.*

Jason spun around and studied the surrounding area, careful not to lose the way he was heading. He no longer saw light anywhere, and although most of the grass was dead, much of it was as tall as him which blinded him even more. He decided he could not continue his search and laid down on the dirt, hoping no creatures would take an interest in him.

Luckily none did. He awoke at first light, and while he only saw mountains far in the distance, at least he now had a light blue sky above him. He continued walking until he reached a clearing in the grass. He could see sticks leaned up against each other close by and a little bit of smoke rising into the sky. He approached the abandoned fire and picked up the ash.

The Ash, while some people took offense to that name, Jason always thought it was fitting. It would remind people that their world was dying. *That's why I'm doing what I'm doing,* Jason told himself.

He examined the area around the fire and spotted three sets of footprints leading further north. This brought a smile to his face. North was good. Just not west, towards his father… at least not yet.

Jason knew what was north. The town of Neverwich sat just beyond these plains on the outskirts of the White Expanse. Jason began to make his way towards Neverwich until he noticed someone on his right. He looked eastward.

He saw a woman cloaked in blue riding a white stallion.

You're not who I'm after, he thought. Just then it appeared as though the woman turned her head and looked at him. She was far in the distance so he was not sure, but it did feel like he was being studied. Suddenly he felt the wind blow stronger and faster around him, it was coming from the Collapsing Hills. He thought about taking cover but knew there was nothing around him. He was vulnerable in an open field. He glanced back towards the woman in blue, that's when he heard it. The flapping of wings.

A dragon came flying over the Collapsing Hills. It had to be sixty feet from head to tail. The black and purple beast soared through the sky with its wings fully outstretched and peered at Jason.

Jason met its gaze, showing no fear of the beast. His red eyes met its purple eyes.

Qualdra, Jason knew its name. It was said to be the largest dragon in the world. Qualdra's claws grazed the ground of the Hissing Plains before it shot back up into the sky. It flew over Jason and turned back around to head east.

The woman in blue turned away from Jason and also headed eastward.

You're not who I'm after, Jason had to remind himself, and continued to head north. Jason watched the sun set in the west as he approached the gates of Neverwich. He had just entered the White Expanse, a great desert which stretched from the western side of The Ash all the way to the eastern sea border. Two guards stepped towards Jason at the gates, they both held longswords and donned dark red armour. Anyone who was loyal to the west would display their red colours proudly. If Jason were at a town in the east, the guards would likely wear dark blue and be his enemy. Thankfully most of the towns and kingdoms in the east are now buried under lava.

"Who approaches?" The guard on the right said in a deep voice.

Jason walked up to them, clearly displaying his black cloak and red eyes. "I am Jarek."

The guards did not have their helmets on so Jason watched

their eyes grow wide. They both knelt before him, "All hail Prince Jarek!"

"You may stand," Jason said. "I'm searching for three vampires."

The guard on the left stepped forward, "I can bring you to Almara, Mayor of Neverwich."

"Very well," Jason said, following the guard through the gates.

Jason didn't understand the point of the gate as it barely protected them. The walls on the other three sides of the town were far shorter and more vulnerable than the one he passed through. He assumed they thought they only needed protection from the main road coming from the Hissing Plains. Everyone in this town obviously felt safe and believed they did not have enemies.

If they're hiding these vampires, then they just let their enemy through their front gate.

He watched the townsfolk stare at him from their porches as the guard led him deeper into the town. He knew some of them were vampires and the others were humans. While the majority of humans were enemies of vampires, some of them have accustomed themselves to the vampire's way of life over the years. No human who dwelt on the west side of The Ash was an enemy anymore.

The guard led him to their wooden church at the centre of town. He walked through the door first and appeared to interrupt a prayer service.

"My apologies, Almara," the guard said. "But this is Prince Jarek, he has come to see you."

Almara was a middle-aged woman but still appeared to

be very youthful. Her flowing red gown and dark brown hair accentuated her red eyes. Jason stepped in front of the guard, "M'lady."

Almara knelt before him, "All hail Prince Jarek!"

The others gathered in the church followed her lead but Jason stopped them. "There's no need," he laughed.

"What can we do for you?" Almara asked.

Aldara watched her sister talk to Jarek through the cracks of the church's floor. She was huddled beside Bassam and Iapetus. She betrayed Jarek. She betrayed her people... but not all her people. The townsfolk of Neverwich vowed to protect her. They no longer wanted to suffer under the control of Israfil. Even the vampires were turning against their king. Israfil was the reason The Ash was dying and Jarek was incapable of saving them.

We need to find a saviour, Aldara thought.

The three vampires hiding beneath the church once considered saving only themselves and travelling further into the United States. If they got far enough Jarek would never find them, but they had to return to The Ash. They could not abandon their people. She could not abandon her sister.

"Neverwich stands with Israfil. We stand with you, Jarek. How can we help?" Her sister said.

"I'm looking for three vampires... three traitors. I know they were headed in this direction, any chance they stopped here?"

"What were their names?" Almara asked.

"Bassam, Iapetus, and Aldara."

"I hear of almost everyone who comes in and out of this town and I don't know these names. I can talk to our innkeeper, maybe they passed through unbeknownst to me," Aldara was impressed by the confidence in her sister's voice. It seemed almost impossible to tell she was lying. As she looked up at her through the cracks, Aldara thought of her as her hero.

"Thank you, any help will be greatly appreciated."

"In the meantime," Almara continued. "It's dark out now and I can't send my prince out in that. How about you stay the night here? We'd be happy to have you."

"That would be lovely," Almara walked past Jarek and headed for the door. Her footsteps sent dust flying off the wooden planks.

"Just follow me and we can get you set-"

"One more thing," Jason interrupted her. "Almara, that's a lovely name."

"Why, thank you," Almara replied.

"I had a friend growing up, his name was Pietari. He had a younger brother, Pietara. I always thought that was so strange. Why would their parents give them such similar names?" Aldara's muscles tensed as she listened to Jarek laugh. "I mean, wouldn't they confuse them? Sometimes when I would call out Pietari's name Pietara would answer, and vice versa. I think it's quite funny actually. Pietari, Pietara. Almara… Aldara," Jarek was not laughing anymore. "Can I ask you a question, Almara?"

"Of course."

"Do you have a sister?"

"No."

"You're not lying to me, are you?"

"Of course not," Jarek took a step towards her but Almara remained cool, although just below Aldara could not stop shaking.

"I hope you're not. Because I always confused Pietari and Pietara. When I find Aldara she's going to be brutally punished. But if I don't find her, I wouldn't want to confuse you for her," Jarek laughed once again as he made for the door. "Almara, Aldara. What a funny coincidence."

Almara followed Jarek out of the church. Aldara, Bassam, and Iapetus all glanced at each other. They were all scared, but at least they were safe… for now.

"So where's this inn?" Jason asked as he led the way through Neverwich.

"Just keep following this road, it's up ahead on the left," Almara replied.

Even though it was after dark, the town of Neverwich was still very much alive. Jason watched as the townspeople were gathered on their porches, caught up in discussion and constant laughter. Jason and Almara walked further up the main road until they reached the inn. It was a rectangular building with six windows at the front. Six windows, six rooms. All of the candles in the windows were still lit.

Jason walked up the steps first and held the door for Almara. "M'lady," he said as he gestured her in.

"Hey, Morton," Almara said as she walked through the door.

"Almara! It's great to see you!" The man named Morton said in a deep voice. When Jason walked in he saw that Morton must have been three hundred pounds. He had short black hair and a patchy beard that was obviously never tended to. He thought he actually saw a fly zip past Morton's brown eyes and wondered if that was due to his smell, but figured it was probably just a coincidence. "Who's your friend?" The massive man asked.

"This is Prince Jarek," Almara replied.

Morton's jaw just about dropped to the floor. "My prince!!!" Morton screamed, if anyone in this town was actually asleep he surely would have woken them up. "What a pleasure!"

"The pleasure is mine, you have a lovely inn," Jason said. At least the people in the church attempted to kneel before him. Morton didn't even try.

"Thank you! Are you staying the night?"

"Yes, he is," Almara answered for Jason. "I noticed a lot of candles were lit, are there any available rooms?"

"Of course there are! I always keep the candles lit even when no one is staying there. I don't want people to think of my inn as a place to sleep, it's a place to party!" Some saliva flew out of Morton's mouth and onto the front desk when he started laughing.

Jason laughed with him, "As fun as that party sounds, all I'm gonna be doing tonight is sleeping, I've had a long day of travelling."

"That's a shame, but hey, as long as you enjoy your stay that's all that matters to me!" Morton said.

"I'm sure I will," Jason replied.

"Before we get him settled," Almara started. "Jarek is looking for three vampires, by the names of Aldara, Bassam, and… what was the other one's name?"

"Iapetus," Jason replied, impressed by Almara. If she was hiding the three traitors she was doing a very good job of acting clueless.

"Yes, and Iapetus," Almara continued. "Any chance anyone with those names came by?"

"No, I don't think so," Morton replied.

"So you haven't seen a group of three at all? Two guys and one girl." Almara continued to question Morton as Jason glanced her way out of the corner of his eye.

"I wish they were here, then I could hand them to you on a silver platter!" Morton laughed, emitting more spit from his mouth.

"Good enough, thanks for the help," Jason then looked over at Almara. "I should really be getting to sleep now, it looks like I'm gonna have a long day tomorrow."

"Yes, of course," Almara replied. "What room is he in?"

"You can take six!" Morton handed Jason a key.

"I'll lead the way," Almara said.

"Don't worry about it," Jason stopped her. "You've done enough already, I'll see you in the morning."

"Okay," Almara nodded. "Have a good night."

"Goodnight, Almara, goodnight, Morton," Jason nodded at Morton as he made his way to the stairs.

"Goodnight, my prince!" Morton continued to laugh as Jason walked up the narrow staircase and through the hallway. "Hey! Betsey!" Jason heard Morton scream right as he got to his room, he assumed Morton and Betsey were going to be partying all night.

The room was simple, there was a small bed in the centre of it and a bedside table. Other than that there was just a small closet to hang clothes in. Jason would not be hanging his cloak though, he blew out his candle and laid down on the bed fully clothed.

Morton and the girl apparently named Betsey were downstairs laughing and screaming. Jason wondered how anyone ever got any sleep in this inn.

It's a place to party! Jason heard Morton say in his head. He would have been annoyed if he actually planned on sleeping, but he did not. He didn't want to join Morton's party… his own party was about to begin.

Almara sighed in relief as she walked out of the inn. She walked casually and did not stop to talk to anyone just in case Jarek was watching from his window. She made her way down the main road and back into the church, where everyone was still gathered.

"How'd that go?" Bryn, who stood behind everyone else, asked.

"As good as could be expected. Can we move the altar?"

Ohti and Felice stepped forward to pick up the altar, which stood at the end of the church opposite the door. They lifted it up and moved it to the side, revealing a hole in the floor. Almara climbed down the ladder and was immediately hugged by Aldara.

They shared a long embrace before Aldara let go. "You did good," she told her sister.

Almara took a deep breath before speaking, "He's in a room at the inn, he made it very clear he needed some sleep tonight."

"So this is our chance?" Aldara now had a smile on her face.

"Yes, this might be our only chance. Give me the knife," Almara held out her hand.

"No, I need to do it."

"You need to stay here, all three of you do. Just in case he isn't sleeping… if he sees you this will turn into so much more than it needs to be," Almara reasoned with her sister.

"Mom and Dad gave this knife to me. They didn't want you to be involved, they knew how dangerous it would become."

"I got myself involved though, didn't I?" Almara said to her sister. "You started this revolt, you brought these people together," she beckoned to Bassam and Iapetus. "You even convinced this town. You've done all the work, Mom and Dad are travelling across the world in search of our saviour, let me finish the job. I need to do this… for our family."

"Almara, it shouldn't be you."

"It has to be me, I can't let anything happen to you," she held out her hand once more and Aldara placed the knife in it. This knife had been in their family for hundreds of years. Almara held it by its golden handle and the ruby in the centre shone in her eye. She had been told that one of her ancestors had mined this ruby in a great expedition beneath the Ash Mountains. This knife had saved her family in the past, and today it would save not only her family, but billions of lives.

In our world and the other world, Almara told herself. She held the knife that would kill Jarek.

"Thank you, Sister," Almara hugged Aldara again. "I'll see you soon. We're gonna put the altar back in place, you three stay down here and don't make a sound until I'm back," Almara began making her way up the ladder.

"Wait," her sister called out to her and they locked eyes once more. "I love you," Aldara said.

"I love you too," Almara replied and continued climbing up the ladder with a smile on her face.

Ohti and Felice moved the altar back in place. "Are you ready?" Felice asked her.

"As ready as I'm ever gonna be," Almara looked at her

people and smiled. They all followed her out of the church and marched down the main road. They were now all traitors. They knew The Ash would surely die under the vampires' rule and would dedicate their lives to finding a new ruler, a new king. Almara's parents had already left in search of that.

Almara and her followers raised their arms as they passed by the townspeople on their porches, motioning them to continue talking. She hoped Jarek was already asleep but if he was not, she did not want him to notice that a once lively town had all of a sudden turned silent. Either way though, Almara could count on Morton to keep the inn loud. As they approached the inn, she saw that Jarek's candle had been blown out.

Good, she thought. They walked through the doors and saw Morton and Betsey at the front desk. She motioned them to laugh even louder which they gladly did. She picked up the spare key to Jarek's room which Morton had placed on the counter. She halted her followers and quietly walked up the stairs. The stairs were squeaky but hopefully not enough to overpower Morton's howling. Almara walked down the narrow hallway, right to the end, until she reached room six. She closed her eyes and took a deep breath while gripping the knife tightly. If she did not succeed, someone in this town would. She told herself that over and over again.

Almara stuck the key into the keyhole and quietly twisted the doorknob. She held the knife above her head, ready to strike. She slowly opened the door, exposing herself to the darkness within the room. The moonlight shining through the window and the faint light from the hallway were her only light sources. The door was now open wide, and she saw an empty bed. She felt her heart drop but realized this was not over. She jumped into the room and pointed her knife behind the door. She stood in front of the darkness, ready to attack, but no one was there. Jarek was not in the room anymore.

She ran back downstairs, "He's not there! We have to get to the church!" Her followers parted as she ran through them. They started running behind her along with most of Neverwich. All the townspeople who had been enjoying their night on their porches now knew something had gone wrong.

Almara charged through the church door, still grasping the knife tightly in her hand. The candles that lined the walls had been blown out. Those who could fit into the church followed her while the others stood in a united crowd outside. She saw the altar had been moved and walked towards the hole, terrified of what she might find. She climbed down the ladder and saw nothing but darkness.

"Aldara?" She called out.

"Almara, Aldara," Jarek snickered but she could not see him. "Not a coincidence then, I guess," he lit a candle beside him and she saw the heads of Aldara, Bassam, and Iapetus on the ground in front of her. Jarek was standing over their bodies on the other side of the room. She felt her heart drop again, for good this time.

"Our red eyes are bright," Jarek said. "Very noticeable when they're peaking through cracks in the floor," he began to laugh. "What? Nothing to say? C'mon Almara, you were so good at talking before. I was actually impressed, you sold your lie quite well."

Mom and Dad, give me the strength to fight him, she hoped they would. She was in shock, she couldn't even think of what to say.

"Well, if you're not gonna talk then I guess we'll just get this over with," Jarek said.

"This whole town will fight you, you can't beat us all," she finally got her words out.

Jarek laughed, "This should be fun. I hope you put up more of a fight than your sister."

CHAPTER TWELVE

Vieno was crouched down, looking under his bed. "Stay here. Don't come out unless I tell you to," he said to his sister, Delia, who was shaking furiously under the bed.

"Stay here with me," Delia begged her brother.

"I'm sorry, I can't. I have to see what's going on out there. But I'll be back, I promise." He slowly pulled his hand away from hers and blew out the candle before leaving the room. He left their house and immediately heard screams in the distance. The town of Neverwich was in an uproar.

"We don't follow you!" Vieno heard someone scream as he neared the crowd. Flames erupted from the church as he set his sights on it. He studied the crowd of people who yelled in revolt as the church slowly burnt to the ground. Nearly everyone in Neverwich joined the uprising.

"You're a false prince!" One man had the courage to yell as

someone was sent flying out of the flames. The crowd parted as he flew out, all of them trying their best to dodge the man. His body collided with one woman, however, and she banged her head on a small rock after being taken off her feet. Vieno saw blood pour from the back of her head and quickly form a puddle around her lifeless body. After eyeing the two bodies, the crowd stepped back over them and once again formed a united front at the steps of the church.

Vieno turned his gaze back towards the burning church, where their enemy now emerged from. Prince Jarek stepped out and smiled at the crowd.

"You're evil!" A woman yelled.

"Yes… I am evil," Jarek laughed. "I'm gonna enjoy this."

Screams came from behind Jarek. Two burning men ran out of the church. Jarek hurled them into the crowd of rebels. The townspeople began to panic as the fire spread among them. Vieno watched numerous horrified faces seize up as the fire started making its way up their bodies. Most of them escaped the crowd and frantically rolled on the ground, while the others decided to charge towards Jarek. The crowd acted like a pack of hyenas, knocking the evil prince to the ground.

Vieno rushed over to join the crowd of people who had just formed a pile on top of Jarek. He started sprinting towards them but stopped in his tracks when a man was thrown out of the pile. Vieno quickly jumped to the left and dodged the man but then froze. He stood still as the man got up beside him. He knew the man. It was Mikula, the town blacksmith. On multiple occasions, Vieno spotted him leaving the forge looking like he was on the verge of a nervous breakdown. His hair was always messy and Vieno had never seen him clean shaven. On top of that, he had numerous burns all over his body. Although, in the heat of the battle, Mikula looked worse than ever. Vieno assumed he was used to getting burnt in his forge but Mikula currently looked like he had been to Hell and back.

Mikula's arm was still on fire as he looked at Vieno. Skin was peeled off half of his face and replaced with sand.

"Fight with me!" The burnt Mikula said to Vieno before he charged back into the pile.

Vieno was horrified. Mikula had gone back into Hell.

Vieno watched Mikula force his way through the pile to get closer to Jarek. He threw a woman out of the pile, giving Vieno a hole to see through. Mikula had charged in with the passion of a brave warrior but clearly did not have the skills of one. Jarek immediately grabbed him by the neck with his left hand and reached into his body with his right. Vieno's mouth widened as Jarek's hand pierced through Mikula's chest and ripped out his heart. In one swift motion, Jarek once again threw Mikula out of the pile before grabbing more people and performing the exact same move. All the while, the townsfolk of Neverwich were stabbing at him furiously, although none of their stabs stopped the powerful Jarek.

As the hole was once again covered, Vieno decided not to join the suicide pile and instead headed towards the burning church. He heard screams of agony coming from the pile behind him. He couldn't make himself look back though, he didn't want to see anymore of his neighbours get massacred. Instead, he crouched beside the fiery wall at the side of the church in an attempt to hide.

In an odd way, the heat of the flames actually helped to comfort him. He closed his eyes and took a few deep breaths.

Upon opening his eyes, he examined the church and noticed the holes which the flames had created in its foundation. He peeked through the largest hole and essentially saw the new graveyard of Neverwich. The hole looked into the basement of the church, a once sacred place, now consumed by flames. Vieno watched the fire erupt around their bodies and knew that Neverwich would not win this battle.

Vieno looked back towards the angry mob. Just moments ago he had heard screams of rage and saw rumblings coming from the pile, but now all was silent and still. He watched intently, hoping anyone would stand up from the pile and declare victory over Jarek. When he finally saw movement, he knew exactly who it was. Jarek made an opening in the corpses and pulled himself out of the pile.

The people who had decided not to join the pile were now scattered across town. Vieno could see a few of them on the street, cowering before the blood-soaked Jarek. It seemed as though they were stuck in place as they watched their enemy approach. Vieno was glad Jarek never looked back and locked eyes with him, as he didn't know if he would have the strength to face him.

Finally, one brave man came out of his trance and charged towards Jarek with his sword held high. Jarek grabbed hold of his hand, making him drop the sword, before sending him flying through the window of a nearby house. He proceeded to attack the other townspeople with the blade. Vieno watched in awe as Jarek leapt from person to person, gracefully killing them with swift swings of the sword. It was as though Jarek was a painter and the sandy ground of Neverwich was his canvas. Blood continued to drip from his sword as he jumped through the air.

After only a few moments everyone on the main street of Neverwich was dead. Jarek's masterpiece was complete. As he walked towards the inn, he grabbed a few torches and flung them into buildings. Smoke polluted the air and blood soiled the ground.

Only moments after Jarek walked into the inn, a large man came crashing through its wall. As Morton laid helpless on the ground, his lady-friend Betsey ran out of the inn on foot. Behind her, Jarek slowly walked out onto the main road.

"Run as fast as you can, Betsey!" Jarek called out to her. "Although, judging by your appearance, you won't make it that far before the firefangs come running," he laughed to himself before locking eyes with Morton.

"Oh, Morton, you really pissed your pants, didn't you?"

"Please, let me go," Morton began to sob as Jarek knelt down beside him.

"I'm sorry, Morton, but you lied to me." In a swift motion Jarek extended his arm and ripped out Morton's throat, causing blood to drench his own face. Jarek laughed as he bathed in the blood, but his smile disappeared as an arrow pierced through his chest.

Jarek quickly looked down at the arrow before locating the shooter. Vieno squinted and managed to move a few steps closer, trying to spot the face of the valiant shooter through the smoke.

"Damn kids," Jarek said as he pulled the arrow out of his chest. Vieno's heart dropped. Some of the smoke cleared and he too spotted the shooter. It was a young girl.

Delia.

"NO!!!" Vieno screamed as the dark prince locked eyes with his sister. Jarek glanced at him and laughed before darting towards Delia. Delia quickly dropped the bow and escaped into the alleyway behind her. Vieno sprinted down the bloody street, following them both. He didn't see either of them in the alley so he kept running. He heard the screams of his sister in the distance and continually shooed the smoke away, hoping he would see her.

"Delia!" He screamed as he stood in a thick cloud of smoke. He had completely lost his sense of direction and couldn't see his surroundings. "Where are you?!" He felt lost in his own town and completely powerless against the threat he was facing.

"Vieno!" He finally heard her high-pitched scream behind him and immediately started running in that direction. After only a few steps he felt the heat of the burning house in front of him. Without any hesitation he decided to take a shortcut through the house. He let out a few coughs before he began to hold his breath. He held onto the hot wall as he guided himself to the back of the house. His throat began to swell up as he forced himself not to breathe and his eyes were boiling. He closed his eyes as he charged through the bedroom door and opened them to the sight of a half-burnt woman crawling towards him.

"Help me!" She screamed at him through a withered throat. She crawled towards him with the speed summoned in a life or death situation. She grasped his ankle with her hand and continued to beg for help. Another scream overshadowed hers, however, and Vieno surprised even himself after he kicked the dying woman off of him and headed towards the window.

"Vieno!" He heard Delia scream again. He grabbed the candlestick which sat on the bedside table and used it to shatter the glass. Vieno hopped out of the window, leaving the screaming women behind. With every scream her voice grew drier.

He raced through yet another cloud of smoke until he finally spotted the sinister figure. Jarek stood with his back facing Vieno and Delia stood across from him, ferociously hissing at her attacker.

"Cute fangs!" Jarek said as Vieno snuck up behind him. Before Jarek had time to react, Vieno raised the candlestick and hit him on the side of the head. Jarek stumbled to the side and without hesitation Delia leapt forward and wrapped her legs around his neck. Jarek moved back and forth, trying to free himself of the young vampire suffocating him, but failed to get her off him. Vieno watched in awe of his sister as Jarek's eyes began to close. They would shoot open for a moment before shutting again. It was clear the all-powerful prince of The Ash was struggling. The whole town of Neverwich had tried to take him down but failed. Vieno would have never guessed that his own little sister would be the one to finish what they started.

Vieno let out a smile as Jarek's eyes remained closed for the longest time yet. He dropped the candlestick and allowed himself a deep breath of relief. That was a mistake. In an instant, Jarek's eyes shot open and this time they were redder, filled with more anger and rage than before. He clenched his fist and sent it flying up at Delia. Her head shook from the punch but she kept her tight grip around him. In a flash, Jarek shot three more punches her way. Delia managed to dodge the first two but the third hit her in the centre of her nose. This punch stunned her, she leaned upwards and looked at the night sky. Jarek took advantage of her vulnerable state and reached up to pull her intestines out of her stomach.

Delia looked down from the sky. She didn't look at Jarek, even though he was her enemy, she looked right at Vieno. The ferociousness that she jumped on Jarek with had vanished. He screamed as he watched her face turn pale before finally falling off the dark prince. In a flash, Jarek grabbed the candlestick off the ground and bashed her skull in. Vieno fell to his knees as Jarek stepped away from Delia. He crawled over to be with his sister's body and held on tight. He felt as though holding her body would save him from the monster who was standing above. It wouldn't. Jarek watched on as he grieved his fallen sister. He was her brother, her protector, but he failed.

"Y- you killed her," Vieno replied, not even looking up at Jarek.

"I'm sorry about that, I really am. The way she leapt at me… no one in this town has been that brave. Good for her."

Vieno immediately stood up and faced his sister's murderer. "How can you say that?! She's dead now!"

"Good for you too… that hit made my vision blurry. Come here, kid," Vieno didn't move so Jarek took a step forward and grabbed him by the neck. "Where are your parents?"

"They died three years ago… they were killed on the way home from Odavell… your home."

"I'm sorry to hear that. But you know what, Odavell should be your home too," Jarek's red eyes looked Vieno up and down. "You seem strong. Why aren't you fighting with us?"

"Your father is the reason this world is dying!"

"So everyone in this town was against us?" Jarek asked.

"We won't be led by the likes of you!"

Jarek laughed, "Good thing I took care of that. What's your name?"

Vieno didn't want to answer but knew Jarek would not accept his silence. "Vieno," he said quietly after a few moments.

"Well Vieno, it might just be your lucky day. If I let you go, will you go east to search for your saviour?"

"I promise you I won't... I'll hide in a corner of this world and you'll never see me again."

"No... I don't want you to do that," Jarek said. "Go east, find your saviour, join that side of the war, but tell them I let you live."

"W- w- why would you let me go?"

"Because you're going to deliver a message for me," Vieno's eyes opened wide as Jarek whispered his message. He had only a moment to look at his sister before Jarek pushed him away. He looked into Jarek's red eyes and began to run eastward.

"Wait!" Jarek called out to him, causing him to turn around. "I want you to know... I truly am sorry about your sister. I'm letting you go today because I know the pain you're feeling. But when we meet again, be better prepared to face me... or you'll end up just like her."

Vieno immediately turned around again and continued to run, knowing the evil prince was laughing at him as he went.

CHAPTER THIRTEEN

Fire lit up the sky. Jason heard footsteps in the distance, they were charging towards him. He knew exactly what was coming. Firefangs, terrifying beasts who could smell blood from miles away. Jason saw the pack of them approach in the firelight. They had no eyes but could smell and hear their prey. Their mouths covered their whole face, aside from a small nose above it. As the pack approached Jason, he saw that they had dark brown fur. The leader of the pack took a few steps forward and hissed at him, revealing its teeth, which held venom capable of burning through skin. They could rip Jason apart in seconds if they wanted to but he knew he was not their target. He was bleeding a little from the girl's arrow and had some blood on his face but not enough to draw them to him. The firefangs began to devour the dead bodies which were lying in puddles of blood. Soon after the pack approached, he heard the flapping of wings and knew bladewings had followed them. Bladewings shared the fire-fang's scorching teeth but also had wings that were sharp enough to slice someone in half. Jason watched as more landed on the buildings to join their friends with four legs in their feast.

Jason saw a horse tied up at the side of a house and walked towards it. The horse was lucky the house had not been part of the fire. He rode the horse past the beasts which had taken over Neverwich and headed west. It was time to go home.

Jason rode through the mountain pass and through the streets of Roguerun as the sun began to rise. The city of Roguerun lived in the shadow of the Odavell Kingdom, the most secure stronghold in the world and home to the deadliest vampire army The Ash had ever known. The citizens of Roguerun never had to worry about anything as they were always protected. Therefore, they spent their time enjoying the pleasures of life. As Jason rode through the city, he heard the joyful screams of women dancing in alleyways and saw men gambling in the streets. Even the guards had their fun, they laughed at and mocked the shop-keepers after children stole pieces of fruit. People did what they wanted in Roguerun, the only rule was to serve their king.

Jason exited the city and approached the gates of the king-dom. The gates stretched fifty feet into the sky. Looming over them, Jason could see the Ten Towers of Odavell. His chambers were in the Amber Tower. This tower was named for the time the Vampire King Aramis defeated the rebel Hermanus in a battle that lasted fifty days on the Hissing Plains. After single-hand-edly killing twenty thousand men on his own and winning the battle, Aramis took Hermanus' wife Amber for himself. Amber was known to be the most beautiful vampire in The Ash. It was said that Aramis was never seen on the way back from the Hissing Plains, he only wanted to spend time with Amber in his carriage. Aramis was in lust, but Amber was not. On their third night together she tried to stab him but he caught the blade. He was so overcome with anger that he dragged her on the back of his horse all the way to Odavell and hung her from the walls. She stayed there, rotting and decaying, for fifty days until Aramis had her taken down. In the end, Aramis thought of her as his trophy from the battle and named this tower after her. Over the next twenty years of his reign, Aramis would take a new trophy every time he went to battle.

The gates swung open and horns began to blow as Jason approached.

"My prince," Feivel, Israfil's messenger, beckoned him through the gate.

"Where's my father?" Jason asked.

"He's in The Fortress. We were not expecting you, my prince."

"I won't be here for long," Jason said as he rode up the staircase towards The Fortress, a wide, circular building which stood in the centre of Odavell.

The Fortress was made up of an outer layer and an inner layer. The outer layer was a hallway which led around the perimeter of the building and had an entrance to the towers on its left and right side. The inner layer was the throne room. Jason walked right past the guards and approached his father. Israfil was sitting proudly on his throne. The seat was massive but the vampire king filled it with ease. Jason's grandmother, Sadia, stood on his left.

"Leave us," Israfil said to his mother. Dark red veins flowed past Israfil's collar and to his forehead. Not the usual markings of a vampire, but Israfil contained more power than a vampire was meant to. The veins throbbed repeatedly, showing Jason that the power coursing through him was strong.

Sadia took her leave without saying a word. She also had red veins running up and down her body.

Jason approached the throne and his father stood up. Israfil towered over Jason. His father grabbed him by the shoulders with a tight grip, "Son, you look hurt."

Jason laughed, "I'm not hurt. The town of Neverwich turned against us. Every single person. I came here hunting four traitors and it turned out they were hiding there."

"Did you handle the situation?" His father sat back down.

"Yes, Neverwich is no more. Almost everyone is dead and half the town is burnt down."

"Almost everyone is dead?"

"Yes."

"Why not everyone?" Israfil asked, this time in a booming voice.

"You want everyone dead? Then do it yourself."

"What did you just say?" Jason and Israfil locked eyes, each with a forbidding stare. It was clear Israfil was waiting for an apology but Jason would not give him that satisfaction. After waiting a few moments Israfil ended the silence, "Why are you here?"

"I need a few more months, then we will rally our army and conquer Earth," Jason had put off the invasion of Earth for a long time and he continued to do so.

"You know, people have started to say that you've come to love the people of Earth, that you've grown soft."

"That's not true. Ask Freya, ask anyone who's there with

me, we're just being careful. This will be the greatest war ever fought in the history of both our worlds. We have the advantage because they don't know we're coming. We could start the invasion today but that would lead to the death of many of our people. That's why I have vampires travelling the world, learning about their weapons. While we will inevitably defeat them, the people of Earth should not be underestimated."

"Okay," Israfil interrupted him. "You don't need to explain yourself to me. I trust you. I know you would never betray your people… especially for a woman."

Jason thought of Monica. "You know, Father, a lot of people would say that you're the one who's actually betraying our people."

"Watch your mouth," Israfil gripped the armrests of his throne.

"I'm there, figuring out a solution for our people, while you're here, hiding in your throne room."

Israfil burst off his throne and grabbed Jason by the neck. "I told you to watch your mouth." Israfil's power dwarfed Jason but he was not scared. Instead he found it funny. "Stop laughing!" His father screamed at him but Jason did not stop. Israfil threw him across the room.

Jason slowly lifted himself off the ground. "Father, you really have to learn to control your anger. Why do our chats always end with us fighting?"

"Because you don't know your place," Israfil charged towards Jason, grabbed him once more and threw him back across the room.

Jason sat at the foot of the throne as Israfil approached. "Okay, Father, I'm sorry. I'm just trying to help you," Jason used the throne to pull himself up. "You claim to be the most powerful king this world has ever seen… but this world is almost dead. Your reign here is almost over. What will become of Earth?" Jason glanced at the throne.

"I will take that world and make everyone bow down to me," his father responded.

"But you're not taking that world, are you? I am."

Israfil laughed. "You think you would be a better ruler than me? Look at you, you're weak," Israfil pushed Jason out of the way and sat back down on his throne. "Don't let the power you have in that world get to your head. Sure, a small group of vampires respect you, but you would never be able to lead the vampires of The Ash. They respect strength, this whole world fears me, and look at you, all bruised and beaten from your fight in Neverwich. No one would ever betray me like they betrayed you. Enjoy the power you have now, Son, because when I enter Earth you will be reduced to the insignificant piece of filth you really are. I don't care if you're my son… you're weak, and I expect you to die long before I do. You will never be a vampire king."

"Why don't you come now then?" Jason said. "Come to Earth, take away my power and take their world, see how that works out for you."

"As much as I would love to come meet your wife and son," Israfil spat on the floor. "Now is not the time, just like you said. I still have unfinished business here."

"You're right, Father. Twenty years ago Neverwich would never dare to turn against us, but now they did. Why's that?"

"You know why."

"The rebellion growing in the east. I thought you said no one would ever dare betray you."

"You know exactly why that rebellion formed! And as always, it's my job to clean up your mess."

"Okay, Father, you continue ruling your dying world while I go back and help us build a new, thriving kingdom," Jason began to walk away.

"Wait," his father said as he made his way towards him. "You're confident enough to say anything to me right now, good for you. You're useful now, but you won't always be, you should remember that for your own sake. You should remember your brother... then maybe you'll think twice about making me angry," Israfil picked Jason up and threw him out of the throne room. Jason flew out of The Fortress and rolled down the stairs.

"You should heed the words of your king," his grandmother stood a few steps above him.

He got up and locked eyes with her. "I really should come visit you guys more often, it's always such fun!"

He led his horse back through the gates of Odavell and the city of Roguerun. He looked back at his father's kingdom before entering the mountain pass. He grew up there, but now was the first time he did not consider it to be his home. He smiled and rode on, back towards the portal.

Time to go home.

CHAPTER FOURTEEN

Sam watched an arrow soar through the air and hit the bulls-eye, joining three other arrows. Chelsea stood beside Sam holding her bow proudly.

"Wow!" Sam was speechless. Even though Chelsea was only twelve she had the skill of a world-renowned warrior.

"Wanna try?" Chelsea held the bow out to Sam.

"Hold on a sec," Abe said, walking out of the house. "That would just be a waste of time. Sam needs to learn how to shoot with a gun, not with a bow."

"It doesn't hurt to try the bow," Chelsea told her grandfather. "I wanna see him try it!" She smiled at Sam.

"Chelsea, no bow. We don't have a lot of time."

"Until what?" Sam asked.

"The end of the world," Abe began to laugh as he headed towards the shed.

Sam let out a yawn as it was only 6am. He was sleeping peacefully in Abe's room, as Abe kindly offered to take the couch, when he was woken up at the crack of dawn.

"Training starts today!" Abe stood over the bed yelling.

They arrived at Abe's house, which was deep in The West Woods, last night. They turned off of Woods Drive and drove down a long, dirt road before they finally arrived at his house, which looked more like a small wooden cottage. Inside there was only a kitchen, living room, and two bedrooms all on the same floor. To the left of the house was a newly built garage, just three wooden walls and a tarp draping over the opening which was nailed to the roof. Beside that was a shed, inside of which sat Abe's most prized possession, a 1967 Mustang. Sam wouldn't know by looking that it was a 67' but Abe had already mentioned it five times.

"Are ya ready?" Abe walked out of the shed and gave Sam a handgun.

"Uhm..."

"Well I don't care if you're ready or not, ya gotta get ready," he pointed to the bottles lined up on the stand just twenty yards away. "Ya see those bottles?"

"Yeah."

Abe smacked Sam across the back of his head.

"What the-"

"Don't see them as bottles anymore. Those are vampires. They're coming after ya and ya have to kill them," he lifted up Sam's arms, making him point the gun in the right direction. "Take your shot."

"I don't-"

"Don't overthink it… just point and shoot."

Sam did not want to disappoint Abe so he focused on one of the bottles. He tried to listen to Abe's advice and think of a vampire's red eyes glaring back at him, but all he could see was the red Coca-Cola label on the bottle. He fired the gun… no glass shattered.

Abe grabbed the gun out of his hand and held it to Sam's head.

"What are-" Chelsea tried to intervene but Abe cut her off.

"You were tackled by a vampire that night. If you were trained and prepared that wouldn't have happened. That vampire is coming at ya again, think about it, nothing else. It's you or the monster," he handed the gun back to Sam.

Sam pointed the gun at the bottle again. He thought of not just red eyes, but the red eyes he saw. The red eyes that could have killed him. He still did not know why that vampire chose not to kill him, all he knew was that he wouldn't give it another chance. He fired… and missed.

Abe kicked him in the shin and grabbed the gun out of his hand again. Sam began to bend down to grab hold of his aching shin but hesitated, not wanting to show weakness.

"Fight through the pain," Abe barked as Sam was already bringing himself back up. He pointed the gun at Sam's head once again.

"Grandpa!" Chelsea screamed.

"You're dead now, Sam! You obviously don't care about your life, ya can't even make a twenty yard shot at something that's not even moving," Abe yelled at Sam.

"Just give me a few more shots!" Sam yelled back.

"You won't get a few more shots! When we're out there hunting these things, they're not gonna stop and let ya kill them!"

"I know that!"

"Then why aren't ya making the shot?!"

"Give me the gun!"

Abe handed Sam the gun, "It's life or death, Sam, make the shot!"

Sam didn't see the bottle. He saw red eyes charging towards him. *Life or death,* he told himself. He glanced at Abe for a moment but then looked away. No distractions. He would use all his anger to make the shot. The vampire came closer, Sam aimed, closer, Sam tightened his grip, closer, now only twenty yards away. Sam shot.

He felt a sharp pain in his other shin and fell to the ground.

"What the hell!" He heard Abe yelling at him.

"Grandpa! Stop!"

"Chelsea, go inside!"

Abe ripped the gun out of Sam's hand and pointed it at him, "Get up!"

I can't do it, Sam felt like lying on that patch of grass forever but forced himself up.

"Like I said, you obviously don't care about your own life. What about your mom's life?"

"What did you just say?!" Sam's fear of getting hit again didn't stop him from screaming at Abe.

Abe pointed the gun at the bottle. "That vampire is coming for your mom, you are the only thing that can save her!" Abe handed the gun back to Sam. "Remember, Sam, you're not just doing this for you, you're doing this to protect the people ya love. That vampire is about to kill the person ya love most. Save your mother!"

Sam looked beside him and saw his mom. *You can't be a*

part of this, he thought. *But I am,* she responded to him, crying. Sam followed her teary eyes and saw the vampire charging towards her. His life did not matter anymore. Her life was his only priority. He pointed the gun at the bloodthirsty vampire and without hesitation fired.

He missed.

"Ya just killed your mom," Abe said to him.

"No I didn't!" Sam yelled.

"Ya killed yourself and ya killed your mom! Who else are ya gonna let die?!"

"No one's dead!"

"Soon everyone will be dead! Unless ya do something about it! Who else are ya gonna let die?!" Abe repeated.

"No one!"

"I don't believe ya!"

"I don't care!"

"Who else, Sam?" Abe paused. "How 'bout Sarah?"

Sam no longer saw the Coca-Cola bottle as a vampire. It wasn't his enemy anymore… Abe was. He turned and pointed the gun at Abe.

"Don't talk about her!" He screamed.

"Sam!" Chelsea switched to yelling at him.

"Why not talk about her?" Abe asked. "Listen to me, Sam, if we don't kill these vampires… she will die."

"No she won't!" Sam screamed but didn't know if he was telling the truth. *Can I keep her safe?*

"She won't if ya protect her!" Abe said. "So point the gun back at the bottle… and kill the vampire."

Sam suddenly lost all his strength and dropped the gun. *I can't keep her safe,* he finally admitted to himself.

"What are ya doing?" Abe asked.

"I can't."

"What do ya mean ya can't?"

"I can't do this." Sam felt a tear running down his face.

Abe backhanded Sam across the cheek, sending him flying to the ground. He hit the ground and couldn't pick himself back up. Soon his mom and Sarah would join him… because he can't protect them. Westwood will be a town of corpses. The biggest graveyard in the world.

"We're all gonna die because of you!" Abe looked down at him, screaming. "You're weak! Just 'cause ya can't make one shot you're gonna give up."

"Just leave me alone! That's all I ever wanted you to do, leave me alone."

"I thought you'd be better. Maybe you were right, Chelsea, maybe we're better off on our own," Abe said as he walked towards his house.

Sam looked over at Chelsea, who was consumed with guilt, then watched Abe as he walked away. Suddenly bullets flew past Sam and he heard the shattering of glass. One, two, three, four, five. Abe stopped in his tracks and looked over at the bottles. None were left standing. Both Sam and Abe looked at Chelsea in awe. She held the smoking gun at her waist, like she was in a standoff in the Wild West.

"You need to get better," she pointed at Sam. "And you," she looked at her grandfather. "You need to grow up."

Chelsea, the archer, Hannah Montana fan, and cowgirl, walked towards the shed.

"So you didn't want me to join you guys?" Abe locked himself in the basement so Sam thought this was the perfect opportunity to talk with Chelsea. Sam sat beside her on a log outside of the shed.

"Don't take it personally," she said. "We have a job to do, we just can't have anyone holding us back."

"You think I'm holding you back?"

Chelsea laughed. "That's a joke, right? I know you're holding us back. It's obvious you are."

"Maybe I sh-"

"But you won't be for long," Chelsea interrupted him. "Don't worry about my grandpa. He wanted you to be perfect, like some kind of war hero," she laughed. "I kept telling him that you were just a kid but he wouldn't listen."

"You kept telling him that I'm just a kid? You're just a kid."

"I'm not a kid."

Now it was Sam's turn to laugh, "Look at you, you're half my size."

"Don't flatter yourself, you're not that tall."

"Fair enough. But still, you're only twelve. No matter what you say, you're just a kid."

"See that water bottle over there?" She pointed to a plastic water bottle sitting on the porch steps.

"Yeah."

Chelsea pulled out her gun and fired a shot which sent Sam jumping off the log. When he composed himself and looked over he no longer saw a water bottle, just a puddle of water forming on the steps.

"Who cares what I look like, how 'bout what I do? So am I still a kid?"

Sam didn't answer until Chelsea pointed the gun at him. "Woah, no, you're definitely not a kid."

Chelsea laughed. "You don't have to be scared, I'm not gonna shoot you. Not yet at least," she winked at him.

Sam let out a fake chuckle but was still a little shaken. He admitted to himself that he was terrified of this little girl. "You said I won't be holding you back for long... what did you mean by that?" Sam sat back down beside Chelsea.

"We're gonna start fighting vampires soon," she smiled. "You're gonna either die or be able to defend yourself under pressure. Either way, you're not gonna be holding us back for long," she winked again and walked away, leaving Sam in bewilderment.

As Sam walked into the basement, a foul stench forced him to plug his nose.

"The Demons are down 9-6 here in the ninth inning," Sam heard the rigid voice of an announcer as he walked further down the basement steps. "A grand slam could win the game," the announcer continued. "All the pressure is on Gonzalez as he steps up to the plate."

The last step creaked as Sam put his weight on it, causing Abe to quickly turn off the tape recorder he was holding.

"What's that smell?" Sam asked.

Abe placed the tape recorder on the table and lifted a tarp, revealing a rotten corpse. Sam stumbled back to the stairs, horrified by the visual of a body missing its legs sprawled across the tabletop. Its head tilted sideways and its dead, familiar eyes stared directly at Sam.

"T- that's th- the vampire that attacked me."

"Ya don't say," Abe responded. "This story is starting to make a little more sense then."

Sam regained his composure and neared the table. "Did you kill it?"

"Someone certainly did… this is the body that fell onto the road that night," Abe replied.

I knew it. No one believed me.

"Consider this your welcome to the team present. Don't say I never gave ya anything," Abe snickered.

Sam remained silent.

"Sorry for trying to joke around a bit. Look… I'm sorry for what happened out there. I just need ya to take this seriously."

Sam finally looked away from the corpse. "You don't think I'm taking this seriously?"

"Ya didn't make the shot. When we start hunting these things, if ya miss your shot you're dead. Even worse, ya put me and Chelsea in danger. I can't have that."

Sam laughed.

"What are ya laughing at?"

"You say you can't have me putting Chelsea in danger, meanwhile you're the one who trained her to hunt vampires."

"Yeah I did… and I trained her well. Do you think she can hold her own in a fight?"

"Definitely."

"Then she's not in danger. She knows what we're up against and she's prepared for that. I wouldn't let her do this if she wasn't ready. I know what it feels like to not be ready."

"What do you mean?"

"Shake my hand first," Abe extended his hand and Sam

shook it. "You've entered a dangerous profession," Abe laughed. "You're gonna get hurt, you're gonna get scared, and we're gonna butt heads. That was our first fight and it won't be our last, if ya can't set aside our differences and focus on our goal I need ya to leave right now," he waited a moment but Sam didn't move. "Good. The first thing ya have to understand is fighting vampires isn't about how strong your body is, it's about how strong your will is. They'll knock ya down but ya have to get up. The moment ya give up is the moment ya lose, do ya understand?"

"Yes."

"So are ya still upset?"

"No."

"Good. Now pull up a stool." Sam sat on the stool across the table from Abe. "Let's talk about your father."

CHAPTER FIFTEEN

"That's him," Ben said to Abe whilst pointing at the man dressed all in black. Clouds began to form above them, it was as if the vampire Jarek used his evil powers to exile the sun. Abe watched as Ben reached behind them and picked up his AK-47.

"Are ya sure about this?" Abe questioned Ben.

"If we don't do this, no one will."

"There's at least ten of them in that cave though, and chances are there's more than we think."

"He took everything from me," Ben looked at Jarek as if he was staring at the Devil. "Are you with me?"

"Of course I am, just one sec," Abe grabbed their pee bottle and began relieving himself. Stalking vampires was hard, patient work so they had to come prepared. After spending almost fifteen hours in the thick bushes of The West Woods, the pee bottle was now almost filled to the brim.

"You gotta do that right now?!" Ben stared, ashamed of his partner.

"If I'm about to die I'm gonna take a piss first. Last thing I wanna do is die with a full bladder."

Ben shook his head and waited for Abe to finish. Abe tightened his belt back up and gave Ben the nod. They both got up and stepped out from behind the bush, revealing themselves to the Devil.

"Ben!" Jarek did not look surprised that they were there, he acted like a welcoming host.

"This ends today," Ben slowly approached Jarek, keeping the gun pointed at his head.

"It's a shame, but I guess you're right," Jarek said. "I like playing with you, feeling your anger brings me so much joy… but all good things must come to an end I suppose," he whistled and a swarm of vampires charged out of the cave. "If you think you know what you're up against, you're dumber than I thought."

Abe saw panic ensue in Ben as he looked from side to side at the wall of vampires which had formed behind Jarek.

"Don't look at them," Jarek took a step towards Ben. "Look at me. Look into my eyes."

"Don't take another step!" Abe screamed, causing Jarek to turn towards him and let out a hiss. Abe's heart felt like it was about to burst out of his chest. He knew they could not take on all these vampires but he wouldn't give up, he would fight and die for Ben.

"You're both scared, I can sense your fear," Jarek laughed.

"I'm not scared of you," Ben whispered under his breath.

"Oh, you're not? You should be… your wife is."

"Don't say that!"

"Don't be angry at me, Ben. You don't have to worry about her, she won't be scared for long. Soon she'll learn to love me and all her fears will go away."

"I'm gonna kill you!"

"Do it then! Stop taunting me with that gun and do it already, pull the trigger."

Without hesitation Ben fired and it was over in an instant. The bullet pierced through Jarek's head and he would collapse at any moment, but he didn't. Abe watched on for what seemed like an eternity but Jarek never fell. When Abe finally let himself blink, he saw the bullet hole in the tree directly behind Jarek. When the shot had been fired, Jarek moved so fast that none of them saw him avoid the bullet. Ben watched in awe but quickly lifted his gun once more. Abe followed his lead and Jarek leapt into the air as they started firing at the wall of vampires. They began to charge both Abe and Ben. Abe continued firing, some vampires fell but most kept coming as if they were unfazed by the frenzy of bullets. Abe couldn't hold them back and got tackled by four of them. As he went down he saw Ben being thrown to the ground beside him. Abe pushed his finger down on the trigger and was determined to never let go. He felt the vampires vibrating overtop him as the bullets flew through them. Finally three of the vampires rolled off of him and he was left to fend off one more. Its fangs were ready to pierce his skin until a bullet flew through its head.

Ben stood over him with a smoking gun. He helped Abe off the ground, "Shooting them in the body is no good, you gotta aim for the head."

Abe looked at the annihilated corpses which had surrounded him. "Yeah, unless we shoot them all fifty times."

Ben pointed his gun at the cave, awaiting more of them, but none came. Abe looked through the thick woods behind them and saw their enemy. Jarek stood fifty feet away from them, completely still. "Ben, we gotta get out of here."

"Leave then," Ben pushed back Abe and walked towards Jarek.

"Ben, don't."

"He dies today," Ben looked back and Abe saw a single tear fall from his eye.

"I don't think he does, Ben… we do. We need to rethink this."

"I've already thought about this enough. I'm done thinking," Ben continued his pursuit and Abe had no choice but to follow.

They were thirty feet away from him. Jarek whistled. Abe looked back at the cave expecting to see more vampires charging out of it, but none came.

Twenty feet. Jarek whistled. Abe looked back again. Ben wasn't concerned, he remained focused on Jarek.

Ten feet. Jarek whistled. Abe looked back. Ben walked forward.

"Ben," Abe remained slightly further back as Ben stood just five feet from Jarek.

"Shoot," Jarek said. Without hesitation Ben fired another shot. Jarek ducked and hit the gun out of Ben's hands before grabbing him by the neck. "Don't!" Jarek screamed at Abe as he held his friend in the air. Abe kept himself from shooting, but his finger remained on the trigger.

"Shoo-" Ben could hardly speak while in Jarek's grasp.

"It won't work," Abe responded.

"Listen to your friend, Ben," Jarek said. "He's obviously got more brains than you."

"Just let him go," Abe begged.

"Okay," he threw Ben across the forest, into the cave, then looked back at Abe. Jarek whistled. He leapt into the air while a dozen vampires fell from the sky. Abe had been looking towards the cave the whole time but they had been in the trees. Before he had time to react, he felt a smack across the back of his head.

Darkness. Darkness surrounded him. But then he saw light.

Abe opened his eyes and saw a red glow. He looked from side to side and through the glow made out the rocky walls of the cavern. His hands were tied behind his back.

"Abe," Ben knelt beside him, also tied up.

"Ben."

"I'm sorry, Abe."

"You've been looking for answers, Ben. Here are your answers," Jarek's voice echoed as he emerged from the red glow. Abe could not make out his facial features but could see his eyes, his red eyes, glaring at them in front of the complementing glow. "This is my home, this is the portal to The Ash." Four more vampires walked through the portal and Abe heard more footsteps approaching from behind.

"ALL HAIL PRINCE JAREK!" The vampires in front and behind them knelt.

"ALL HAIL THE ROYAL FAMILY!"

"Who are you?" Ben asked.

"Prince of The Ash," Jarek laughed. "And you thought you could beat me."

"What's The Ash?"

"I'd love to show you but you're not gonna be that lucky. I

just thought, after all the energy you've wasted trying to destroy what I've built, that you deserved some answers before you die."

"You won't win," Ben said.

"I already have won. Bring me his friend." Two vampires picked Abe up and threw him at the feet of their prince.

"No!" Ben screamed. "Help!"

"You can scream all you want, Ben. No one's going to hear you. Anything you want to say to your friend before I rip his head off?" Jarek's warm hand gripped Abe by the back of his neck.

"Kill me. He didn't do anything wrong… let him live."

"I'm afraid I can't do that, nor would I want to. Seeing the pain in your eyes is far too fun."

Ben began to cry, "You won't win."

"You can keep saying that, but look around."

"You won't win."

Jarek pushed Abe to the ground and approached Ben. "I won. I'm gonna kill your friend, then I'm gonna kill you. Then your wife and son will join me."

"No they won't!" Ben screamed as he met Jarek's gaze.

Jarek grabbed Ben by the neck and picked him up. "If they don't… then I'll enjoy killing them too," he threw Ben back to the ground.

Abe felt the cave floor shake as Jarek walked back towards him. He watched the confidence in Jarek's eyes turn to fear. The ground was shaking. It didn't stop. Jarek turned around. Abe felt something moving beneath them, from the portal towards Ben.

"Grab him!" Jarek yelled, pointing at Ben. Rocks fell from the cave's ceiling. The shaking didn't stop. The vampires rushed towards Ben but were too slow. Whatever was moving beneath them had entered Ben. Abe watched as the red glow was diminished by a blue glow. The blue glow flowed through Ben as he burst out of his bindings and shot upwards, launching the vampires into the walls of the cave. The glow made it all the way up Ben's body and entered his eyes. His gleaming blue eyes met Jarek's red eyes, which did not seem as bright anymore.

Ben let out a scream and Jarek hissed. They both leapt towards each other and met in the air. The vampires scattered. Those who had not already been knocked over by Ben either escaped through the portal or followed the path leading out of the cave. Ben collided with Jarek. Blue collided with red. Abe flew back and hit the wall behind him. He was blinded by a bright flash and watched through squinted eyes as the two figures met in the air, before they both fell. All that was left was the red glow of the portal.

"Ben," Abe didn't know who was who but saw someone crawling towards the portal. Red eyes looked up at him. The red eyes of Jarek. But they were no longer the eyes that were determined to kill him. Jarek was fighting for breath… he was in pain. He grabbed hold of the stone of the portal and pulled himself through. In an instant he was gone.

"Ben," Abe stumbled towards the body which laid on the ground. "Ben?" No answer. "Ben?" A cold, faint breath escaped his mouth but he was not moving. "Stay with me, Ben," Abe picked him up and wrapped his arm around his shoulders as he led him out of the cave.

He didn't know where he was. He passed by the occasional torch but it still felt like he was wandering through a dimly lit maze. All he could do was grasp the wall and follow where it led him. He walked so far up that his legs felt like they were about to collapse. He reached an opening and put Ben down. He could see daylight through an entrance in the distance.

"Ben, ya have to wake up." He didn't.

"I can't carry ya any further." No movement.

"Ben," Abe fell to the ground beside his friend.

Just as Abe's eyes began to close he felt a gust of wind. He felt movement. He jumped up and saw Ben's eyes open. He saw his familiar eyes, not the glowing blue ones he had seen deep in the cave.

"Ben!"

"Abe, where are we?"

"In the cave, almost out of it now," he held out his weak arm and pointed at the light.

"Where is he?"

In another world, Abe thought. "Ya hurt him. Ya hurt him bad. But he's not gone, just far away. We have to get out of here, so we can live another day."

"No, we have to end this today."

"We can't. Ben, please listen to me. We have to live another day… so we can come back and kill him. We're gonna come back and kill all of them." That was a promise Abe intended to keep.

Abe and Ben walked out of the cave, into daylight. Their fight was not over though. They heard a hiss. One vampire scampered out of the cave behind them. Then two. Then three. Then ten.

"Go," Ben said to Abe.

"What do ya mean?"

"We both know who they're gonna come after."

"I'm not leaving ya."

"You have to."

"I won't."

"You will," Ben looked at Abe. "Please, I'm begging you. Who else will protect Sam and Monica?" He moved to his right, leading the vampires away from Abe.

"Please don't!" Abe screamed. Only two vampires crept towards him.

"Goodbye friend, and thanks," Ben began to run. That was Abe's cue, the vampires began to charge him and he ran too, abandoning his friend.

Abe swatted a fly away from his face. "I ran and didn't stop running. Luckily, I made it to Woods Drive and there was some traffic. The vampires didn't follow me onto the street, they wouldn't risk being caught."

"That was the last time you saw my dad?" Sam wiped a tear from his cheek.

"Yeah… I went back to the woods that night to look for him. That's when I found him at the bottom of the cliff. I didn't tell anybody, I couldn't."

"Didn't you think you should warn the police? The military?"

"Ya think they would believe me? Of course they wouldn't. Your dad wanted me to protect ya, so I had to be around to do that."

"Does that mean you've been watching me for the last fourteen years then?" Sam asked. "How? I've never noticed you until recently."

Abe's gaze remained on the body of the dead vampire in

front of them, "I've made a lot of mistakes, and I haven't always kept the promise I made to your father. But I'm here now, and I'm not going anywhere."

Abe focused entirely on studying the vampire on the table. Sam watched intently as Abe pointed out its red eyes, fangs, and nails, the three distinguishing points of a vampire.

"Are they at all similar to the vampires from the stories? The ones that suck blood and can't be near garlic?" Sam asked.

"No," Abe replied. "The vampires we're dealing with are different... they're stronger."

"Have you ever tried to use garlic, or even a wooden stake?"

Abe looked over at the tape recorder he was listening to when Sam first walked into the basement. "Yes, I have," he said longingly.

"So they can only be killed by shooting them in the head?" Sam asked.

"As far as I know, yeah. I assume any significant damage to their brain would work, whether from a bullet or another weapon, anything that can penetrate their skull."

"Are shots to the body just useless then?"

"They still feel pain but a shot to the head is the only guaranteed way to kill one... that's why ya need to hit the bottle."

It was dark when Sam left the basement. He stepped over the water bottle which Chelsea had shot earlier and walked to the edge of the property. As he investigated the dark forest that seemed to go on forever, he imagined his father's fear. Sam had only faced one vampire and stood no chance against it, his father was forced to face dozens. He looked out into the abyss of The West Woods and imagined seeing all those sets of red eyes.

I have to get better, he told himself. He had to fully commit.

He pulled out his phone and texted Sarah, "Can we meet up?"

CHAPTER SIXTEEN

"Where's Sam?"

"Gone."

Jason and Monica stood on separate ends of the kitchen. Jason had only arrived home from 'Seattle' ten minutes ago but was already questioning her.

"Is he at Sarah's?"

"No."

"Then where is he?"

"He's just gone. You should've known this would happen eventually. Did you think he would stay here forever? After everything that's happened, did you really think he would never look deeper into his father's death?" Monica was shaking.

Jason inched across the kitchen, eyes growing redder with each step. He grabbed hold of his wife and tried to resist his anger but could not. He let out a scream and threw her against the fridge. Monica fell to the floor, revealing a dent in the door of the fridge.

"Did you tell him?!" Jason stood over her.

"No!"

"Why's he gone then?"

"I don't know! I don't know what he found out or how he found it out. I just came home yesterday and he was gone."

Jason studied Monica. "He's gonna die. You know that, right? I don't know who he's working with… but they'll all die." Monica grabbed hold of the counter and pulled herself up, crying. "I leave for a few days and you let this happen. Do you have anything to say?"

"No."

"Then get out of my sight," Monica left the kitchen and Jason's eyes locked onto a picture which had fallen off the fridge. A picture of him and Sam.

Who is he working with? Jason remembered Dishon telling him about the old man, disguised as a police officer from Quarryview, who had been searching for the body in The West Woods.

But they told me they killed him.

Jason blinked and saw a flash of blue. He opened his eyes and was back in the cave, right beside the portal. He was about to kill Abe but then heard the rumbling. It was coming from the portal, something was moving beneath him. The rumbling stopped when it reached Ben. Jason watched as the blue shine entered Ben's body. It moved through his veins and Jason felt fear for the first time since he had come to Earth. He collided with Ben in the air and felt all his power get sucked out of him.

He wasn't Prince of The Ash. He wasn't Jarek. He was just

Jason. He knew what it felt like to be a human. He was powerless.

He had survived. But barely.

Jason blinked again. He was back home, looking at the picture of him and Sam.

I have to beat him.

He was now scared for the second time since coming to Earth. He had to do something now. He walked out the back door.

Monica was curled up in a ball on her bed, an all-too-familiar position. She could do nothing but watch as her life fell apart in front of her. She knew the end was coming. The end of her. The end of Sam. The end of everything and everyone.

She heard the back door slam.

Monica rushed to the backyard and swung open the door, "Where are you going?"

"Get back inside!" Jason turned around and pointed towards the house.

"It's only nine. Why are you leaving?" They almost never met unless it was the middle of the night. In the early days they met during the day but quickly learned they had to be more discrete.

He turned around, ignoring her. "Jason!" She called out.

"Shut up!" He stopped walking and faced her again. "You let this happen. You let him leave and now he has to pay."

"No!" Tears formed in her eyes as she ran towards him. She grabbed hold of his arm, "No, Jason, please no." He pushed her to the ground. "No," she begged him.

"Get up," he commanded but she didn't listen. "Monica… please get up. You know I have to do this. I have no other choice."

There was nothing Monica could say in response. She knew what his duties were. They had been made clear to her. She had learned to look past his violent nature. Hurting others was part of being a vampire… but this was her son. Jason grabbed her by the arm and helped her to her feet.

"Go inside," Jason said before fleeing into The West Woods. She walked inside her home, her prison, and sat back down on their bed.

Monica could do nothing to save her son. She was completely powerless, more powerless than she had ever been before.

We made a deal. You help me and I keep your family safe, she remembered Jason telling her.

Liar.

Either way, whether I turn him or kill him, I'll enjoy myself. Everything she had done was to keep her family safe. But Sam was going to die tonight. She failed. It had all been for nothing.

You told me he would be safe. For fourteen years, you told me he would live, she looked at the picture of herself and Jason on the bedside table.

Liar.

She smacked herself repeatedly on the head. When the throbbing became unbearable she stopped and laid down.

Monica was curled up in a ball on her bed, an all-too-familiar position. She could do nothing but watch as her life fell apart in front of her. She knew the end was coming. The end of her. The end of Sam. The end of everything and everyone. But what if she could stop it?

She forced herself to get up. The end was coming, but the

end of what? Monica reached under the mattress and pulled out a handgun.

The end is coming.

"What?!" Sam and Sarah stood on The Cliff.

"It's over," it was hard for Sam to remain emotionless as he spoke. "There's no room for you in my life anymore."

"What are you talking about, Sam?" Sarah grabbed his hand, just like she had the last time they spoke, only this time she squeezed it with all her might.

"I know I should give you more answers… but I can't. So much has changed in my life and I can't stop any of it."

"So now what? You're just gonna forget I exist?"

"I'm gonna be gone for a while, maybe a long time," Sam broke eye contact and looked at the ground. "You have to move on with your life and I have to move on with mine."

"Where is this coming from?!"

"I never wanted this to happen. But like I said, I have no choice."

"You have to tell me what you're talking about!" She put both her hands on his shoulders and began to shake him. "What are you hiding from me? What's going on?"

"I can't keep you safe!" He immediately felt bad for how loud his yell was. "Ever since the accident-"

"I can take care of myself, Sam. You don't have to worry about me," Sarah cut him off.

"No, you can't. No one's ready for what's coming. That's why I have to do this."

"Sam, just tell me what you're hiding."

He looked into her eyes once more. There was pain in

them, but they were also so compassionate and understanding. Sam wanted to tell her everything, he owed her more answers than he was giving her.

"You can trust me, Sam."

He opened his mouth to speak but stopped when he felt the cold metal of a gun on the back of his head. He watched Sarah's mouth open wide as she trembled at the figure who had just emerged from the darkness behind him.

"Ya better not say another word."

"Abe?" Sam turned around and Abe lowered the gun.

"Sam! Who is that?!" Sarah stumbled away from him.

"Don't move!" Abe yelled, pointing his gun at Sarah.

"Get that gun away from her!" Sam screamed at his new ally. "It's okay, Sarah. There's nothing to be worried about."

"Ya didn't tell me you were leaving," Abe said.

"I didn't think I needed your permission."

"Well ya do. Did ya tell her anything?"

"Sam, who's this?!" Sarah interrupted.

"No, I didn't," Sam avoided Sarah's question once again.

"Good," Abe said before raising the gun once more and pointing it at Sarah. "Listen to me, sweetie. As far as anyone knows, ya never left your house tonight. Ya never saw Sam, and ya definitely never saw me. Got it?"

"I told you to put the gun down, Abe!" Sam yelled.

Instead, Abe took another step towards Sarah, moving the barrel a few inches closer to her skull. "Got it?"

"Y- yes," Sarah said.

Abe lowered the gun. Sarah looked at Sam with the face of a horrified child who just saw the boogeyman. Sam chose to focus his sight on the scar across her face. As much as it hurt him, he knew he was doing what was best for her. As long as she was out of the picture, she wouldn't be put in danger again.

"You're gonna get in your car and drive straight home," Abe said. "Sam and I are gonna walk down to my truck at the bottom of The Cliff. We're gonna follow you to make sure you get home, alright? So don't even think of going anywhere else."

"O- okay, yeah, of course."

Sam didn't say another word to Sarah. She looked at him after answering Abe but he looked away. They followed her home and watched as she drove through the gates of The Connelly Estate. Sam didn't know if he would ever see her again.

Sarah's hands couldn't stop trembling as she drove down the long driveway to her home. She remembered being worried when Sam forgot to finish that pointless assignment, that seemed so long ago now. She never expected to be broken up with, or have a gun pointed at her for that matter. She wasn't sad, she wasn't worried, she was only confused.

Who was that man? She remembered Sam calling him Abe. *What is Sam doing?* She didn't know the answer to this question but knew it couldn't be anything good. She needed to discover what he was hiding and felt like she couldn't do anything else until she knew. She didn't even know where to start and doubted someone with all the answers would simply come knocking on her door.

She parked her car and approached the front door.

"Hello, Sarah," she couldn't make out a face but a shadowy figure stood on her porch. A man in black. A man with all the answers. "Just the girl I've been waiting for."

Sam's somberness continued to grow as they drove down Woods Drive. Abe suddenly braked, sending Sam reeling forward. They were stopped in the middle of the road and their headlights shone on four figures. Four sets of red eyes stared at them.

Abe handed Sam a flip phone, "Call Chelsea, tell her it's code red." He revved his engine, "You guys wanna play? Let's play." Suddenly they heard rustling all around them. More were coming, and they were coming quick. Abe stomped on the gas and sped towards the vampires.

"Chelsea!" Sam screamed as the four vampires jumped out of the way of the truck. They heard a thump over their heads. "Chelsea! Are you there?!" Sam couldn't make out what she was saying but heard her voice. "Code red! Chelsea, did you hear me? Code red!" The call was ended, but not by Sam. "She hung up, I don't know if she heard me."

"She heard ya, she'll be ready," Abe said just before slamming on the brakes, sending the vampire on top of the truck flying back onto the road. Sam looked behind and saw countless vampires chasing after them. It was so dark he could not see their bodies, but their eyes shone bright like dozens of tiny blood moons. The vampire in front of their truck stood up and grinned, Sam recognized him.

When you're hunting with the Wilson's, there'll always be a catch! Todd Wilson, suspected of murdering his own brother. *He did it,* Sam now knew. *And now he's gonna try to kill us too.*

Abe sped at Todd once again but Todd did not jump this time, he did not even flinch. Instead, he extended his arms and stopped the car. Abe kept his foot pressed hard on the gas but they couldn't get past Todd. His veins popped out of his neck as he hissed at them.

"Grab me the gun on the back seat!" Sam reached back and grabbed the shotgun. He saw dozens of vampires even closer to them now.

"You gotta make this quick or else we're gonna be surrounded!" Sam said as Abe grabbed the gun out of his hand. Abe pointed the barrel at Todd but didn't have to fire. Todd's arms gave out and he fell beneath the truck. They heard his bones crack underneath them as they made their way further down Woods Drive.

"Shouldn't you be driving faster?!" Sam noticed that Abe let off the gas.

"Don't need to. I don't know why that one tried to stop us, he probably didn't know the plan. The other ones don't wanna stop us here, they want me to lead them back to wherever we're camped out. They wanna make it so that we can never go back there." Sam looked back and could see the vampires were now running slower. "Trust me, if they wanted to kill us here, we'd be dead already."

"So we can't lead them back to your house, we can't let them know where we're living."

"The time has come, Sam. They know we're after them, we can't hide anymore," Abe hit the brakes and Sam looked back.

The herd of vampires had stopped as well. One vampire emerged from the pack, however. Sam didn't think someone could be that tall. "He's not from our world."

The tall vampire at the front of the pack let out a screech that echoed through The West Woods.

"Ya want a fight, ya got one," Abe kept driving. "They're in for a surprise," Sam saw a slight smile on his face as he continued to drive towards his home.

Monica heard the screech as she sped down Woods Drive. The scream hurt her ears. She wanted to stop, she wanted to turn around and go home. She would be safe there, but she could not live a safe life anymore. It was time to fight for her freedom. She kept driving but stopped when she saw a body on the road.

Sam?

She pulled over and ran towards the mangled body. She turned it over and was met with red eyes. This wasn't Sam. She jumped away and watched as the vampire's bones cracked back into place.

"T- Todd?"

Todd hissed at her and ran into the distance. As he disappeared into the darkness, Monica looked up and saw smoke rising from the trees. She looked through the forest and saw a glow in the distance. Fire.

I'm coming, Sam. She pulled her gun from the back of her jeans and grasped it tightly as she ran into The West Woods. It was best to go on foot from this point on.

As Abe sped down Woods Drive, the vampires matched his speed. They were leading the monsters back to the house where the battle would commence. Sam feared it might be his first and only battle but hoped Abe and Chelsea had some tricks up their sleeves. It now appeared as if fifty sets of red eyes were following them. Sam looked back at their pursuers as Abe drifted right, sending him flying into Abe's shoulder. Abe pushed him off as he tightened his grip on the steering wheel. Mud flew in the air as Abe sped down the dirt path. They were almost there. Sam could see the lights on in the cabin and a figure standing on the porch. Chelsea stood defenseless. They got closer, speeding towards her, but she didn't move.

"Why is she just standing there?" Sam yelled but evoked no response from Abe.

Sam watched the speedometer go from forty to fifty to sixty. They were charging towards Chelsea, they were going to hit her. But they weren't. Sam now spotted something in her hand. Something that was flashing.

Abe reached the end of the road and stomped on the brakes. Sam turned back and saw the vampires flying through the sky to match their speed.

"Now!" Abe shouted.

Chelsea pressed the flashing button and the vampires were sent to where they belonged… Hell.

The ground around the perimeter of Abe's yard collapsed and fire shot up. Sam listened to their screams of agony as they fell into the pit of fire. Abe jumped out of the truck and Chelsea threw him a gun.

"It's now or never, Sam!" He yelled out.

Sam followed his lead. He caught the assault rifle Chelsea threw to him and joined them on the porch.

"Remember, aim for the head," Abe said to him as he began firing at the vampires who avoided the pit.

Sam had no idea what he was doing but had to figure it out soon. He pulled the trigger and felt the heat of the bullets flying out. It flung him backwards at first but he recovered quickly. He stood his ground and kept firing.

The night sky turned red. The fire spread and the grass around them withered. It consumed their sanctuary. Abe had trained Chelsea there and hoped to train Sam there too but that would not be possible anymore. Sam leapt off the porch as two vampires came crashing through the roof of the cabin. He got to his feet and fired at the red eyes stalking him. The more he looked around, the more red he saw. Sam backed away from the red eyes and ran under the tarp, into Abe's garage. Now there was only darkness. He heard a noise behind him and quickly turned but it was only a hammer falling off a shelf. He kept moving until his back was up against the wall. He kept his gun pointed at the tarp, anticipating his enemies. He stood no chance but would fight until he could fight no more. The tarp moved and Sam held his gun tighter. A hand began to lift it up, revealing four sets of legs, but in an instant four gunshots popped off and one by one they fell.

"Need some help?" Chelsea walked through the tarp.

Sam smiled. Feeling relieved was his first mistake. "Tha-" a pair of hands crashed through the wall behind him and pulled him outside.

Sam was being held up by the vampire who stood at the front of the pack, the one who towered over all. "There you are, boy."

Chelsea charged through the wall but the vampire back-handed her, sending her flying into a tree. Sam watched her struggle to get to her feet as he was thrown to the ground.

Vampires formed a circle around him, through their legs he saw three creating a perimeter around Chelsea as well.

"No," he reached out to her but had no more strength.

"Don't worry, boy," the tall vampire said. "You won't die yet, he wants you alive."

Who? Sam remembered the man who Abe said his father fought. *Jarek.* He was going to be brought to him and he would die just like his father. He was not ready to face him yet. He looked on as the vampires taunted and hissed at Chelsea.

"I need more time," he told himself as he pressed his head against the ground.

"What's that, boy?"

"I need more time." But now was the time.

Suddenly he felt the ground beneath him shake and knew the vampire was walking towards him. Sam closed his eyes. He felt a sharp, stinging pain in his feet before it made its way up his body. He didn't know what was being done to him, but he had never felt anything like this. He turned over and looked up but no vampires were near him.

Then what is this pain?

He let out a scream that drew the attention of every vampire in the area. He looked down and saw his ankle shining bright blue.

"Grab him!" The tall vampire screamed but Sam shot up and they all took a step back. He stood in the middle of the horde of vampires as they looked on in fear. He felt so much power... then he heard three shots and looked to his left. The vampires who surrounded Chelsea were shot down. A woman emerged from the forest with a smoking gun held out in front of her.

"Mom?"

"Sam!"

He felt all the power leave him and all he saw was darkness.

Abe fired three shots. One hit the tall vampire in the eye, but he was quick enough to dodge the following two bullets. Covering his bleeding eye with his hand, he stumbled into the forest as Chelsea began firing at the other vampires, who scattered. Abe watched Monica get tackled to the ground as Chelsea ran towards Sam.

"Go start the truck! I'll be right behind ya," he said as he approached Sam and Chelsea.

Abe picked up Sam and followed Chelsea through the garage and out to the truck. He threw Sam into the cargo bed and hopped in with him. "Go! Go! Go!" He banged on the back window and Chelsea drove off.

As they drove through the flames and away from his home, Abe saw a black cloak blowing in the wind. He knew whose cloak that was… they escaped just in time. Abe knew two things as he held Sam in the back of his pickup truck: that wasn't his home anymore, and they would be seeing the monster in the black cloak soon.

Hopefully not too soon though. He needed to keep the man's identity a secret as long as he could…

Monica was being dragged to the front yard when she heard the sound of sirens approaching. She was thrown at Jason's feet. He looked down at her and smirked.

"Drive the car out of the garage and take it to Garry, let everything else burn."

As one of Jason's servants drove off in the 1967 Mustang, Monica looked on at the destruction that took place. Half of the house had been burnt to a crisp, and the remaining walls were covered in scattered bullet holes. Jason's vampires had come and conquered.

But you didn't win, she looked up at her husband.

"They're gonna be here in a minute, everyone scatter and meet at the cave in an hour." Several vampires stared blankly at Jason. "Get out. Now!" He shouted, watching them all scurry.

Monica caught glimpses of red and blue lights through the trees. "Hi, honey," Jason said. "You're a little dirty, let's get you home and cleaned up."

CHAPTER SEVENTEEN

Once the sun was out and a new day was upon them, Abe parked outside of the Quarryview Outlet Mall. It wasn't much to get excited over, aside from the newly built Walmart the mall consisted mostly of old thrift shops and an outdoor market. But Abe wasn't here for the shopping selection, he just needed to drive to the most public place he could think of. The West Woods was now the most dangerous place in the world, especially for them. But as long as they surrounded themselves with civilians they could not be harmed.

Sam woke up just two minutes after parking. "Just in time," Abe declared. "They'll be lookin' for this truck, we gotta leave it behind."

"Hey, sleepy," Chelsea was sitting beside Sam in the cargo bed of the truck. "How are you feeling?"

Sam looked into Chelsea's dark brown eyes, then towards

Abe, then to his left. Someone was standing by the truck.

Mom? He remembered everything from the night before. He remembered feeling the excruciating pain and seeing the blue shine, but when he looked up and saw his mom all the pain went away. Her figure vanished.

"Mom?" He said aloud. "Where's my mom?" He squeezed Chelsea's hand.

Abe broke in before Chelsea had a chance to speak. "What are ya talkin' about?" Chelsea shot a quick glance at her grandfather.

"I saw my mom last night… just before I passed out."

Abe glanced back at Chelsea, "We didn't see your mom, kid."

"She was there though."

"With all due respect, I think we would've noticed your mom if she was there. Ya had a tough night. If ya saw her, I think it was just a hallucination."

Sam took a deep breath, it must've all been in his head. "What happened to me last night?"

"Good question," Abe said. "What do ya think happened to ya?"

"I felt a pain… it started in my feet but it worked its way up my body. I've never felt pain like that before."

"And then your foot started shining blue," Abe continued Sam's diagnosis. "I'd say whatever happened to your dad that day in the cave happened to you last night."

What am I?

"I can't tell ya what happened last night, I don't have those answers," Abe continued. "But I do know one thing for certain… they were scared. They may be the ones hunting us but now they realize we're stronger than they thought. As long as they're at least a little scared of us, we have the upper hand," his smile was contagious.

"So where do we go from here?" Chelsea asked.

"There's a motel nearby, we'll ditch the car and go there on foot. We can stay there temporarily while we plan our next move," Abe took a stack of bills out of his pocket and shoved them in his backpack, which also held some of their other backup supplies.

"Before we start walking… how 'bout we go shopping?" Chelsea smiled from ear to ear.

Chelsea managed to convince Abe that her and Sam should be allowed to go shopping while he took the truck into the forest to hide it. Abe was not easily convinced but she had a way of getting what she wanted. He handed Sam a handgun to hide underneath his jacket before walking off.

"I really like that jacket by the way. It gives me an idea!" Chelsea took Sam by the arm and led him through the market. As they passed through, she made sure to swipe two apples from one of the stands. She moved so quickly that Sam barely saw her do it, never mind the shopkeeper.

Sam's eyes remained fixed on the ground, clearly preoccupied.

"Hey," Chelsea spoke up. "Everything's okay, we made it through the night," she reassured him as she chomped on her Granny Smith.

They finished their apples right as they walked into one of the thrift shops. The walls of the store were lined with the worst fashion the 1980's had to offer. Chelsea's hand brushed past brightly coloured tights, jumpsuits, and puffy pants as she made her way to the jackets. By the time Sam got there Chelsea already had her hands on what she wanted.

"Are you sure about that?"

"Yeah!" She replied. "What do you think?"

"It looks great!" A smile erupted on Chelsea's face. She charged towards the cash register without even taking it off.

"I'd like to buy this please!"

"Wow! It looks fantastic!" The girl behind the counter, who looked like she belonged in an 80's roller rink, complimented her. "That's gonna be forty-seven ninety-nine, pretty lady."

"No problemo!" Chelsea said as she pulled a fifty-dollar bill out of her pocket.

"Where the heck did you get that?" Sam asked, wondering if Abe paid her under the table for her excellent vampire hunting.

"I stole some from grandpa," she winked at the worker.

"That's the way to do it, girlie! Come back soon!" The worker called out to them as they were walking out. "You'd rock any of the outfits in here!" Chelsea walked out of the store with a newfound swagger. Sam, in his jean jacket, and Chelsea, in her brand new, slightly oversized black leather jacket with flames running up its sleeves, were surely a force to be reckoned with.

Sam sat on the curb as Chelsea strutted back and forth, showing off her jacket to everyone who passed by. They finally saw Abe approaching far in the distance, kicking a can across the searing pavement.

"That blue magic of yours sure did scare those vampires last night!" Chelsea laughed.

"I don't even understand what that was," Sam said.

"Well it sure sounds a hell of a lot like whatever magic your dad had way back in the day. I guess it runs in the family!" Chelsea proclaimed excitedly.

"I guess so," Sam laughed. He didn't normally like speaking about his dad, but it was hard to be too grumpy around Chelsea.

"So is that why you broke up with Sarah? 'Cause you learned about how your dad really died?" Sam glared up at her. "Sorry," Chelsea said. "My grandpa filled me in on the gossip while you were still passed out."

"Of course," Sam smirked at her before pausing for a moment. "I guess it is why I broke up with her. I just can't believe my dad knew about these vampires and died trying to fight them. What dragged him into all this in the first place? Are the stories I heard about Mia even true?" This last question seemed to come out of nowhere. Chelsea stopped her strut.

"Who's Mia?" She asked quickly.

"She-" Sam hesitated. "She was my sister."

"You have a sister?"

"I had a sister."

"Oh," that was all Chelsea could think to say.

"I guess Abe never filled you in on that gossip?"

"No, he never mentioned anything about that. What happened to her?"

Sam looked at her, not knowing what to say next, not knowing where to even start. "I don't know if I can talk about that right now."

"Sam," Chelsea sat beside him on the curb. "I watched my parents die, I was hiding under their bed when it happened. I have some horror stories of my own."

Sam's face showed more horror than hers, "I'm so sorry about that."

"Life goes on, right?"

"I guess so," he said. "You really want to hear the full story?"

"If you want to share it, then yeah." Something about Chelsea really calmed Sam down. He knew it was finally time to get something off his chest.

"I was only four, but to be honest I still remember the day perfectly. We all woke up early in the morning, my mom was taking Mia shopping so my dad decided to plan something fun for me. I had no idea where we were going, he just started driving. Before I knew it, we were at the beach. I swam and played in the sand all day, I swear I've never been more tired in my life," Sam let out a chuckle, although tears were slowly beginning to run down his face. "While I was having fun, my mom and sister were driving home. They got in an accident. The car flipped and my mom blacked out. When she woke up she tried to save Mia but it was too late." The tears were uncontrollable, they forced Sam to pause for a moment. He took the chance to wipe his nose with the sleeve of his jacket.

"I remember being at the beach and seeing two police officers walk over to us. They started talking to my dad, and he just dropped onto the sand. They took us to the hospital to see my mom. I remember sitting there until it got dark, my mom was awake and okay but my dad still wouldn't leave her. My mom had to force him to bring me home so I could sleep in my own bed," Sam allowed himself to smile for a second. "They actually had an argument about it. My mom was in the hospital with a broken leg and a concussion… but she was still stubborn enough to argue with my dad," Sam's smile faded and he looked down at his shoes. The excitement in his voice was lost. "They argued a lot after that. Then three weeks later, they found him."

Sam paused for a moment and composed himself. "I always thought he was sad, depressed, and that's why he did it. But it wasn't him who did it."

Chelsea suddenly lunged herself at him, hugging him as tightly as she could. After their hug she got back up. She lowered her hand to help Sam off the ground. He took it, even though she wasn't nearly strong enough to pull him up. "Thanks for sharing that with me," she said whilst holding out her fist.

"If you ever want to talk about anything, I'm here for you," he said while they fist-bumped.

Chelsea glanced at Abe, who neared them. "I'll tell you everything when the time is right, let's try not to get too depressed right now," she laughed.

"Fair enough," he laughed with her.

"Hey," Chelsea looked back at Sam before Abe approached. "You're strong, Sam. It seems to me you're much stronger than you think. We're gonna get into more trouble like that going forward, do me a favour and keep using your powers."

"I'll try my best," Sam responded.

"Have you been crying?" Abe asked as he walked up to Sam.

"There's nothing wrong with a man crying, grandpa," Chelsea defended Sam.

"You're absolutely right, sweetie," Abe pinched her cheek, causing her to flail her arms in the air and blush at Sam. "Are you guys ready to go?" Sam and Chelsea nodded and they set off for the motel.

We're gonna get into more trouble like that going forward, Chelsea had told him, and as he walked he knew that was true. He just hoped his powers would help him. He didn't need to understand them but as long as they saved him and his friends, he would be grateful. He walked and hoped, he hoped and prayed. He prayed but figured there was no God listening. Only The West Woods listened, and the demons that lay within them.

CHAPTER EIGHTEEN

A swarm of flies flew past their heads as they approached the coyotes. Chelsea screamed as she shooed the flies away. Sam found it funny that Chelsea showed no fear when facing a pack of vampires but was brought to her knees by a few harmless flies. Three coyotes laid dead on the ground before them. Sam and Chelsea stood back as Abe examined their wounds.

"Claw marks," he pointed at the belly of a coyote. "And fang marks," he moved his hand up to its neck. They all performed a scan of the area around them but whatever killed the coyotes was gone. Although there was no danger in sight, Sam still felt uneasy standing in the open field. The West Woods were just to his left and anything could be watching them from within.

"Should we keep moving?" Sam asked.

"Yeah, I found our trail," Abe pointed at footprints leading into the distance.

"Are you sure we should follow those? If anything shouldn't we be avoiding that path?" Sam looked around him once more, feeling even more on edge.

"There's just one set of footprints," Abe smiled. "Only one vampire, we can take on one vampire."

There was no point in him arguing with Abe. Whether Sam liked it or not they were vampire hunters now, it was their job. They needed to reach the motel for safety but they could not pass up this opportunity. This one vampire could be responsible for hundreds of deaths if they did not get to it first. So Sam remained silent and obediently followed Abe and Chelsea across the field. He tried to avoid looking down, partly because he wanted to stay aware of his surroundings but also because he didn't want to look at the vampire's footprints. They were more than double the size of Sam's foot. He felt like he was in Jurassic Park, seeing the gigantic footprint of a Tyrannosaurus Rex for the first time.

Sam silently debated whether he'd rather hunt vampires or dinosaurs. *At least you can see a dinosaur coming,* he chuckled to himself.

They walked for another hour before hearing voices in the distance. Abe immediately put up his hand, halting both Sam and Chelsea. They were the screams of children, not scared screams though, playful ones. Sam saw a house through the trees in the distance. They snuck towards the house and took cover behind some trees.

Two kids, a boy and girl, ran up their porch to their father, who was cleaning his gun.

"We wanna come, Dad!" The son said innocently.

"Someday soon you'll be able to come with me, but not yet," the father replied.

"Why not?!" Both kids yelled out in unison.

The dad laughed. "I would love to bring you guys! But if I did I would never hear the end of it from your mother," he smiled nervously, hoping they would not repeat that to their mother.

Just then the mother came out of the house, "What did I just hear you say?"

"Nothing, honey, nothing at all," the dad laughed. He was caught red-handed. His wife pouted for a moment, hands on her hips, before swatting at him playfully. Sam thought of Sarah. This family seemed to live such a peaceful life in the middle of nowhere, away from society and responsibilities.

"Are you lying to me?" His wife said back to him.

"I would never lie to you, honey," they both looked at each other and smiled. "C'mon guys, back me up here."

"He's not lying, Mommy," the daughter spoke up. "He was just telling us how much he loves you!" She ran to hug her mom's leg as she looked back and smiled at her dad.

"So it's settled now!" The dad hopped out of his chair. "I was just telling them how much I love you." He kissed his wife then his kid's foreheads before walking down the porch. "I'll be back before it gets dark, you guys be good for your mom!" He walked away, gun in hand, as his family went back inside.

They'll be safe inside, Sam was relieved. *But will he be safe?* He would soon learn the answer to that question. No one was safe in The West Woods anymore.

Chelsea smiled at the sight of the happy family, but her smile soon faded from her face. Abe pointed at the ground, just ten yards away from them. They followed him over and saw the massive footprint in the dirt.

"It was here," Abe said. "It was watching them too." The loving husband and father who was embarking on a hunt was anything but safe. The hunter would become the hunted, but unbeknownst to the vampire there were more hunters in the woods.

They continued to follow the vampire's trail but it eventually ended. Sam hoped that was a good sign but still sensed it was lurking in these woods.

"Hello," Abe called out as they caught up with the hunter, who turned around quickly.

"Who are you?" The hunter asked as they approached him.

"I'm gonna need you to go home, get back inside and stay with your family."

"Why?"

"It's not safe out here."

The hunter chuckled, "I'm in these woods almost everyday. Thanks for your concern but I think I'll be fine," he continued walking.

"What's your name?" Chelsea called out.

The hunter turned around, looking puzzled. "What's your name?" She asked again.

"Rick."

"Rick," Abe said. "There's something dangerous out here, something we can't explain to you."

"Well you better try to explain it."

"Rick," it was now Sam's turn to speak. "You wouldn't believe us even if we did explain it. We need you to go home to your family now."

"How do you know I have a family?"

"We saw them," Abe said. "They seem happy, you seem

happy with them. Now look, there's something dangerous out here so ya need to go home and be with them while we take care of it."

"What is it?" None of them knew what to say, forcing Rick to ask again.

"A beast," Abe said in a menacing tone. "A beast that we know how to kill, but you don't. For your own safety, please just go home."

Five minutes later the four of them were walking through The West Woods together. Rick was stubborn and wouldn't go home. Even more so though, he was protective. Protective of his family, protective of his property, protective of these woods.

"If there's a beast out here, near my house, I have to help kill it," he had told them. No matter how hard they tried to convince him to go home, he wouldn't.

"Do you have a family?" Rick asked Sam while Abe and Chelsea were further ahead.

"What?"

"You guys know I have a family, now I wanna know if you have a family."

"I have a mom… and a stepdad."

"Where's your real dad?"

Sam didn't respond, Rick had received his answer.

"I'm sorry for your loss. Is your stepdad a good man?"

"Good enough I guess."

"That's good. It's a man's responsibility to take care of his family," Rick smiled and patted him on the shoulder. "So why are you out here?"

"What do you mean?" Sam responded.

"I get the sense that those two are related but you seem like the outsider in this trio. Plus, you're young, not as young as the ten-year-old with the gun, but still young."

Chelsea quickly turned her head. "I'm twelve!" She said before storming forward.

"Why are you in these woods and not back home enjoying your life?"

"It's more complicated than you think. I guess I have to be out here… I don't really have a choice."

"You always have a choice."

Sam's only response was a chuckle.

"I'm serious. If there's one thing I've learned in life, it's that you never have to do anything you don't want to. Other than taxes… you always have to do your taxes, Sam. Anyways, there's almost always a choice, remember that."

Sam nodded and walked ahead. He appreciated Rick's words but didn't know if he believed them.

They continued their patrol until nightfall. The sun lowered through the thick trees of The West Woods, emitting a golden glow around them as they climbed up a small hill. They heard rustling in the trees and they all looked up. This was more noise than they had heard all day, for the duration of their hunt the forest had been silent. However, even through the silence, Sam had a feeling they were being stalked. The wind started to pick up and the rustling leaves around them grew louder. The sun was lowering, the darkness was taking over, and with the darkness the monster would come. They stood in an opening at the top of the hill with their backs to each other.

There would be a rustle and they would all turn towards the noise, but then there would be nothing for minutes. Another rustle, then silence. This pattern seemed to go on for hours, although Sam knew it had only been a few minutes. As the forest darkened, he found himself becoming more worried about Rick. He had told his family that he would be home by dark but he seemed dedicated to seeing this through. Sam found himself worrying more and more about Rick's family. He desperately hoped they wouldn't come searching for him.

I'll get him home soon.

Sam wanted the vampire to strike. He could not wait anymore, he was ready to fight. Just then a shadow emerged from the trees, it towered over all of them. The vampire who stood at the head of the pack the night before returned to finish the job.

"I am Batraz, the mightiest vampire The Ash has ever seen." The one-eyed Batraz stood over them. A fresh patch of pink flesh covered where his eye used to be.

"I am Saija," a woman approached from Sam's right.

"I am Cassander," a man approached from Sam's left.

"And I am Todd," a voice came from behind Sam. He turned his head and looking over Chelsea's shoulder saw Todd's red eyes.

When you're hunting with the Wilson's, there'll always be a catch! Sam had seen the television-host-turned-vampire the night before. *I thought you died.* They ran him over but obviously that was not enough to kill him. Now he stood with the pack of vampires, in one piece and ready to strike.

Sam looked back at the tall vampire, Batraz. They were surrounded. Four against four, but they had the disadvantage. His opponent was Batraz, Abe would face Saija, Rick would face Cassander, and Chelsea would take on Todd.

"You've made a grave mistake traveling these woods," Batraz declared.

"Ya don't know who you're up against," Abe said. He either had some misplaced confidence or was just trying to scare the vampires.

Batraz laughed. "We are the most powerful beings in both our worlds. We are one. Together, we can never be defeated."

"You're wrong," Chelsea said.

"Let's find out," Batraz leapt in the air and didn't come down. He chose to spectate.

The other three vampires charged at their prey. Sam watched as Abe was thrown down the hill. Rick was slammed against a large rock. Chelsea put up more of a fight against Todd but soon enough was hurled against a tree and fell, unconscious, into the nearby bushes. Batraz descended from the sky. He stood at the front of his pack, they all looked down at Sam. The others were just obstacles, Sam realized that he was their real prey.

Sam was powerless. But then he felt a pain emerge in his foot. Soon it worked its way up his body, quicker than before. Just moments after he initially felt the pain it was already in his neck. He felt the veins popping in his neck and when it reached his head everything went black. The last thing he saw was Batraz's eyes open wide. Then, he felt hope.

The vampires were scared, they were no longer hunting a human, they were hunting something else. In those few seconds Todd, Saija, and Cassander leapt towards Sam while Batraz remained motionless.

While the vampires leapt towards him, the darkness Sam saw began to diminish. Stars formed around him and he realized he was in the sky. He was floating above The West Woods. Just a moment ago he was vulnerable in those woods but now he was free, except he wasn't. He couldn't control his body, he tried to go back into the woods but was unable to. Instead, he started flying through the sky. He flew over the canopy of tall trees until he reached the open fields leading into town. He soared over the town he grew up in. He once felt so insignificant, but now had access to power beyond his wildest imagination. He was on top of the world. He focused his attention away from Westwood and looked towards the horizon. To his right he could see the whole of the Pacific Ocean. His vision had never been clearer, he could see all the way to Hawaii and beyond. To his left, he saw his whole country, every town and city that made up the United States, all the way to the Atlantic Ocean.

Then he looked back down on his town. This town was his life, it was all he knew.

"Not for long," a voice said to him, he knew the voice.

He finally reached his home and fell. He wasn't scared that he was falling though, he felt the power that flowed through his veins. He landed in his backyard and faced his back door. He tried to walk towards the door but couldn't, he still didn't have control over his body. Instead, he was forced to turn around and what he saw shocked him.

He saw himself. Sam, not Sam the powerful being who flew through the skies, but Sam the human. He was watching the encounter between himself and the vampire in his backyard.

"You are trespassing!" The speaker above his back door called out.

"This was just the beginning," the familiar voice said.

Sam, the god, watched as Sam, the human, was tackled by the vampire. He wanted to run over and save himself but couldn't do a thing. He watched his head slam against the ground and remembered how much that hurt. He remembered how scared he was, he thought he was going to black out and lose control but didn't. He had recovered from that blow to his head and fought off the vampire. But none of that ever happened. When his head slammed against the ground he tried to scream but couldn't. Instead, his eyes closed and the vampire opened its mouth, revealing fangs as sharp as blades, and bit him.

"No!" Sam, the god, now had control of his mouth. "That's not what happened! I didn't get bit!"

"Yes you did," the familiar voice spoke.

Sam watched as the vampire removed its fangs from his neck. Just then Sam, the human, opened his eyes and began fighting back again. The vampire began pushing down harder on Sam's chest.

"You are trespassing!" The vampire hissed.

"You are trespassing!" It continued to pound.

"You are trespassing!" The defenseless boy used all his strength to fight back.

"You are trespassing!" Sam, the god, watched as the strength began to fade from his human self.

"You are trespassing!" The vampire hissed at the speaker before jumping up.

"Beat him," the vampire said as he stared deeply into the human's soul.

After engaging in a stare down the vampire ran away into the night. At the time, Sam thought he got lucky and the vampire decided to leave him alone. He couldn't have been more wrong. By the time he reached his back door the bite marks on his neck had faded.

Sam was not a god after all. He was a vampire.

Sam, the vampire, watched himself walk into his house

before he got sucked into his basement. He stood against the wall opposite from the window, once again an observer. He watched himself lie in bed until he was woken up by a noise.

"You are trespassing!" Sam turned away from the window.

"You are trespassing!"

This is the dream, Sam realized. *The dream where I see my dad.*

"You are trespassing!" Sam watched himself turn around and face the window.

Probably just a squirrel or something, he remembered thinking. *That's not a squirrel… it's your dad.*

"You are trespassing!"

Your dad's a vampire.

"You are trespassing!"

"There's nothing there!" He heard himself yell out.

"Yes there is," Sam said but the Sam lying in bed couldn't hear him. "Your dad's there… and he's a vampire."

"No I'm not," Sam looked to his right and was shocked to see his father already standing in the room. This was the voice he had been hearing the whole time. He looked back to himself in bed but that Sam was now frozen. The light outside had turned off and not come back on. Everything was frozen. Time stood still.

"Dad?"

"Hello, Son."

"You're a vampire."

"I'm not, I'm just a vision… but you are."

"No I'm not."

"You are," his dad smiled. "You have an extraordinary amount of power, now you have to learn to use it."

"I don't want to have this power."

"You have no choice. You have joined me in the fight against the vampires, now you must defeat them."

"I don't know how to use these powers… I can't!"

"Yes you can! You have to learn!"

"I don't want to!"

"You must!"

"I don't want to!"

"Join me!" His dad's face grew redder as his anger intensified.

"Join me!" Sam didn't know what to say anymore. He was scared of his own father.

"Join me!"

"Stop!" Sam wanted this to end. He wanted to go back to the night he first saw the vampire and not check his backyard. He wanted to be back with Sarah. He didn't ask for any of this.

"Join me!" His dad screamed once more. His face was now black. He had no perceivable facial features anymore, just two red eyes. Two eyes of evil.

"Join me!" The shadowy figure that was once his father revealed its fangs and leapt towards him.

"Join me!" That was the last thing Sam heard.

Darkness. Darkness surrounded him. But then he saw light.

He opened his eyes as the three vampires leapt towards him. It had only been a few seconds since he closed his eyes. He was a vampire… and he had to fight.

He grabbed Todd first and sent him flying into a tree. He heard Todd let out a scream as the tree began to tip over. Seconds later he caught Cassander, who had lightning-fast reflexes but was still not quick enough, and pummeled his face with his free hand. Saija launched herself into him and he dropped Cassander. Both vampires jumped on top of him and began clawing at his skin. Sam watched as the vampires scratched at his body, waiting to feel the inevitable pain, but nothing came. His wounds seemed to heal instantly, he felt stronger with every chunk of flesh that flew off of him. He channeled his anger and flung them both twenty feet in the air. He jumped up as well, catching Cassander and launching him far into the distance. Sam landed gracefully, grabbed Saija by her ponytail, and threw her towards her master. Batraz was still standing in the same position, watching the show. Batraz caught Saija by the throat with ease.

"Disappointing," he said to her before chucking her in the distance. "You're strong," Batraz said to Sam. "But then again, they're weak. Their strength is nothing compared to others."

"Show me your strength then," Sam's hatred and anger grew by the second. He used it to fuel his power. He felt like he could do anything with this power flowing through his body. He wanted Batraz to attack him, he even welcomed it. He was making a huge mistake.

Batraz charged and Sam extended both his arms out in front of him. Batraz hit them both down and pushed Sam into a rock. He shot up quickly but was immediately knocked through the rock by Batraz's right foot. He picked up Sam by the neck, who once again felt powerless, and held him high in the air. Just moments ago Sam was unstoppable. His body was performing actions before his mind could even comprehend what he was doing, but now it felt like that power left him. He became too confident, too reckless, and that would be the death of him.

"You're just a boy, don't think of yourself as anything else,"

Batraz squeezed the life out of him. As Sam's vision became fuzzier, he heard a scream. It was his father, all those years ago, screaming as he was killed by the vampires. He had failed and now Sam had failed.

"No," his father said to him.

Sam's eyes opened once more and he realized the scream was not his father's, but Rick's. Rick was standing twenty feet away from them with his gun pointed at Batraz.

The hunter will kill his prey. Sam smiled as Batraz dropped him. Rick fired the gun. He had one shot, one chance, and he made it count. It felt like time came to a halt as Sam watched the bullet blast out of the gun and fly towards their enemy. But Batraz ducked, missing the bullet by a centimetre, and Sam's smile faded. A split second later Batraz's claws pierced through Rick's stomach and he fell to the ground.

Batraz raised his claws again as he leapt towards Sam. Rick's blood was dripping off them but Sam knew they would not taste his blood. Not today at least. He shot out his arm and caught Batraz in the air. Batraz was incredibly heavy, but Sam held him up like he was just a child. Sam's outstretched claws drew blood from the tall vampire's neck. He looked deeply into the red abyss that was Batraz's eye. Fear, that was his greatest weapon.

But, as suddenly as he had regained his power, he began to lose it again. His arm grew limp. He started to shake but could not let Batraz know he was shaking. He needed to keep him afraid, as long as he was afraid then Sam had the advantage. If he dropped him now Batraz would know there's a limit to his power. Tonight will not be the end of Batraz. They will meet again.

I'll be waiting… I'll be ready.

Sam let out a scream as he threw Batraz off the hill. He had won the battle, but he did not feel victorious. He stumbled to the ground and crawled towards Rick. Sam reached out and put his hand on Rick's chest. He was a loving husband and father, he had no place in this story, but he made the ultimate sacrifice so Sam could survive. Sam would not forget that.

I'll be ready.

His hand remained on Rick's chest as his eyes closed.

CHAPTER NINETEEN

Darkness shrouded The West Woods. Only the full moon peering through the clouds created any sort of light. Sam felt completely devoid of all humanity. He felt blood running down his arm and assumed all his insides were seeping out of his body. He felt cold, his blood was not warming him anymore. He would continue to look up at the stars as he froze to death in this forest. But then his hand twitched and he realized it was not his body that was lifeless, but Rick's.

He quickly leaned over and vomited on the grass beside him. *I guess I'm still alive,* he reassured himself. His eyes opened wider as he began to regain consciousness. He was alive, he just didn't feel human.

"Sam!" Chelsea knelt beside him before turning her attention to Rick.

They were both speechless. Chelsea helped Sam up. Well,

she pretended to help him up. She was at least fifty pounds lighter than him and in no condition to lift him, but she reached out her arm while Sam did all the actual work. It's the thought that counts.

"I have something to tell you," Sam said as he looked over the hill. He couldn't see anything, but he liked it that way. It made it so that he couldn't see the destruction he had caused. He was one with the darkness, a vampire, this was all his fault. Rick's death was his fault.

"It's gonna have to wait," Chelsea replied. He couldn't see much of her but he made out a tear running down her face. The moonlight glistened off the droplet as it made its way to the ground.

They shone their flashlights as they made their way down the steep hill. Chelsea had done her best to prop Abe up against a tree, although he had already begun to slide down. His shirt had gotten stuck on a small branch sticking out of the tree so Sam had a clear view of the scratches on his back as Chelsea shone her flashlight on Abe. He was an old man, but Sam had never viewed him as one. Sam thought Abe could do anything, but in this moment that facade began to fall apart. He heard Abe moan after making the slightest of adjustments. He watched his purple, chapped lips quiver with every sip of water. Then there were the scratches, the dark bruises, the blood. Abe looked like an old man on his deathbed.

"How ya doing, kid?" Abe tried to laugh but it quickly turned into a series of coughs.

Chelsea knelt beside him and held his hand, comforting him through his cough attack. There was nothing she could actually do to help him, but again, it's the thought that counts.

"Help me pick him up," Chelsea said once the coughing finished.

"Are you gonna be alright?" Sam wasn't sure if picking Abe up was the best idea.

"Kid, I've been through worse, I'll be fine."

Sam was not about to argue with him. Not only was he trying to avoid any form of discussion, but he was frankly terrified to go on without Abe. He was their leader, their guide, they had no hope without Abe. He needed to survive.

Sam bent over and helped Chelsea pick up her grandfather. Abe let out a pained grunt as they picked him up and released some spit which landed on Sam's leg. They only made it three steps before Abe collapsed. Neither Chelsea nor Sam were strong enough to hold him up once he started to fall.

"You need to rest, we can't move you anywhere right now."

"Ya need to get stronger," Abe laughed, allowing some more spit to drip out of his mouth. "Get Rick over here, it'll be easier with him."

Neither of them responded.

"Shit."

That was all Abe needed to say. He agreed that he needed rest but said they could not stay there. If Rick's family started to look for him, they could eventually end up finding their camp. They couldn't be seen by anyone. An innocent man died tonight and if anyone found them they would surely be questioned. So, Sam and Chelsea fought through the pain of holding Abe up and made their way from the battleground. Knowing who was really responsible for Rick's death didn't relieve much guilt, it wouldn't help them sleep any better tonight. They couldn't even give Rick a proper burial. By the time someone found him he would be eerily pale and covered in bugs. It wasn't fair, but it was necessary.

They walked for about half an hour before Chelsea and Sam gave up. Actually, Chelsea had given up ten minutes prior and at this point was just pretending to help. Sam didn't blame her though, she was just a little girl, lifting this weight for even twenty minutes was impressive for her.

They reached an opening in The West Woods and Abe, who was beginning to doze off as he was being carried, woke himself up for long enough to scan the area and tell them to set up camp. Chelsea began to light a fire, which impressed Sam because he could not have done it himself, while he made a makeshift pillow for Abe out of any spare clothing and a pile of leaves. He gently lowered Abe's head onto it and Chelsea began to wet an extra shirt to clean Abe's wounds.

"Thanks, guys," Abe mumbled before drifting off. "Thank you." It seemed to Sam that Abe's pain ceased as he fell asleep and knew things would be okay. At least he hoped things would be okay.

"So what did you have to tell me?" Chelsea asked as they both sat in front of the campfire. Sam had already forgotten he had to tell her anything. He became so focused on helping Abe that he did not think about himself. He liked it that way. The less he thought about himself the happier he was. Even though Abe was in terrible pain, Sam was at peace. But Chelsea had just broken that peace.

"I know what's wrong with me."

"I assume you used your magical blue powers again tonight?" She smirked.

"It's not just that, it's something worse... I think I'm a

vampire, Chelsea." That wiped the smirk off her face. Before he could react, she grabbed her gun and pointed it at him. He sat there, defenseless.

"What are you doing?" She asked.

"What do you mean?"

"If you're a vampire you should've jumped into the sky then back down to grab my gun. You should've jumped from tree to tree to make it impossible for me to shoot you. You didn't do any of that, so why should I believe that you're a vampire?"

"You don't have to believe it, but I had a vision-"

"Are you gonna try and do something to prove it to me?"

"I don't know how to control it yet."

"So you can't show me anything?"

"Hold on," Sam said as he ripped off the bandage he had on his arm. "Remember when I cut my arm after you guys almost ran me over?"

"Yeah."

He finished ripping the last piece of bandage off his arm. When he looked down he saw just what he expected to see. Nothing. "See, no cut." While he was at it he decided to take off the bandage which had been covering his ribs for the last few days, ever since the car accident. "And once again, nothing," he said. "Plus, I have no scratches from any of our battles. They've all disappeared."

Chelsea took a long pause. "Is everything alright?" Sam spoke again.

"Yeah... I guess so. It's just-" she stopped herself.

"What?" Sam asked.

He noticed her grip on her gun tighten. "I've spent almost my entire life thinking about vampires. But I've never actually known one, or even talked to one for that matter. Are they all like you?"

"What do you mean like me?"

"Are they all nice?" Chelsea spoke slowly, thinking deeply about every word she spoke. "Are they good?"

Sam watched as Chelsea's lips began to subtly quiver. He took a moment to properly word his response. "Not the ones we've been fighting. They want to hurt us, and other people too. There might be good ones out there, but our job is to stop the bad ones."

"Yeah... okay." Chelsea responded hesitantly.

"I promise, you can trust me, Chelsea. We're gonna beat these guys, together."

"Okay. I believe you." She smiled. "You're a vampire... but you're one of the good ones! And you're going to use your powers for good!"

"That's the plan," he responded.

"Our chances to beat them just increased then!" She jumped up and shone her flashlight in his face. She examined his mouth, nails, and even did an impromptu eye test to confirm that no vampire features were showing. There were no noticeable signs that he was a vampire but that did not falter her newfound excitement.

He finally got her to lie down after about ten minutes of constant claw checks. He didn't think she would ever calm down but the suggestion that she might wake Abe up finally convinced her to. They laid on opposite ends of the fire but through the crackling Sam could still hear her singing to herself.

"My best friend's a vampire," she laughed.

"We're best friends?" He asked.

"Of course… at least you're mine. Am I yours?"

He laughed and even felt himself blushing a little, "Of course you are."

Chelsea seemed happy but through the firelight he spotted one thing that sent his mind whirling. As she laid down, she still kept a tight grip on her gun. They laid in silence for a few moments but Sam had to ask her something before falling asleep, "Are you still up?"

"Yeah!"

"How will your grandpa react when I tell him?"

He heard the rustling of a few leaves and decided to keep his eyes closed. The wind began to hiss and whirl but he decided to keep his eyes closed. He heard a branch crack and fall off a tree. The thump it made when it hit the ground sounded close to them. Sam opened his eyes and shot up. Chelsea and Abe were still sleeping and the fire was almost completely out. He looked all around him and saw nothing but heard more rustling and cracks of branches. He knew what was there. He stood up and gazed further in the distance. The sun hadn't begun to rise and the sky was a deep blue, but that did not stop Sam from spotting the shadowy figure moving through the trees.

He looked for more but did not see any. This vampire was without its pack, completely vulnerable. Was it Batraz or one of the others? He was able to fight Batraz, the tallest and strongest vampire he had seen, and not lose. He didn't win either… but at least he scared him. Sam looked down at Abe and Chelsea and watched on as they peacefully slept. Abe was injured and in no condition to fight and Chelsea had been through enough already. Sam was now the strongest in their group, if he could awaken his power this lone vampire wouldn't stand a chance. He grabbed a gun just in case and followed the shadow alone. He could do this, he would do this for Abe, his teacher, and Chelsea, his best friend.

Sam ran as fast as he could. He didn't care if the vampire heard him coming, he was ready for a fight. He ran through the dark woods until he reached an open field. He squinted in the distance and saw a figure sitting in the field full of dying grass. He ran and under his feet the dying grass turned to coarse dirt. He traversed through the dry field, towards his enemy who sat alone and unaware, devouring a freshly-slaughtered squirrel.

Sam's powers had not been awakened yet but that was not going to stop him. His hands tightened into fists as he pushed himself to run faster.

He approached the vampire and slowed down his pace. Cassander turned and faced him.

"You," Cassander said.

Sam was determined those would be his last words. He did not hesitate to pull out his gun and fired three quick shots. That was for Rick. Cassander was not the one who killed him but he was part of it. He was pure evil and now he would face his end. Sam missed two of his shots, only connecting with the last. Still, it was enough to temporarily handicap Cassander, who looked down at the bullet wound in his thigh.

Cassander looked up at him and hissed. Sam fired another shot and hit his other thigh. Cassander leapt at Sam with all the strength he had left and threw him to the side. Sam flew twenty yards and bounced off the rough ground. He immediately rolled around to face Cassander, whom he expected to be charging after him, but he was wrong. Cassander was fleeing… and he was slow. Sam jumped up and resumed his sprint towards his enemy. Cassander was Sam's prey and he knew it. Sam had to take advantage of that fear.

Cassander looked back at Sam and tried to force himself to run faster but couldn't. Vampire's wounds regenerated quickly so Sam needed to end this soon. The chase continued across the barren field until Cassander reached a fence leading into a trailer park.

Rusty Ralph's Campgrounds. Growing up, Sam had always felt bad for the families living in these trailers. When he pictured a campground, he pictured large fire pits surrounded by tall trees. Sprawling rivers ran through them and whenever you looked into the water you could see an assortment of fish enjoying their swim. Rusty Ralph's Campgrounds did not match that vision. Instead of lush greens and vivid blues, all you saw when you looked at this trailer park were dull browns. The once white RV's now matched the dead ground which they lie on.

Cassander slowly and clumsily climbed the rusted fence. Sam watched the sun rise in the background, as if it was shining a spotlight on Cassander's obvious pain. It was now morning, the families who lived in these RV's would soon be awake. Sam looked down at his gun, knowing he only had one bullet left. He had to take his shot and get out before he was seen.

Sam also hopped the fence, making it look graceful compared to Cassander, and followed the helpless vampire onto the dirt road.

"Stop!" Sam yelled out just before Cassander collapsed. Sam was exhausted, he wiped the sweat off his brow with one hand as he raised his gun with the other. He locked eyes with the broken vampire.

"Please… don't." Vampires did get tired, they could not fight forever. Sam had won this battle without using his powers. He won… for Rick.

Sam would not allow Cassander to plead for his life anymore. He fired his shot. The sound of the bullet seemed to echo off the aluminum of every trailer in the park. Sam ran away as Cassander dropped to the ground.

It was 5:05am. Sam escaped before the sun woke up the world. But Bill Hygens didn't wake up with the world. Bill had been living in a beat-up trailer in Rusty Ralph's Campgrounds since he was a boy. His dad left when he was only four, his mother chose to destroy any evidence of his existence so Bill barely remembered the man's face. She did her absolute best to provide him with everything he needed, but work wasn't always the easiest to find in Westwood. Bill grew up and, lacking supervision, got into things he probably shouldn't have gotten into. He dropped out of high school early after getting the neighbour's daughter pregnant. Her parents didn't take the news well, but Bill and Alex were overjoyed. They were excited to raise a family together, they were excited to do something right for the first time in their lives. Alex passed away a few years back, leaving Bill a single father of two beautiful little children. He worked as hard as he could every single day to give them the life they deserved, but it wasn't easy. Working construction took a toll on his body, waking up early every morning and going to bed late every night. He wasn't sure how much longer he could go on. He just needed to get his kids out of Rusty Ralph's, out of Westwood. He had an aunt who lived in Jersey and he liked the idea of not sweating through his shirt every day. But until he got a raise at work, Jersey was only a dream. This morning he rolled out of his single bed and went outside to vape. He finally quit smoking two years ago but it was still difficult to resist the temptation. Vaping was his relaxing little ritual that prepared his mind for a gruelling day of work. He walked out of his trailer and expected it to be like every other morning in the campground, completely desolate. But this morning he saw two men on the road, one on his knees and the other standing over him.

Bill had dropped his vape on the ground. He hoped it didn't break. The gunshot echoed through the trailer park. He watched one man fall to the ground as the other began to run away. He pressed the red button on his phone, ending the recording. He wasn't particularly good with technology but his kids had taught him how to record a video. He rushed inside, ignoring his potentially broken vape. He sat down at the table and held on to the edge to stop himself from shaking. As he watched the video, he realized he caught everything. He was worried he would mess something up but he didn't. He clearly saw the killer, just a young man.

News outlets would pay good money for this footage…

New Jersey never seemed closer.

CHAPTER TWENTY

What have I become?

Todd had tried to crawl away from the tree the boy threw him into but in a moment of weakness lost all his power. His legs began to feel numb and his arms stopped working. The tree had collapsed on top of him and he was wedged in between its trunk and the ground. He watched Batraz hold the boy high in the air. He saw the other man stand up and point his gun at Batraz before Batraz noticed… he chose not to call out to his leader. He could barely look while Batraz butchered the man, but felt some sense of hope when the boy threw Batraz off the hill. The boy then collapsed and Todd regained enough power to slightly raise the tree and crawl away. Would he help the boy? No. Would he find Batraz? No. He fled.

He ran through the night until he couldn't run anymore. He hadn't slept in days, they were so focused on finding the boy that Batraz didn't allow them that luxury. At least he didn't have to worry about Marissa looking for him. He told her he was going to LA for a few days to meet with the network executives, he thought that was a good excuse. He collapsed and crawled towards a tree. He rested his head on the trunk as his eyes began to close. For a little while he would be at peace. When he awoke he would be in Hell again.

What have I become?

"When you're hunting with the Wilson's, there'll always be a catch!"

"Cut!" Their director yelled and the whole crew clapped. Todd looked away from the camera and at everyone else on set. He felt admired, adored, it was amazing.

"We did it, Brotha!" Skipper grabbed him by the waist and picked him up. Todd couldn't keep himself from laughing even though he felt uncomfortable being hoisted up. Skipper grunted loudly as he brought him back down to his level and they embraced each other.

"Everyone, that's a wrap on the pilot!" Julian Folino, their director, said. Todd and Skipper became really good friends with Julian while working on the first episode of the show. Todd's favourite part of each day was eating lunch with them and talking about future ideas for the show. Of course, many of those ideas were never implemented. Kaleb Bond fired Julian after the first season of their show because of "creative differences". Kaleb had differences with all three of them early on but he couldn't fire his two stars so Julian became his victim. But as of now the three worked happily on their project, blissfully ignorant of what was to come.

"We gotta go celebrate!" Skip said to the two of them while the rest of the crew were still packing up all of the equipment.

"I don't know about that, Skip, I gotta get home to the wife and kids," Julian looked at Todd and laughed.

"Yeah, me too," Todd agreed.

"C'mon guys, we just made a freaking TV show! Don't make me get drunk by myself."

And so they went. All three of them. Todd and Julian were both a little nervous to call their wives, but how could they be mad? Like Skipper said, they just made a freaking TV show!

It was 4am and Skipper was still hogging the pool table in Fireside Pub. Every time he sunk the eight ball he would cheer and shout like he just won the world championship, causing Malcolm, the bartender, to send another grimace his way. They were the only ones left in the bar, Skip was still full of energy but Todd and Julian were half asleep in their booth. Julian still couldn't see straight but Todd felt completely sober. He took it upon himself to be responsible and call them a cab.

"Skip! Time to go!" Malcolm finally smiled after hearing those words.

"Just one more game, c'mon man!"

"C'mon Skip, you've had your fun." It seemed like Skip was going to keep arguing but he finally dropped his cue and walked over to the booth without putting away any of the balls, wiping the smile off Malcom's face.

Skipper skipped out the door as Todd guided a clumsy Julian behind him. Malcolm never locked the door quicker than he did that night.

"We did it!" Skip ran out onto the road and screamed.

"Get off the road, Skip!"

Skip turned around to face his best friend. "Brotha! We made a freaking TV show!" He proceeded to scream once again but this scream quickly turned into vomit. This woke Julian from his daze and caused him to vomit as well. Todd let Julian drop down to his knees and proceed to flush out his insides and went to grab Skip.

"You good?"

"I'm great!" Skip said with a smile which gave Todd an all too thorough look at the old pieces of regurgitated food stuck in his mouth. Approaching headlights shone a light on Skip's pale, joyful face.

"Looks like the taxi's here, c'mon guys. You can both stay at my house tonight, as long as neither of you have anymore puking to do."

Todd was worried that they would puke in the taxi the whole way home. Skip kept dry-heaving just to scare the driver, who in turn kept threatening to charge Todd three hundred dollars if he made a mess of his new vinyl interior.

"We just made a TV show! We can pay you whatever you want!" Skipper said to him repeatedly.

Luckily, they managed to keep the taxi clean and their fare down to just twenty dollars. Julian puked once more on Todd's lawn but after that they were both able to sleep peacefully on Todd's living room floor. Todd made them both take a few sips of water before turning off the lights for good. Within minutes Julian was snoring so loud Todd thought his whole family would wake up, but he was far too exhausted himself to worry about the noise too much. He sat down on the couch and closed his eyes, not having enough energy to walk upstairs. He didn't mind staying on the couch, he liked it down there. His best friends were down there.

Todd was just about to doze off when he felt someone grab his leg. He quickly jumped up but it was just Skipper, who had crawled across the floor to him.

"Hey, Brotha," Skip whispered.

"Hey, man," Todd replied.

"I just wanted to say thanks for taking care of me tonight."

"Of course, anytime," Todd smiled.

"I love you, man."

"I love you too," he smiled even more.

"Brothers for life."

"Brothers for life," Todd repeated as his eyes closed.

But then they opened. Todd was still sitting in an upright position on his couch. It was still dark outside, it couldn't have been more than an hour since he fell asleep. Darkness was all he saw, but there was something in that darkness. A ghostly figure moving towards him. Todd tried to stand up but he felt frozen in place. A face began to reveal itself to him. He knew it wasn't Skip or Julian, they were both asleep on the floor. He hoped one of them would hear the man walking around the house, but they wouldn't. Only Todd heard, only Todd saw. The figure came closer to him and he saw who it was. Kaleb Bond. One half of Connelly and Bond Studios. Kaleb stood in front of Todd and smiled.

What have I become?

Todd's eyes shot open. He had fallen asleep against the trunk of the tree. He had a terrible dream, not a dream though, a memory. He saw the same face in front of him. Kaleb continued to smile, Todd knew it wasn't real but still locked eyes with the spectre of Kaleb.

What have I become?

"You did this to me," Todd said aloud to Kaleb, who continued to smile as he faded away. Todd was no longer looking at his former employer, now he just stared at the grim forest which lay in front of him.

Now feeling stronger than before, he stood up and began to walk through the forest.

What have I become?

He hated his life. He hated the powers that had been bestowed upon him. He hated doing the terrible deeds his masters commanded him to do. He would flee. If they found him, he would die a gruesome death but he had to take that risk. He would take Marissa and the kids and run. Even if they had to be on the move forever, that was better than living in this waking Hell. He had to lie to his own family. Even though these powers brought back his confidence and saved his marriage, it wasn't worth the things he had to do. He remembered holding the boy's car on Woods Drive. He looked into his eyes and saw not a warrior, but a scared young man. The boy didn't ask for this life and neither did he. They both have an immeasurable amount of power, and with that power comes a constant voice in your head to bring pain and destruction everywhere you go. What if he could fight that voice? He didn't know if he could, but in this moment it felt amazing to feel sympathy instead of hate. He made it through the forest and to an open field. He would go home, pack his bags, and leave Westwood forever. There was nothing here for him. He could be happy somewhere else. He believed that.

First, he had to eat. He walked across the field and made it to a road. In the distance he saw a sign. It was a tall sign with a sunny side up egg on top of it with two wide eyes and a smile in the yolk. A speech bubble was coming from the egg's mouth. "Eggciting Times!" Below the egg read the words, "The best bacon and eggs in Northern California!" Todd had been here before, and while it was definitely not the best bacon and eggs he ever had, it was a solid 8/10. As Todd walked down the road towards the restaurant, he embraced feeling the sun on his skin. In The West Woods he felt so trapped. The forest was so dense it was hard for the sun's beams to find their way through the leaves. That wasn't the case anymore, though. He enjoyed his walk down the open road. He was finally free.

Todd sat at a booth in the corner of Eggciting Times. He sat facing the wall so he didn't have to look at anyone else in the restaurant. More importantly though, no one else would see him. He ordered three glasses of orange juice, three eggs, scrambled, with a side of bacon, home fries, and two pancakes as well as the spotlight item on today's menu: the "Eggciting Breakfast Burrito".

As he waited for his meal, he stared at the painting which hung on the wall in front of him. It featured Eggcited Eggy, the mascot of Eggciting Times. In this painting he was playing the drums but the cymbals, snare drums, and bass drum were made of sunny side up eggs. Of course they were. As Eggcited Eggy slammed his drumsticks down the yolks splashed up and smeared the white wall behind him.

He had been sitting impatiently for about ten minutes waiting for his food to come. He had already finished the three glasses of orange juice and anxiously awaited the server to deliver him more.

"Oh my gosh," he heard his waitress say behind him. He

glanced back and saw her watching the television which hung above the cash register. He saw his orange juice on her tray.

Hurry up, he thought. But she wasn't in a rush to go anywhere. She grabbed the remote and turned up the volume on the television. It was now so loud everyone in the restaurant could hear, a few even got up to get a better look. Todd watched from his seat in shock and awe.

He saw the words "BREAKING NEWS" appear on the screen in big red letters and watched a man shoot another man inside a trailer park. Todd did not need to watch twice to identify the people involved. The shooter was no man, he was the boy. The victim wasn't a man either, he was a vampire, Cassander.

Todd lost his appetite.

CHAPTER TWENTY-ONE

Sam arrived back at their campsite and was able to lie down for an hour before it was time to get up. Half of that hour was spent restlessly twisting and turning, regretting what he just did. He killed a man, but he had to tell himself over and over again that that was no man. Cassander was a monster. He did what he had to do and now he had to live with it. But the guilt wouldn't leave him alone. He was worried that this feeling might keep him up forever.

By the time he opened his eyes and forced himself off the ground, he saw that Chelsea and Abe were both up and packing up their belongings. It brought a smile to his face to see Abe up.

"I just needed a good night's sleep, that's all," Abe said. He was still moaning and groaning but Sam could immediately tell he was feeling much better.

Sam was eternally thankful that Abe was back on his feet.

Their goal was to make it to the motel by mid afternoon and Sam didn't even want to imagine the physical toll it would entail to have to hold Abe up the whole way. Abe was walking fine and in just over an hour they cleared the woods and made it onto the nearest road. After following the road south for a few miles they noticed a sign in the distance. As soon as Chelsea got a good look at the sign she roared with laughter until they reached the restaurant. Chelsea loved Eggcited Eggy and convinced Sam and Abe that they needed a freshly cooked meal to start their day. It didn't take much convincing on her end, however, by the look on his face Sam could tell Abe was starving just as much as he was. So, they decided to have the best bacon and eggs in Northern California.

They walked in and Abe immediately claimed the booth closest to the door. Sam sat opposite to him and Chelsea decided to sit beside her newly named best friend. All three of them were covered in filth and scattered specks of dried blood, but the restaurant was filling up too quickly to freshen up. Abe didn't want to draw any of the unnecessary attention that came with even a simple trip to the washroom.

Just before their waitress came over, Chelsea surveyed the restaurant and burst out laughing once again. "Aw, I wish I sat on your side, grandpa, then I could look at that funny painting over there," she pointed to a painting of Eggcited Eggy playing the drums. Sam looked for a second but didn't pay attention to the details of it. None of them noticed the man sitting alone in front of the painting.

Sam and Chelsea both ordered orange juice then Abe, feeling like he desperately needed a boost, ordered two orange juices and two coffees. "We're gonna be out of orange juice before the day's done," their waitress said to her co-worker as she walked away.

"So, grandpa, as much as I would love to keep looking at Eggcited Eggy all morning, Sam has to tell you something." This was the part he was dreading.

Sam kept glancing at the ridiculous paintings of Eggcited Eggy as he discreetly told Abe the news. He looked deeply into Eggy's wide smile and for a second thought he was being laughed at. Eggy definitely thought this story was way too absurd to be true.

You know nothing, Eggy.

Abe's reaction was the polar opposite of Eggy's. He held a straight face the whole time Sam spoke and remained silent even after he finished.

"So, what do you think?" Chelsea spoke up, breaking the awkward silence.

"How are ya feelin'?" Abe finally asked Sam.

"Good."

"Ya haven't felt any... strange temptations recently?"

"No, what do you mean?"

Abe stared at Sam sternly for a few moments but managed to give their waitress a slight smile when she came over.

"What can I get for you guys today?" She said with a smile as wide as Eggy's.

Chelsea was about to speak up but Abe interrupted. "We're all gonna have the 'Classic Eggciting Times Breakfast'. Scrambled eggs for everyone, white toast, and bacon on the side. We're kind of in a rush so can ya try your best to bring it out quickly?"

"I'll try!" Her smile began to fade.

"Thanks, darlin'," he smiled back but his stern expression

returned as soon as she walked away. "I've seen vampires do some treacherous things, Sam. Ya know some of the things I've seen."

"I do know, and that's why I want to kill them all."

"How can I trust ya? Not just around me but around Chelsea. We're vampire hunters… it doesn't really make sense for us to work with an actual vampire."

"You should know I want to stop the vampires as much as you do, I thought I've proved that to you."

"You've proved that to me. But I recruited Sam, the boy who lost his father and had a reason to be in this fight, not Sam, the boy who didn't know he was a vampire."

"How could I have known? I didn't know I had powers, I didn't know how to control them."

"And now ya do?"

Sam thought about Cassander. He wanted to unleash his powers in that fight but couldn't. He still managed to kill him though, although now was not the time to reveal that. "No… but I will."

"And then what?" Abe continued to question him. "Will ya be on our side still or will ya turn against us?"

"Abe, stop. You already know the answer."

"Do I? You're powerful, Sam, and with that much power comes a lot of risks. Your powers could be the end of all of us."

"But they could also be the end of the vampires. Like I told you, I fought Batraz and saw fear in his eyes. I'm the weapon we need to destroy them all."

"You're just one vampire though, against who knows how many? The odds aren't in our favour."

"Were the odds in our favour when we were just three humans?" Abe didn't know what to say to that. "I believed you when you said we had to try to beat them. I put my trust in you… now I need you to put your trust in me."

"I trust you!" Chelsea put her hand on his shoulder and smiled. "You're not like the other ones, you're good." That made Sam smile.

"Are ya good?" Abe asked.

"I don't want you to doubt me. If you doubt me this won't work."

Abe sat silently for a moment before finally nodding his head and sipping on his orange juice. Abe's approval took a weight off Sam's shoulders. Sam believed in himself. He believed in them.

"Oh my gosh," Sam heard their waitress say. He looked over and saw her watching the television above the counter. She turned up the volume so that everyone in the restaurant could hear. People started crowding around her to get a better look. Sam, Abe, and Chelsea all stayed seated.

The words "BREAKING NEWS" appeared on the screen in large letters and Sam's heart dropped once he saw Rusty Ralph's Campgrounds. He saw Cassander on his knees, and of course, he saw himself. Everyone in the restaurant jumped when the gunshot went off. A millisecond before the bullet entered Cassander's skull, the video paused. Sam saw Abe's jaw drop in his peripheral vision and Chelsea was shaking beside him.

None of the people in the restaurant could take their eyes away from the television as a reporter began talking immediately following the video. "The shooter in the video appears to be Sam Sparks, an eighteen-year-old boy born and raised in Westwood. Also, this morning, police found a car abandoned on the side of Woods Drive with two dead bodies inside. The bodies of Parker

Smith and Lucas Armstrong, two local young men who both went missing a couple days ago. The car they were found in was registered in local recluse Abe Hannington's name. In a shocking turn of events, local Westwood police officer Dishon Williams spotted Sam Sparks leaving town around six o'clock this morning with Abe Hannington and his granddaughter, Chelsea Hannington. Police are now on the hunt for the presumed serial killers."

Before Sam could register what he just heard, Abe was grabbing him and Chelsea by the arms and pulling them away. He pushed them outside and quickly led them to the back of the restaurant before shoving Sam to the ground.

"What did ya do?!"

Sam didn't know what to say.

"Ya killed a man this morning?!"

"That wasn't a man! It was Cassander, one of the vampires who attacked us."

"Well he sure looked like a man in that video. I don't care who or what he was, ya killed a man and someone saw ya do it!"

"I didn't know anyone was there," Sam put his head down.

"That doesn't really matter, does it?! Now you're a wanted murderer. I'm a wanted murderer. They're even looking for Chelsea."

"I didn't mean for this to happen!"

"But it happened, Sam, it happened." Abe's face turned bright red as it tensed up. "The Sam I know wouldn't have done what I just saw," Abe said.

"Abe, I-" Sam couldn't find the words.

"Chelsea said she believed you're good... that you could use your powers for good. I thought ya could too. I believed in ya. Ya told me you were fine, that ya weren't feeling any strange temptations, but that was a lie."

"What do you mean?" Sam still couldn't find the strength to stand up.

"Vampires use hate and anger to fuel their powers. In that video I saw both in ya, for all I know Chelsea and I could be your next victims," a tear began to trickle down Abe's cheek.

"I didn't know this would happen," Sam also began to cry.

"I believed in ya. Now I don't know if I can trust ya anymore."

Abe trudged away, towards the forest.

Chelsea looked at Sam but didn't know what to say. She followed Abe.

Sam was left alone, but he couldn't stay by himself for long. He followed thirty yards behind Abe and Chelsea. He didn't have anywhere else to go. Soon everyone he loved would see what he did. His mom, Sarah, Jason. All of their lives would change because of this. He had to go with Abe and Chelsea. He needed them, and even if they didn't know it at the moment, they needed him too.

CHAPTER TWENTY-TWO

Todd thought he must have been the only person who didn't join the huddle beneath the television. It had been twenty minutes since they played the video on the news and people were still standing up, nervously talking about it. Thankfully, his waitress was forced to go back to work and finally brought him his orange juice. After he finished those three glasses, he ordered six more, thinking that was more efficient than having to bother her again. Based on how long it took to get his food, it was clear that the cooks also stopped to watch the news.

"Not much of a news person, are you?" His waitress asked when she finally brought him his colossal breakfast, the smell of which brought his appetite back.

"There's too much going on in the world nowadays, it's hard to keep up."

"Can't argue with that," she smiled as she walked away.

He cleared his entire plate in no more than five minutes then looked around at the other tables in the restaurant. Judging by the amount of untouched, rapidly cooling food on everyone else's tables, it was obvious the crowd was far too distracted to eat. He had a sudden urge to steal all of their food, but resisted the temptation. As he was turning around to face the wall once again, he made eye contact with a man standing at the counter.

No, he thought.

He would not turn around again. He should have never turned around in the first place. Todd faced Eggcited Eggy and prayed the man did not recognize him. He sensed someone approaching from behind and put his head down. He listened as the footsteps grew closer, but to his relief they continued past him to the bathroom. Todd thought about leaving but wanted to wait until the crowd dispersed.

Don't you people have anything better to do with your lives? He questioned, but realized they probably didn't. *All your lives are pointless.* He immediately told himself he was wrong. He didn't want to think these thoughts but it was hard not to. In reality, he envied these people. They may be wasting their time talking about the news but at least they were with their friends and family. They were part of a community.

He remembered the people he had quickly seen when he looked back. Two families sat in booths. A happy couple sat in one and what appeared to be a less than happy couple sat in the other. Each couple had a set of rambunctious children. In the far corner sat three girls who looked hungover, two of them even kept their sunglasses on. Sitting at a table in the middle were a group of men who acted like they were on a first name basis with every employee. They probably came here every Sunday before going golfing or fishing. He assumed the man in the bathroom was with them. Two older couples sat on stools at the counter. The fire in their relationship was long gone but at least they had friends to keep them company. Todd remembered what it was like to have friends. He was the only one who sat alone. He was not a part of their community and he knew that. He was technically still a part of a rather exclusive community, but he didn't want anything to do with them anymore. Yet the power still flowed through his veins. No matter how badly he wanted to rid himself of those powers, he couldn't.

Todd quickly bowed his head when the man exited the bathroom. He looked down at the yolk dripping off the side of his plate, hoping the man would simply pass by, but he decided to stop. Todd chose not to look up until the man uttered his first words.

"Hey, I know you."

Todd slowly raised his head, "I don't think you do."

"You're the guy from that TV show!"

Todd faked a laugh, "I wish I was on TV."

"No, I'm positive, you are on TV. When you're hunting with the Wilson's, there'll always be a catch!"

Todd glanced behind him and noticed a few other people looking his way.

Don't, he thought.

"I can assure you, that's not me."

"That is him!" One of the man's friends said as he walked over. Both men were wearing freshly pressed khakis and almost matching baby blue dress shirts.

Please don't, but he knew they would. The man's friend even bent over to get a better look at Todd.

"You're Todd Wilson."

Todd didn't dare to look back again but sensed more people walking towards him. There was no stopping it now.

"Oh my gosh," one of the fathers said.

Now there must have been six people standing around his booth. "Okay, yeah, I'm Todd Wilson. Now if you don't mind, I'd like to get back to my breakfast."

"But you're done," the father said.

"Uh, yeah, I'm actually heading out now."

"Were you watching the news just then?" Another one of the man's friends asked. He was wearing the same damn baby blue button up but mercifully had a pair of black jeans on.

"Yeah I was, what about it?"

"You're lucky no one recorded you killing your brother."

Todd looked the man right in the eyes and only now noticed his greasy haircut which must have cost at least a hundred dollars. "What did you just say?"

"It's obvious you killed him. How could you do that to your own brother?"

"I didn't kill anyone."

The man laughed and the others joined in. "You may be able to fool Ben Pines but you can't fool me. You're not lookin' so hot, was hiding evidence too tiring this morning?"

"You better watch your mouth."

"You know, I used to like your show," the father said. "I can't believe I put more money in your pocket," he cleared his throat before leaning over and spitting on Todd's plate, causing even more laughter to erupt in the restaurant. Laughter at Todd's expense.

"Hey, Billy! Todd here is gonna pay for all our bills today!" Another man yelled out.

"I'm not doing that," Todd didn't even have enough money for himself, he was planning on walking out.

"Uh, yeah you are," the father looked at the others and laughed. He had now joined the group of snobby men who were currently making the worst mistake of their lives.

The laughter overwhelmed him. It was all Todd could hear, he even saw his waitress chuckling behind the counter. He looked at the man's family. Two kids, both blonde with blue eyes, were smirking at their father's joke. His wife looked less impressed by his humour. Behind them he could see glimpses of the other family. The mother and two kids were standing further back but the father was up on his tippy toes looking over the shoulders of the other men. The three hungover girls now looked more awake and were even chatting with the two waitresses behind the counter as they all watched the show. The two older couples were still sitting in their seats at the counter. Todd was grateful they didn't join the group, but saw that they still laughed at all the jokes. Two cooks were poking their heads out of the kitchen, they kept glancing over at each other after every comment was made. Then there was the group of four men standing in front of him. They invaded his booth and laughed at each other's verbal daggers. He could handle their comments but it was the laughter that got to him. Everyone kept laughing. It was never-ending. He was able to study all of them while they were distracted, tears even ran down a few of their faces. He counted at least twenty-two people.

"You may be jobless now but we know you still have money, get the bills, Billy!" More laughter, so much laughter. It reminded Todd of Skipper's laughter. Skip would make a joke at Todd's expense and laugh for minutes. No one he had ever met could make people laugh more than Skip could make himself laugh. Years ago, he used to love Skip's laugh, but over the years it changed. It evolved from joyful to menacing. The show changed him. Kaleb Bond changed him.

More laughter. Todd tried to drown it out but he couldn't. He looked away from them and at the painting in front of him. But now it was no longer Eggcited Eggy playing the drums, it was Kaleb Bond's face, smiling with his own menacing grin.

This was why Todd could use his powers so effectively. His powers fed on hate and anger and Todd had so much of both. The vampire found him at a point when he was the angriest with Skipper. Even over a month after Skip's death, Todd still felt that anger. And right now, it was being directed at every single person in the restaurant.

More laughter. He wanted to beg them to stop but knew they wouldn't. He didn't want to succumb to his power but it was flowing so strongly through his blood. He felt himself begin to slip away. He looked at all twenty-two of them and prayed he wouldn't do anything to harm them. They weren't dangerous, just ignorant. He knew this ignorance was the biggest mistake of their life, though. His powers fed on his hate and anger, and now he was beyond the point of control.

His powers overtook his body. Fathers screamed and mothers held their crying children. Rapidly the screaming began to fade, one voice at a time. They never had a chance.

CHAPTER TWENTY-THREE

Sheriff Ben Pines sat in silence with Monica Sparks and her husband Jason in their living room. He didn't know what to say but he had to say something. Jason had his hand on Monica's thigh in an attempt to comfort her through this tough time, although Ben imagined there was nothing anyone could do to comfort her today. He had two kids himself, Lucy and Henry, and couldn't begin to imagine being in Monica's position right now. He devoted his life to protecting this town from those with no sense of morality. If one of his children decided to kill someone, it would be the biggest betrayal he could imagine. He did not know Monica Sparks well, but remembered feeling terribly sorry for her when she lost her previous husband and daughter all those years ago.

What was her name? He was ashamed to ask himself whilst sitting right across from Monica. He remembered her husband,

Ben, but couldn't think of her daughter's name.

Shit, he felt even guiltier after considering the fact that he only remembered her late husband's name because it was his name. He began to sweat and felt blood rush to his face but hoped that was not obvious to Monica and Jason.

He cleared his throat and finally decided to speak, "I know this must be a terribly hard time for both of you. I can't even begin to imagine the emotions you must be feeling, and quite frankly, can't think of anything to say to try and comfort you."

"I don't need comforting," Monica interrupted him. "I need to see my son."

"Well I need to see your son too. I hope you can understand that my number one priority is to protect this town. Right now that means finding your son. If you have any information you can give us-"

"My son is not a murderer!" Monica began to cry, making Ben even more uncomfortable.

"Ma'am, as a parent myself, I'd like to think my kids are the salt of the Earth. But you have to understand, someone caught him on tape. I've watched the video maybe fifty times myself and as much as I hate to say it, that's your son in the video."

She began to cry even more as Jason tightened his grip on her thigh.

"Like I said, ma'am-"

"My name is Monica!" She snapped at him.

"I'm sorry. I know it is. You know, before I became sheriff I went to see your husband after he- after his accident. I feel for you, I truly do. I remember being devastated when I saw him. I didn't know him but he was part of this town. He was part of the community I promised to protect and I couldn't protect him.

Now, I know I can't help everyone but sometimes I like to think I can. So you have to understand I would love to help your son, but before I do that I need to protect the rest of Westwood. They come first, then him. I know it sounds harsh but that's what I need to do. So, Monica, while I do sympathize with you, I need to ask you a few questions about Sam," he took a deep breath, feeling exhausted from his speech.

Her tears had already dried, she tried her best to compose herself. "What do you remember about my husband?" She asked while looking him dead in the eye.

Jason jumped in before Ben could answer. "Okay, let's not dwell on the past," Ben noticed his grip tighten again. "We have to talk about Sam. Ask away, we'll answer your questions to the best of our ability."

"Okay, has Sam been acting strange around the house recently?"

"Actually, Sam hasn't been home in a few days," Jason said, causing Monica to shoot a glare at him.

"How many days has it been?"

"Just two," Jason responded.

"Did he tell you why he was leaving?"

"I was actually away visiting some family, but Monica was here and she just let him go."

"Monica, did he say anything to you?" Ben turned his body slightly, he focused all of his attention on Monica.

"He's eighteen years old, he's old enough to make his own decisions," Monica's voice sounded cold.

"Have you ever had any reason to worry about Sam? I mean, has he ever acted out in the past?"

"No," Monica said. "Like I said, my Sam is not a murderer, he's a good kid."

Ben glanced towards Jason and heard him let out a sigh. "Monica, I truly do understand why you believe that, but Sam murdered someone this morning. Obviously something has happened recently which caused him to do that."

"Something has happened. Something is happening. You're just too oblivious to see it."

"What do you mean?" Ben and Jason leaned forward and studied her in unison.

Monica let out a laugh. She looked at Jason, then at Ben and kept laughing. "You say your first priority is to protect this town. If you think my son is the most dangerous thing in Westwood then you're oblivious," she continued to laugh. Ben didn't know what to say. "Hear my words, Ben, you are oblivious."

Ben's heart began to race, so much so that his ringtone almost made him jump out of his seat. "Excuse me," he mumbled as he got up and turned his back to them. Normally he would not take a call during this kind of meeting but he wanted any excuse to get out of Monica's line of fire. "This is Ben Pines," he said. Barry Pickett was on the other end of the call. He was a good kid, Ben could even see him taking over as sheriff one day. He smiled when he heard Barry's voice, but only briefly.

"You gotta come down here, boss."

"Down where? What's going on?"

Barry took a long pause, "Twenty-four people were murdered at Eggciting Times this morning."

Ben's phone fell to the floor.

Monica stayed silent on the couch once Ben left. Neither of them heard his mumbles as he walked out the door but it was obvious he was in a rush to get somewhere. Jason stood up and walked down the hallway. She hoped he wouldn't come back in but knew he would.

"What were you gonna say to him, Monica?" He asked as he charged back into the living room.

"Nothing."

"Nothing?"

"Yes, nothing."

"What were you referring to when you said something is happening in this town?"

She lifted her glance from the floor and met his gaze. "You know, sometimes I see a hint of red in your eyes. It's hard to see, to be fair, but I've looked into your eyes so many times that I've come to immediately recognize it. It's always when you're angry."

"Monica, what were you gonna say to Ben?"

"Nothing. You know me, Jason, you should know better."

"It didn't sound like you were gonna say nothing," he grabbed onto the top of the chair beside him and she noticed his grip immediately tighten.

"If I say anything, I die and my son dies. I know that. You know that's why I've stayed quiet all these years."

"You called him oblivious. You told him something is happening in this town."

"Yeah, I did. You had my husband killed years ago, I know the consequences of turning against you. I won't say anything, but everyday I pray someone else figures it out. I pray someone else sees that hint of red in your eyes and starts to put the pieces together."

Jason lifted the chair and threw it against the wall behind her. She ducked out of the way and landed on the floor. "You think this is a game?!" He shouted. "You think you can just leave little hints and have your fun at my expense?" He picked up the coffee table in front of him and sent it flying across the room. "You can't beat me!"

Monica ducked again. She knelt down in the corner of the room, completely defenseless, although she felt like there was nothing he could possibly do to hurt her. She met his gaze and laughed. "Your eyes... they're redder." He grabbed the television and tossed it into the corner. She rolled forward and felt pieces of the splintered coffee table stabbing into her legs. Even through the shattering of glass behind her, she continued to laugh. "Keep it coming! The angrier you get the redder those eyes become!"

He stormed across the room and lifted her by her neck. "Do you want to die?" She didn't answer, instead she just kept laughing. She knew every second of laughter sent a new dagger flying into his heart. He held her up in the air, she knew this could be the end. But it was not her time yet. Jason dropped her onto the shattered glass.

She backed up and leaned against the couch. "You're pathetic," he said.

"You know," she looked back up at him with no tears in her eyes, she would not give him that satisfaction. Not anymore. "I was heartbroken when Sam left. I knew he was going to face you and I knew he would end up dead. But then I saw him that night, and I saw the fear in your people's eyes," she chuckled. "I think even you're scared, and you should be. I don't know what's going on with Sam, but I think he can beat you." He walked over to her and sent his fist flying into her face. Blood immediately flew out of her mouth and stained their white couch. She no longer had the strength to feign a smile.

She coughed out more blood onto their floor. "If he doesn't beat you, I will. I promise you that. Your days are numbered, Jarek."

He walked out of the room, escaping her laughter. But he could never escape it completely, it would follow him, and continue to feed his powers. He would conquer this world. That was his destiny. No one could stop him.

No one, he was surprised to feel tears running down his face.

Ben had never seen so much blood. There were still puddles of blood forming underneath the corpses. Ben saw gashes on their necks, chests, arms, legs, and even across their faces. Blood was splattered all over the walls. He noticed one painting in the far corner of the restaurant, it was of Eggcited Eggy playing the drums. The egg yolk which once drenched the painting had been replaced by blood.

Barry approached and looked like he was about to say something but Ben raised his hand, stopping him. He knelt down beside two children, a brother and sister. The brother's arm was still covering his sister's eyes. They were completely innocent but that didn't matter. The demons of this world still rose up to feed on the innocent.

This was his town. How could he let this happen?

"What kind of person would do this?" Barry asked, struggling to get the words out.

"A monster," Ben replied. He looked up and saw the colour

rush out of Barry's face. The young officer promptly stumbled out of the diner to vomit. Looking out the window, Ben observed the rest of the police force and forensics team. He had sent them outside when he arrived but they were all still looking through the window. He thought they would want to get away from this bloodbath but they could not keep their eyes off of it. He looked into every single one of their eyes. Brown eyes, blue eyes, green eyes, he could even see a hint of red in Dishon's eyes and wondered if he had been crying. He knew the diner, the blood, and the children, would live on in all of their minds forever.

A monster, he thought. It was his job to catch that monster.

His phone rang, once again making him jump. He hesitantly pulled it out of his pocket. He didn't recognize the number but answered it anyways.

"This is Ben Pines."

"Hello, Ben."

"Who is this?"

"It's Todd. Todd Wilson."

CHAPTER TWENTY-FOUR

San Francisco was too crowded for Todd. As he drove across the San Francisco - Oakland Bay Bridge he already felt uncomfortable, and not just because he was sitting in a puddle of blood. The blood that drenched his seat had dried up after the five-hour drive. After the incident at the restaurant he reached inside the pocket of one of his older victims and grabbed their car keys. Todd was running on auto-pilot at the time, but he had since grown grateful that he happened to steal a Mercedes-Benz. He drove to San Francisco in style, although he immediately reduced the value of the car the moment he sat on the leather seat. But it didn't matter, the previous owner didn't have to worry about that anymore.

He spotted a thrift store about an hour into his drive and stole some clothes. He did not try to hide the fact that he was stealing. He walked in, told the cashier he had an accident before grabbing a pair of jeans and a white shirt which read "Here Comes The Sun", and walked out. He also grabbed another shirt to clean the blood off the seat. The cashier gave him a few choice words as he walked out but didn't bother exiting the store to chase after him. That was a smart move, Todd was appreciative he didn't have to hurt him too.

He was worried he would get tired during his long drive, but surprisingly he didn't. Killing all those people gave him an adrenaline rush that seemed never-ending. Plus, he was looking forward to the job he had to do down south. Just visualizing the hours to come kept him awake and aware.

He drove with all four windows rolled down the whole trip. Every other time he'd driven to this city for the past half-decade he would get depressed. It just meant that he had to meet with the executives at Connelly and Bond Studios. He thought about those times in his life and laughed. He didn't have any control during those years, now he had all the control, and soon everyone would know it. Still though, once he crossed the bridge and entered San Francisco he felt a sense of dread. He remembered all the good times he had with Skipper and knew this was the city that destroyed him. Sure, as their show took off Skip started flying to LA to party, but this was where everything started. This was the city where they had that first meeting with Kaleb Bond and Colton Connelly. This was the city where Kaleb began to take Skip out to bars and sway him to his side. This was the city where Skip betrayed Todd. Todd never forgave him for that, but it was all Kaleb Bond's fault.

This was the city where Kaleb Bond would pay for everything he's done.

Todd arrived at Connelly and Bond Studios at 1:13pm. He

immediately saw the red Rolls Royce and knew Kaleb was in the office today. He parked three spots away from the tacky car and waited. He had about four hours to kill. He didn't mind waiting though. He sat in his car and proceeded to think about Skipper. There were moments where he laughed, moments where he cried, moments where he grew so angry he thought he would charge up to the top floor of the building and get it over with. But he didn't do anything, he knew waiting and visualizing what he would do would only make the moment more satisfying when it came.

It was 5:28pm when Kaleb strutted out of the building. Most of the other employees left about fifteen minutes ago, but as the co-owner of the company, Todd expected Kaleb to come out later than the rest. That was perfect, it meant the parking lot was empty for him to meet with Kaleb. It had been too long since they had seen each other.

This is for you, Skip.

"Todd," Kaleb's eyes were glued to his phone and he didn't see Todd until he was just ten steps away.

"Hey, Kaleb." Kaleb was always a big man, but his height helped offset the extra weight. He had maintained bleached blonde hair for all the years Todd had known him and now even had a matching goatee. He stood across from Todd, dressed in his usual blue suit with a bewildered look on his face, but suddenly smiled widely.

"It's been too long, Todd, are you here to talk about season four?"

"No."

"I hate to hear that, we really do have some amazing ideas for it, you gotta trust me on this one."

I trusted you before and you ruined my life.

Kaleb waited for Todd to respond but when he didn't, he made his way to his car. "If you're staying in the city come by my office tomorrow, that way we can sit down and have a longer talk about it."

"Actually," Todd said. "I'd like to talk to you now." Todd followed Kaleb to his car and Kaleb hesitantly unlocked the doors.

"Want me to go somewhere?" Kaleb asked. "We can grab dinner or something."

"No thanks, I want to stay right here," Todd opened up the passenger's door and sat in the car.

Kaleb laughed nervously as he followed him into the car. "I'm not gonna lie, Todd, this is getting a little weird."

"Do you have a brother?" Todd asked, completely ignoring Kaleb's worries. He fiddled with the rear view mirror.

"No, I don't," Kaleb shooed Todd's hand away from the mirror.

"I don't either. I always wanted one growing up, and I finally got one in Skip. But now he's gone and I'm all alone again."

"C'mon, Todd, you're not alone, you've got a lovely wife and kids at home."

"Yeah, but to be honest, I've been going through something strange lately and I can't tell them about it."

"I'm sorry to hear that, anything I can do to help? You know, if you sign on to make a fourth season, I can give you so much money you could do anything you want. Travel the world, buy a new house, find a way to get rid of your problems."

"It's always been about money for you, hasn't it?"

Kaleb chuckled, "Well, Todd, I am a businessman after all, that's just the way the world works."

"You know nothing about this world."

"Woah, don't come at me here, buddy, I'm just trying to help."

"You can't help me."

"How 'bout this?" Kaleb responded. "I get you the best hotel room in this city. You can do whatever you want tonight, go party, blow off some steam, or stay in and relax. Then tomorrow we can meet up and talk when you're feeling better."

"Is that what you did for Skip? Did you get him the best hotel room in this city?"

"What do you mean? I did a lot for Skip, I love you guys."

"No, you loved him because you could control him," Todd looked at Kaleb and could see the sweat dripping down his face. "You and I both knew he had problems, but you took advantage of them. You ruined his life, Kaleb. I always wanted a brother, and I loved him, but then you took him away from me."

"I didn't take anyone away from you, pal, it's not like I'm the one who killed him."

"It doesn't matter who killed him, you started to kill him years before he actually died. After he got close to you he became a completely different person. You made me hate him… and you're going to pay for that."

"Is that a threat, Todd? What are you even here for?" Kaleb leaned out of his seat, as if he was getting ready to strike Todd.

"I'm here to kill you."

Kaleb chuckled even louder this time and that infuriated Todd. "So it was you. You hated Skipper so you killed him. Wow, I didn't want to believe it but it makes sense."

"I didn't kill Skip."

"Then who did?"

"Batraz."

"Who's Batraz?

"A vampire. Probably the strongest one I've met, other than our master."

"Are you high or something?" Kaleb leaned over and looked closely at Todd. "Yeah, your eyes are a little bloodshot there, Toddy," he laughed.

"The angrier we get, the redder our eyes become."

"What do you mean by we?"

"The vampires."

"I want whatever you're on right now," Kaleb leaned back and laughed some more. "I'll tell you one thing, Skipper would've loved whatever you're on," he laughed so hard that he began to cough.

Todd looked at him with red eyes. Not just bloodshot eyes, these were the red eyes of a vampire entering battle. He smiled, revealing his fangs, and reached over to dig his claws into Kaleb's thigh. Kaleb yelped loudly, before his face froze in horror.

"It takes time for a vampire to learn to fully control their powers. Sometimes, I still can't control them," it was Todd's turn to laugh. "Earlier this morning I killed over twenty people in a diner. I didn't want to do it but I was just so angry. My powers wanted me to do it."

Kaleb opened his quivering mouth to say something. "Don't talk," Todd took the hand that wasn't an inch into his thigh and covered Kaleb's mouth. "I like seeing you squirm. You think you own this world, you think you can do anything you want to anyone you want, but you can't."

Kaleb started mumbling, his eyes bulging out of his head. Todd soaked it all in before removing his hand from his mouth.

"A- and what about you?" Kaleb asked.

"What about me?"

"You're saying I think I can do whatever I want, but you're the one who's lost your mind and gone on a killing spree!"

Todd laughed and took a moment before responding. "Do you believe in the grim reaper?" Kaleb didn't answer, instead electing to spit at him. Todd nonchalantly wiped his face. "It's weird, my whole life I never gave the grim reaper any thought. That is, until we started filming the show. After we finished the first episode, me, Skip, and Julian went out to celebrate. They were both hammered so I let them stay at my place. That was one of the best nights of my life. I sat on the couch, smiling, while my best friends in this world fell asleep, but then I saw something. I saw you, Kaleb. I saw your face in the darkness and ever since that moment I knew who the grim reaper was. It's you. Ever since then you've done everything you can to ruin my life. I figured out that every person has their own personal grim reaper, haunting them until they breathe their final breath. So, you're my grim reaper, and I'm yours." Todd removed his claws from Kaleb's leg and stuck both hands into his chest. Kaleb let out a loud gasp and shot back in his seat. Blood immediately spewed out between Todd's fingers and coated the windshield of Kaleb's precious Rolls Royce.

After a few moments of Todd carefully observing the pain on Kaleb's face, Kaleb tried to speak. "Y- y-" Kaleb let out a cough and began gasping for air. It took him a few moments to regain his breath and find the strength to say his last words. "You're acting like I'm the villain," he coughed three more times. "But look at what you've become. You are pure evil."

"I know," Todd smiled and continued to watch as Kaleb's

skin grew paler and paler. "I'll be better soon, I just had to do this first," he lifted his claws once more and stuck them into Kaleb's jugular.

That was for you, Skip. It felt good, it felt right, it felt like justice.

Todd left Kaleb's body in the car for his employees to find in the morning. His job was done. But, as he walked down the street he began to cry. That was unexpected, killing Kaleb was supposed to help. He slayed the spectre that had haunted him for years, he shouldn't feel bad about it. But he did, he felt empty. A war was coming, the humans would face the vampires, and Todd found himself questioning what side he would be on.

Throughout the entire drive down from Westwood, he had said it was his powers that were making him do it. But now he realized his powers were just an excuse for him. His powers allowed him to murder Kaleb, but they did not fuel the hate inside of him. Powers or not, Todd wanted Kaleb dead. Todd, the human, held onto all his hate in that moment. His tears clouded his vision until he could barely see a thing. He escaped into a nearby alley and made a home beside a dumpster. He broke down more as he realized he had become one of the monsters he escaped from.

The vampires may catch him and he may not be able to escape these powers, but he would try.

What will I become? He hoped he was capable of shaping his own life.

He took his phone out of his pocket and began dialing a number. He hesitated before calling, but knew what had to be done.

"This is Ben Pines."

"Hello, Ben," Todd saw his reflection in a puddle beside him. He looked past his disheveled, bloody appearance, and tried to see the good inside of him. There had to be some left.

"Who is this?"

"It's Todd. Todd Wilson. Do you wanna know what really happened to Skipper?"

CHAPTER TWENTY-FIVE

Sam still maintained a great distance between himself and Abe as they neared the motel. Chelsea walked in between them, playing the role of their non-verbal mediator. Sam even decided to stand outside as the two of them went into the office of Campfire Inn to book their room. The motel was a standard L-shape but had the added touch of trees painted onto the walls, fitting perfectly with the theme. Each car was parked right in front of a room and at the far corner of the lot was a surprisingly well-kept pool. Attached to the fenced-in pool was a campfire with a few chairs around it. It looked nice but Sam knew he wouldn't get any use out of it, he didn't imagine Abe or Chelsea would be eager to share s'mores and tell stories around the campfire.

There were only two cars parked in the lot so Sam assumed it was not going to be a busy night for the motel, at least he hoped it wouldn't be. The less people they came in contact with, the better. Sam was entertaining himself by kicking a pebble back and forth across the parking lot when Abe and Chelsea walked out. Sam frowned when he saw Abe. As pathetic as it was that he found great joy in kicking the rock, it took his mind off of everything going on.

Abe tossed a key at him and continued walking away, "Try to get some sleep. We'll see ya in the morning."

Sam did not catch the key at first, he flailed his arms in the air as it bounced from one hand to the other but then knelt over to pick it up off the ground. When he looked up, Abe was already almost at their room and he made eye contact with a weary Chelsea. She shrugged her shoulders at him and kept walking as well. "Wait," Sam called out to Abe. "We're staying in different rooms?"

"Yeah," Abe said quietly while unlocking his door.

"Don't you think that's a bad idea?"

Abe already had his door open but looked back at Sam, "No, Sam, I think it's a fantastic idea. You're all the way down at that end so if you decide you wanna sneak away in the middle of the night, no one will stop ya! Doesn't that sound wonderful to you?"

Sam didn't know how to respond to that and Abe was obviously not patient enough to wait for a reply. He slammed the door and Sam locked eyes with Chelsea. "Just give him some time, he'll get over it," she said.

"Did you know he would react like this all along?" Sam asked her.

"I didn't think it would be this bad. To be fair though, I didn't know you were gonna go kill some dude either." That could've been perceived as a jab at Sam but the smile on Chelsea's face made it clear she only meant it as a joke.

He wanted to smile with her but could not, "I'm sorry, Chelsea, I really am."

"Don't worry about it, Sam," she replied.

"So you're not mad at me too?"

"Of course not! Cassander was bad and you're good."

"I don't know if your grandpa's so sure about that."

"Look, when you told me about your sister, I wasn't ready to tell you about my parents," she paused.

"Chelsea, you don't have t-"

"I want to," she cut him off with a slight smile on her face. They walked over to a bench in front of the office. "After everything that happened with your dad and my grandpa, I guess the vampires followed him. He managed to lose them for a while, he even convinced himself that he lost them for good. So, when he finally thought he was safe, he came to New Orleans, where I lived with my parents. He stayed with us for a long time. He even gave me a note with his phone number on it and told me to call him first if I was ever in an emergency. One day, about a year after my grandpa showed up, he wasn't home and some people broke into our house. My parents thought they were just intruders. They were vampires, of course. My parents hid me under their bed and left the room. Before going under though, I grabbed the phone. I called him and called him and called him. My grandpa never answered and my parents never came back in the room. In fact, I never saw them again. I was so scared to crawl out from under the bed that I stayed there for hours, I don't even remember how many hours. My grandpa eventually came back and found my parents. The vampires never found me."

"I'm so sorry," Sam noticed that Chelsea didn't shed a tear while she recounted her experience.

"It's okay," she said. "My point is, no one's perfect, least of all my grandpa. We all make mistakes, Sam. He'll forgive you eventually."

Chelsea began to walk away but Sam called out to her, "Hey, Chelsea, did your grandpa ever find the vampires who did that?"

"Yes."

"What did he do to them?"

Chelsea looked down at the ground before turning around and walking to her room.

Chelsea solemnly walked into her room and looked at Abe, who was sitting on the bed. "What were you two talking about?" He asked her.

"I had to convince Sam that you would forgive him eventually."

He chuckled. "Ya like that kid, don't ya?"

"We're a team," she responded. "Of course I like him."

"It doesn't feel like we're a team right now."

"No, it doesn't, but that's not because of Sam," Chelsea said, causing Abe to look up at her.

"What's that supposed to mean?"

"We haven't talked about it yet, but you lied to Sam. That day at the outlet mall, you told him his mom wasn't actually there the night we fought the vampires."

"I have my reasons for that."

"You may have reasons but I don't. You brought me in on

a lie that I don't want to be part of. I don't know why you insist on lying to him but that's not the type of teammate I wanna be. He's gonna find out, grandpa, that's the type of lie that comes back to bite you." Abe continued looking at her but didn't know what to say. "Sam's not the one destroying our team. You are."

Chelsea's words gave Sam some much needed perspective. Maybe it was because of her age, but for some reason she never seemed stressed out, even in the most serious and life-threatening situations. Perhaps she had unlocked one of the secrets of the universe; when you look at the big picture most things don't matter and therefore we should not spend more than a second worrying about them.

Sam entered his room and laid down on his bed. He fell asleep and dreamt of flying through the sky, just as he had on the hill the night before. It was exhilarating to soar through the night sky, everywhere he looked shooting stars pierced through the clouds that surrounded him. He wanted to make a wish upon a star and knew exactly what it would be. He wanted to see who he saw the night before.

Take me to my father.

Suddenly the wind grew stronger and he lost control of his body. He tried to regain control as the wind carried him over the tall West Wood trees and into his backyard. He landed beside his firepit and nearly threw up.

He turned around and saw his father. All he could do was smile but his father didn't look pleased. Sam took a few steps forward and looked closer at his face. Last night when Sam saw his father, he looked like he did before he died. Now he looked aged, not just physically but emotionally too. He watched as his father trembled.

Sam's smile faded as he asked his dad what was wrong. His dad didn't answer so he asked again, but suddenly his dad was nowhere to be found, like he vanished into thin air. In fact, nothing was around him anymore, he was just staring into a black void. He looked above him and noticed the fan from his motel room spinning around and around. It took him a moment to realize he was back in the real world.

"What's wrong?" He asked again, despite knowing he was alone. His head was spinning as fast as the fan.

"Nothing's wrong, Sam," he shot up to locate the source of the voice. It was the news anchor on the television, who to Sam looked oddly like his father, only older.

"What did you say?" Sam asked.

"Twenty-four people were brutally murdered at the popular Eggciting Times restaurant this morning." Sam snapped out of his vision. He must've turned the television on before he fell asleep.

Sam, now fully awake and cognitive, listened intently as the anchor described the situation at Eggciting Times all-too-vividly. It happened only a few minutes after Sam, Abe, and Chelsea left. Sam had so many questions, he didn't even know where to begin, but one stood above the rest.

What's wrong?

"Sorry, folks," the anchor paused, grabbing his earpiece. "We have some more breaking news."

"What's wrong?"

The anchor paused for a few moments before continuing. "Sarah Connelly, daughter of successful business man Colton

Connelly, has now been missing for over thirty-six hours. Police urge anyone who might have information on her whereabouts to come forward as soon as possible."

Sam was sent into shock. He thought of the rock he kicked around in the motel parking lot. That rock had no power over him. He could kick it in whatever direction he wanted and it could not resist. He could pick it up and throw it into the sky and it could not resist. That rock's life depended entirely on him. But that is about the only thing he had power over. He tricked himself into believing he had power over Cassander. He murdered him in cold blood and now he had to face the consequences. Even after watching the clip on the news, Sam believed Abe and Chelsea would understand. He was a vampire after all, he was the only one who could save them in the battles to come. But just because he thought they should understand his actions doesn't mean they have to. He does not control their lives as he does the rock's. As a vampire he possessed an immense amount of power, but that did not mean this world revolved around him. Sam thought he could do anything he wanted but was gravely mistaken. He enjoyed having control over other people's lives. He was their judge, jury, and executioner. His powers had begun to consume him. He thought they could keep people safe, but it was his behaviour that put the people he cared for most in danger.

Sam shot out of his self-reflective state and stared at Sarah's picture on the television. It made her green eyes appear to be shining. He looked at his own hazel eyes in the mirror and prayed they would turn red soon. He didn't simply want to feel the rush of power. He just wanted one more night, one more chance, to end it all.

Sam rushed out of his room only to see Abe already walking towards his door. Sam didn't even notice Chelsea at first because she was blocked by Abe's body, as if he was protecting her. She was struggling to hold up a bag, Sam didn't understand why Abe wouldn't carry the bag for her but that's when he saw it. Abe raised his gun and pointed it at Sam.

"Get inside," Abe said sternly.

They're leaving, Sam thought. *They're leaving without me.*

"We can't do this right now. It's Sarah, she's in trouble," Sam pleaded.

"Get inside! Now!"

Sam did not dare disobey. He backed inside his motel room with his hands above his head. Abe followed him with the gun held high and ordered Sam to sit on the bed.

"You're making a mistake," Sam said. He imagined unleashing his powers and killing Abe to save his own life, but there was no way his powers would cooperate with him. His powers only seemed to work when he was angry. As he sat on his bed with a gun pointed at his head, he didn't feel angry, just sad. "We were supposed to work together," Sam continued. "We were supposed to be a team. I want to end this tonight."

"We're not a team, not anymore," Sam looked past the gun and into Abe's hardened eyes.

"I need to help Sarah."

"Then help her," Abe flipped the gun so it was no longer pointed at Sam and held it out to him. Sam hesitated. He didn't exactly understand what was happening, but Chelsea's nod of approval was all he needed to know they were still on the same side. For now at least. "We've got company," Abe declared.

Sam and Chelsea watched from his window as Abe drunkenly stumbled across the motel parking lot. His loose hood swayed back and forth across his head but it was necessary to conceal his face. Just moments ago this seemingly drunken fool grabbed the bag from Chelsea and unzipped it on Sam's bed, revealing a fine assortment of firearms. He informed Sam that he was sitting by the unlit campfire, enshrouded by darkness, when he saw Batraz walk into the motel office. After an encounter with the manager, Batraz retreated back into the field across from the motel, leaving a bloody trail behind him.

"I think he went to get the others," Abe had said, and believed they would be back any minute.

Now they were back. Sam saw two shadows pass under the motel's neon sign. Batraz was easy to recognize as he towered over the other, but Sam figured he knew who the vampire beside him was too, Saija. Their hunters had found them, but it surprised Sam that there weren't more vampires. At least, from what Sam could see they were not being followed. Who knew what lay in the darkness beyond the motel?

Sam was so focused on the two vampires that the glass shattering made him jump. Abe had fallen to the ground and dropped the beer bottle he was holding, perfectly encapsulating the drunken character he assigned himself to play.

"Don't mind me, I'll be just fine," Abe said as he walked close to the vampires, two of the most powerful beings in this world.

"You ready?" Chelsea said as she looked up at Sam.

He quickly inspected his gun. "Yeah, are you?"

"Always," she smiled. "And don't worry, we're still a team."

Sam gave Chelsea an uneasy smile before he turned his attention back to Abe, who was still making a fool of himself.

Abe fell one more time on his way to the vampires, who were now just watching him in shock. "You guys wanna partay?" He asked them.

The two vampires looked at each other. "I don't think you're gonna have too much fun tonight."

"Oh really… well I think you're wrong," Abe immediately pulled his gun out of his back pocket and fired three shots into Saija's skull. Sam and Chelsea charged out of the room, guns held high, as her lifeless body fell to the ground.

Abe tried to fire a few more close-range shots at Batraz but he moved too quickly and knocked the gun out of Abe's hand. He raised his claws once more, ready to strike Abe down, but a bullet pierced through the centre of his hand. Batraz hissed and launched himself into the sky as Sam and Chelsea ran up, guns smoking. The three of them looked up into the darkness. Sam glanced at Abe but Abe did not return a look. He looked back up at what seemed like a dark void, the only source of light was the motel's flickering neon sign. They could hear sounds above them, then beside them, then the sounds merged together and made it sound like they were surrounded. People began to come out of the other two occupied rooms at the motel. A family of five ran out of one, the father's arms extended to shield his wife and children. An old man wearing only a tank top and a tight pair of underwear came out of the other with whom Sam assumed to be his mistress, a woman who had to be at least twenty years younger than him in a short purple dress.

"Go away!" Abe yelled at the people as he ran towards them. "Get your keys, get in your car, and go! Ya don't have time to pack up." The father immediately followed his orders, leaving his terrified family at the doorway as he ran into their room.

"Who do you think you are?!" The old man was more re-sistant.

"You have to listen to him, you have to go!" Sam yelled out, causing Abe to send a scowl his way.

The old man brushed past his mistress and took a few steps closer to Abe. "I'm no-" Just then a monster fell from the sky and landed on his car, completely crushing its roof in the pro-cess. This sent the old man into a panic, quickly running past his mistress and back into his room. He shut the door behind him, prompting the woman to bang on it frantically.

"Never mind him," Abe called out to the girl. "Hide in their room!" He turned his attention to the family as the vam-pire, above them all, sent a menacing hiss his way. "Take her with you, get inside and don't come out!" They all immediately obeyed. The vampire did not even turn to face them, obviously too focused on Abe.

Just then another vampire fell from the sky, crushing the roof of the family's minivan, and sent another hiss their way. The vampire hopped off the van and approached Abe while the other pursued Chelsea. They both moved quickly, grabbing their vic-tims and launching them into the air. It seemed like they were trying to avoid Sam, who sprinted towards the spot where Chel-sea was taken. Just before Sam reached the neon sign, Batraz fell from above. His tall body was illuminated by the pink neon light as his glowing red eye focused on the real target.

"Hello, Sam."

Sam looked past Batraz and saw Chelsea struggling on the ground. She had dropped her gun and was crawling towards it but the vampire grabbed her leg just before she could reach it. In one swift motion, the vampire wrapped its arm around Chelsea's neck and picked her up, holding her hostage. Sam scanned the rest of the motel, hoping to see Abe running to their aid, but there was no sign of him anywhere.

"Your friends are weak, Sam. It's just you and I."

As he continued looking around the motel, he spotted the children looking out of their room window. When he saw them they immediately closed the blinds, as if they were afraid of him.

Why are you afraid? I'm on your side. But then he looked at his reflection in the window of the motel office. He couldn't see much of himself, but the red eyes stood out. He screamed in pain as his powers began to flow up from his feet. He knelt down on one knee, clenching his fists tightly. His claws formed while his fists were closed, causing him to cut his own palms. He screamed louder than ever as his power flowed into his face, causing his fangs to burst out of his gums. He fought through the pain and rose again. The children closed the blinds because they saw him for what he truly was... a monster.

"There's the real you," the monster who stood across from him said.

"Let her go!" Sam yelled whilst pointing at a squirming Chelsea.

"Do you feel powerful?" Batraz asked, ignoring his plea.

"I only feel hate and anger," spit flew out of Sam's mouth as he continued to breathe heavily, desperately trying to fight through the pain.

Batraz laughed. "Yes, of course. Hate and anger are the two strongest powers in the universe. They're what feed our powers. If we let go of those feelings we grow weak."

"Don't listen to him, Sam!" Chelsea yelled, causing the vampire to tighten its hold on her.

Sam looked over briefly before turning his attention back to Batraz. "What if I want to be weaker?"

"You don't. If you're weak you'll die with the rest of this world. You'll die just like your friends are gonna die tonight."

"They're not gonna die."

Batraz's laugh turned into a smirk. "I can tell you really believe that, but you're wrong. They chose the wrong path and tonight is their night to pay for that. I know that's hard for you to accept right now but I promise you, you'll get over their deaths. You have a long life to live in this world, Sam. Give it a hundred years or so and they'll be nothing more than a memory," his smile grew wider.

"A hundred years?"

"Yes, Sam. You'll be around long after your friends."

"Why? You're not here to kill me?"

"Of course not, Sam. I'm here to bring you to my master, Prince of The Ash, Jarek."

"The vampire my father fought?"

"Yes, Jarek ordered his vampires to kill your father."

Sam clenched his fists, "I'm gonna kill you, then I'm gonna kill Jarek."

Batraz laughed once again, "I like to see that, the hatred in your eyes. Draw on that hate. Whenever you're in a battle think of what happened to your father and you could be one of the mightiest warriors in the universe. You'll be a true vampire."

"I don't wanna be one of you!"

"Look at yourself, it's too late."

A shot fired. Batraz's smile faded as he bent over, grabbing his shoulder.

Sam looked over to see a hunting knife sticking out of

Chelsea's captor's skull. She held her smoking gun out in front of her. He raised his own gun and fired five more shots into Batraz's stomach before charging towards him and catching the vampire as he fell to the ground.

"Why didn't you aim for my head," Batraz struggled to say.

"Don't worry, I'll finish the job before your wounds heal. I just want you to feel the pain. This is for Rick," Sam pulled out his knife and stabbed him in the chest, easing the mighty vampire to the ground.

"You're a foolish boy."

"I'm gonna kill your master. Then I'm gonna kill every vampire, every one of your people. I want you to know that before you die."

"Go find my master then," Batraz struggled to laugh. "You'll see who he really is, and you'll learn he's already been haunting you for a long time." Sam looked down at Batraz, he froze as he gazed into his enemy's red eye. He was pulled out of his trance by a booming gunshot. Batraz's head exploded beneath him and Sam's ears began to ring. He looked to his right and saw Chelsea, who delivered the killing blow. She raised her other hand and pointed at the pool. All the life looked like it had been sucked out of her eyes. His ears still rung, and his vision was slightly blurry, but he could make out two figures falling into the pool through the dim light above. Abe and his opponent.

The water that rose up to meet Abe felt like cement. He had two large cuts across his back, so the crash sent a shivering pain through his body and for a brief moment he lost control of his legs. He let out a few coughs and more water rushed into his mouth. He almost reached the bottom of the surprisingly deep pool before he flung his arms out to escape the darkness of the water. He struggled to extend his arms again, his body aching more than it ever had before, but he was almost free, almost out of the water. He saw the light above the pool, it was faint but still acted as his guide. With that light came fresh air. He fought to push himself upwards once more but just as he was about to reach the surface, he felt resistance. It was as though he was in the ocean and got caught on a long piece of seaweed. As a kid he was always terrified of seaweed, he hated feeling it on his feet when he swam. There was never actually anything to be scared of, of course, but this wasn't seaweed.

His fingers burst through the surface of the water but he could not pull himself up any further. Abe looked below him and saw the bright red eyes. The vampire was like a sea monster hunting its prey in the deep ocean. Abe kicked as hard as he could but the vampire kept pulling him down. He kicked again and again and again, but to no avail. With every kick he wasted the energy he needed to fight for his life. He was pulled down so deep he couldn't even see the light above anymore. The vampire moved its claws up his leg until he reached his torso. It wrapped its arms around him and slammed him against the bottom of the pool, sending another sharp burst of pain through his spine.

It took slamming Abe two more times against the bottom of the pool for his vision to become blurry. On the fourth slam he couldn't see at all. He was surprised to find himself still conscious. Even through the immense pain of the vampire's claws digging deep into his sides, there was some part of him that had to continue fighting. He brought his knee up and connected with the vampire's stomach, which he knew did no damage, but while doing so he reached into his boot and was thankful to discover his knife had remained in his sock. This immediately gave him some adrenaline and he used all his strength to shove the knife into the side of the vampire. His sight momentarily returned and he saw blurry air bubbles escape from the vampire's mouth as its eyes grew wide. Abe repeatedly stabbed into the side of the vampire, hoping it would let him go for even a second. It retaliated by slamming him once more and shoving it's nails even deeper into Abe's side.

Abe's body went numb. As more blood poured out of him, he began to feel completely lifeless. He had been struggling to breathe for so long but now decided he didn't have to. He accepted it all. The vampire defeated him. The seaweed defeated him. He even smiled, thinking about how foolish he was to believe a grown man with a fear of seaweed could defeat an army of vampires. In his final moments his vision finally returned to him. He saw what he always thought he would see as he died… a demon. Red eyes, sharp nails, it might as well have had horns sticking out of its head too. He looked at it, scared at first, but he decided he wouldn't fear this monster. He would be free soon enough. His eyes closed. He was at peace.

Water came shooting out of his mouth. Abe gasped for air and this world gave him all that he required. Fresh air had never felt so good entering his body. For a few seconds he thought he was still in the pool and feared seeing the demon again. But he saw the stars, before Chelsea's not-so-innocent face blocked his view of them. She smiled at him and he smiled back. He reached for the fresh bruises which plagued her neck, but she eased his arm back down, indicating she was okay. He smiled, looking back up at the stars again, realizing she was his saviour.

His twelve-year-old granddaughter had saved him.

"He jumped in and saved you, grandpa!" Chelsea said to him, wiping the tears from her eyes.

Abe slowly leaned up and looked at the pool. No one was there. The two of them stared at the black water, neither saying a word for at least a minute. Then someone rose from the pool and turned towards them. It had red eyes. And behind this red-eyed monster rose another body, although this body remained faced down and floating. Abe noticed Chelsea smiling beside him but could not match her enthusiasm. Sam emerged from the pool and locked eyes with Abe.

"He did it!" Chelsea celebrated.

Abe now knew Sam had saved his life, and he knew he would have been face to face with him at the bottom of the pool. He asked himself which vampire was the demon he saw. As he looked at Sam, he didn't know the answer.

Before Sam could take his first step towards them, the sirens began. They seemed far away at first, but neared them rapidly. Before they had time to react they saw two cars speeding down the road, turning the dark fields around them into fields of red and blue.

"Get behind the cars," Abe finally managed to get some words out. He ran and picked up his gun before joining Sam and Chelsea behind the cars.

As the police cars pulled into the motel parking lot, the father walked out of his room.

"Help is here!"

His excitement waned as Abe pointed his gun towards him. "Get back in the room!" Abe shouted at the man.

"What are you doing?!" Chelsea yelled at him.

"We're wanted by the police. They think we're murderers. Do ya think we can just leave here peacefully with them?" Neither Chelsea nor Sam responded. "I'm not turning myself in. There are still vampires out there. We're not done yet."

"I'm not done yet," Sam said as he looked at Abe, his eyes still red. "This isn't your fight anymore. It's mine." Abe knew his powers were still flowing through him, guiding every decision he made.

"This is our fight," Chelsea responded.

"No," Sam said, still looking at Abe. "We're not a team anymore."

"Come out with your hands above your head!" One of the policemen said over their speaker.

Sam stood up. "Boy, put your hands above your head!"

He looked at Abe, then at Chelsea. "I'm sorry. I need to face their master… alone."

"Sam, ya don't want to do that! Ya have to trust me!" Abe tried to stop him but it was too late. Sam leapt into the air and escaped into the field behind the motel.

Abe and Chelsea were stuck between the motel and the police. There was nowhere to run. "I repeat! Come out with your hands above your head!" The speaker sounded louder than before. Their red and blue lights continued to flash. Abe looked down at his granddaughter.

"What are we gonna do?!" She was scared.

He thought about how he felt under that water. He accepted his death. His story had come to an end. He was at peace. After all these years, he finally found peace. But then he woke up. Hiding behind these cars, he knew he was in Hell. He smiled at his granddaughter, who he loved more than anything in the entire world, and for a second everything disappeared. It was only them. She smiled back. His clarity returned. His resolve was strong, he knew what he had to do. His story wasn't over yet. This was still their fight.

He fired his first shot.

CHAPTER TWENTY-SIX

Sam could see the flames from far across The West Woods. Fire spewed from two rows of torches, each row extending about thirty yards, and formed a pathway leading up to their cave. He knew they were waiting for him. This was not an ambush, but a greeting. He jumped down from the treetop and began walking on foot. He felt comforted and whole in his dad's jean jacket. Despite how drastically his life had changed, he told himself he was still the same Sam. He hoped that if he repeated it over and over in his head, he'd eventually believe it.

As he neared the path, the flames illuminated the dark figures that stood beside each torch. Once he took his first step onto the path he would be trapped, surrounded by death on all sides. Sam refused to be intimidated, he walked past the first set of torches with his head held high and looking straight ahead. He focused his attention on the mouth of the cave, not worrying about the vampires that could attack him at any given moment. They wouldn't lay a hand on him, their only job was to lead him to Jarek. That is why Batraz never intended on killing him. He was merely a servant, just like the rest of them, all pawns in their master's plan.

Sam wondered if they knew that. Each of these beings possessed an extraordinary amount of power, but they would never truly be free to use those powers.

Sam felt the heat of each flame as he walked down the path. It lit up his eyes even more, the hate inside of him burned bright. All of the vampire's heads were down. His were the only red eyes visible in these dark woods. As he approached the halfway mark he saw a being walk out of the cave. The master. He couldn't see the master's face but was met with another set of red eyes. They were a darker shade of red, more experienced, more cruel. Sam made his way to the end of the path and stood just five yards away from Jarek, Prince of The Ash.

Another vampire emerged from the cave. Unlike their master, Sam could see this one's face. She had long dark hair and her jet black cloak made her pale skin ever more ghostly.

"You are in the presence of Jarek, Prince of the Ash," the vampire spoke.

"ALL HAIL PRINCE JAREK," Sam was startled by the uproar of the vampires behind him.

"Bow before your prince," the female vampire spoke again.

"I will not bow for anyone."

"You will," their prince finally spoke. It was a voice he had heard before.

"Who are you?"

The prince laughed a familiar laugh. "Sam Sparks, the boy

vampire. Who knew we were both hiding things from each other," Jarek lifted his hood, finally revealing his identity.

Sam saw a flash and he was back in his living room. His mom wanted to take pictures before he left to go on his first date with Sarah. He acted like he was impatient to leave but in reality he wanted to stand beside her forever. He was so nervous for the date but his mom comforted him. Then Jason asked to take a picture with Sam. His mom hesitantly agreed and Jason placed his arm around Sam. He felt awkward taking pictures with Jason. But he looked up and noticed how happy Jason was and that made him feel more at ease. He even saw his eyes light up. There was a hint of red in them. Of course he was happy. He was relishing in his power over Sam, over his mom, over everyone. Sam's whole life had been a lie.

"Where's my mom?"

"She's at home. I'll deal with her once I'm done with you."

"It was you all along, Jason."

"My name is Jarek, Prince of The Ash. Master of the vampires. Master of you."

"My father is dead because of you!" Sam felt like he needed to cry but no tears fell from his eyes. Instead, hate and anger raged inside him.

"Your father was weak, Sam. He wasn't worth my time. I would've taken no satisfaction in killing him myself. But you on the other hand, I'm gonna enjoy killing you, Son."

"You've lied to me my whole life," Sam continued to fume.

"I have, and I've enjoyed every second of it."

"I'm gonna end this. Tonight."

"Sam, you're just a boy, and you're foolish. You're directing all your hate and anger at me and you're not looking at the bigger picture. Do you think I'm the only one that's lied to you?"

Sam didn't respond. He just looked deeply into the dark red eyes of Jason. The same eyes he had seen glimpses of over the years, but had never put it together.

"Your mom, the woman you love most, has built her whole relationship with you on a lie."

"No... you're wrong."

"Do you think she didn't know what I really was when she married me? Oh, Sam, you're so innocent, too naive to accept the truth."

"She would never lie to me."

"She loves you, Sam, I'll give her that. She loves you a lot. So much so that she agreed to help me infiltrate your world in exchange for your safety."

"Stop talking!" Sam screamed at the top of his lungs.

Jason just laughed, "I can also sense your fear, Sam. It weighs you down, makes you weaker. You can't kill me. You won't kill me."

"I'll kill all of you!" Sam extended his claws and spit flew out of his mouth.

"Then what?" Jason asked him in a calm manner. "This is going to be over soon, Sam. I've already won. Tonight is the end of you. And once you're gone, your whole world will fall. Your mom will die... but not before we take care of your little girl-friend."

Another being emerged from the cave. It was Doctor Allen, dressed all in black, his eyes as red as the rest of them.

Go for it, you'll regret it if you don't, Sam remembered Doctor Allen telling him to ask Sarah out. That same man who inspired him not too long ago, now dragged the girl of his dreams by her hair out of the cave behind him. He threw Sarah down onto the ground. She was scarred, bruised, and broken. Sam struggled to hold back his tears.

"You see, Sam, I knew I could always use your mom against you, but she was all I had. That is, until Sarah came along," Jason started moving towards Sarah. "I personally think you two make a gorgeous couple," he caressed her face.

"Get away from her!"

"But I was never able to form a close enough relationship with you to talk to you about your little crush. I guess I'm just not good enough at connecting with humans," he shrugged his shoulders. "But Doctor Allen, he was the perfect man for the job!" Both Jason and Doctor Allen smiled.

Sarah looked at Sam through two swollen eyes.

"It's okay, Sarah," Sam consoled her. "It's gonna be okay."

"Is it okay, Sam?" Jason asked. "Are you sure it's okay? Let me ask you something, Sarah, do you really know who Sam is? Do you know the things he's done?"

"Everything I did, I did to protect my friends," Sam responded.

"So that's why you murdered Cassander?"

"He would've done the same to me."

Jason continued to smile. "But what about Wyatt Jessings?"

"What are you talking about?"

"What about Parker Smith? What about Lucas Armstrong? Did you kill them to protect your friends too?"

"I- I didn't kill them."

"It's as I expected," Jason laughed. "You see, I keep a pretty close eye on my vampires. When one of them steps out of line, I find out. You were turned by a vampire who disobeyed me. Don't worry, I've already dealt with him. So when I heard those three boys went missing, I thought it had to be one of my people. But that wasn't the case. I interrogated everyone and was confident that it wasn't any of them. It made no sense. But then Batraz told me what you really were, then a few hours later I saw you murder Cassander on the news. It all clicked. Wyatt Jessings was found with red eyes, he had to be killed by a vampire, but no one did it. It was you, Sam, you killed those innocent boys."

Lookin' good, Sarah, how bout you ditch him and come home with me later? Sam remembered how embarrassed he felt in that moment, but it was more than just embarrassment. It was hatred, anger.

"Our powers are strong. If you don't learn to control them soon enough, they can overpower you. After your lovely first date you escaped the hospital, found the boys, and killed them. And you probably don't remember a thing."

Sam looked at Sarah, who couldn't stop shaking. Was she scared of Jason, or of him?

I can't keep her safe. I've never been able to. Sam fell to his knees.

"The police ended up finding Wyatt, with red eyes and all," Jason continued. "But they didn't find his two friends, so I sent my vampires searching. These are our woods, Sam, we know every inch of them. It didn't take long to find Parker and Lucas. They came in handy, we planted them in Abe's car to turn you and him into wanted murderers," Jason paused and studied Sam, who was speechless. "Speaking of your old pal Abe, my vampires were reckless and he managed to find a body in these woods. The same body which fell in front of your car the night of your accident. I didn't know if you would end up joining him. My plan was to coerce you and your mother into obeying me. But you are your father's son, and I knew there was a chance you would want to rebel. So I thought, maybe if you and Abe joined forces, then I can have you both killed. Let me ask you, were my vampires able to kill Abe tonight?"

Sam didn't say a word.

"You're smart not to answer. But something tells me he's still alive, and his granddaughter too. It's not a problem though, after I kill you, they will die too. Like I said, Sam, we control these woods, soon we will control this world, and everyone you love will die."

Sam would not give Jason the satisfaction of a response. Even if he wanted to speak, he wouldn't know what to say. Sam always tried his best to think of himself as a hero, but he was a villain. Maybe he was not as evil as Jason, but he was evil nonetheless. He thought he was strong enough to control these powers but he wasn't. He was a murderer. He finally admitted it to himself. There was nothing left to do but accept defeat. Jason had already won.

"After fourteen long years, you finally know the truth," Jason declared. "I can see your pain, and I take great pleasure in knowing you're going to die a horrible death."

Sam locked eyes with Jason and saw the same face he had seen at home at the kitchen table, at Little League games, at restaurants, and at school to pick him up when his mom was feeling sick. It was a face he never seemed to be able to understand, and now he finally knew why.

"I'm ready to be with my father," Sam took one last look at Sarah. He had failed her, he did everything wrong and this was his punishment. Now, as hundreds of vampires stood in between them, he was out of her life for good. He was out of everyone's life for good. The world would be a better place without him.

Jason smirked once more before striking. With one push he sent Sam flying down the path he had just walked. He was face down against the ground, spitting dirt out of his mouth. He looked up and saw Jason walking down the path slowly, savouring every step, every moment. The red in Sam's eyes had faded as he submitted to the Prince of The Ash. The vampires he was surrounded by all expected a fight but he refused to give them that.

Sam stood up as Jason neared him. "Fight back," Jason commanded.

"No," unlike everyone else in the forest, Sam would not be Jason's servant. Jason sent a piercing punch to Sam's face, sending him another five feet in the distance.

"Fight me!" With each crushing blow, Sam continued to disobey. Each time Sam would look up and see Jason approaching him again, not giving up, waiting for a fight that would never happen. Pain finally started to shoot through his body. He liked it, it was exactly what he wanted. Something, anything, to replace the emptiness.

"You're weaker than I expected, I thought you would at least give me a challenge," Jason picked up Sam by his shirt and slammed him right back to the ground. "After everything I've done to you, everything I've done to your mother, you're just gonna give up," he picked him up again and sent him flying back down the aisle of vampires. "That's not the boy I know. The boy I know became ever so curious about what was going on in this town. Now when you finally discover it, you lose interest." Blood spewed out of Sam's mouth as Jason struck him again.

Jason picked Sam up and held him by the neck, his claws

stabbed through his skin. Sam's body went numb. It's not what he wanted, he wanted to keep feeling the excruciating pain but at some point, that pain had to go away. As Jason held Sam over his head, Sam realized that death didn't mean eternal pain. It's made up of that emptiness, that numbness, the same feelings he was trying desperately to escape from. It was too late now though, Sam felt too weak and knew Jason was far too strong. The last thing he saw as all of his life left his body was a demon. Not just a demon, the Devil. He looked deeply into Jason's red eyes and felt scared. Not scared of Jason, but scared of leaving this world. He expected to feel at peace, but instead his breaths grew heavy, he panicked. He wanted to scream and squirm but he couldn't. It was too late. He let the Devil win.

Jason laughed, "I really broke you, didn't I?"

"You want a fight, boss?" Sam heard Doctor Allen say behind him. He looked back at the vampire, who had a tight grip on Sarah's neck. "I have an idea," Doctor Allen outstretched his claws and brought them flying down into Sarah's stomach.

"NO!!!" Sam spit out blood as he screamed for Sarah. She looked up at him as her hands tried to cover her stomach, blood oozing through her fingers. There was no hope, however, she was dying. She continued looking into his hazel eyes as she faded out of consciousness, but those eyes quickly turned red.

"NO!!!" He screamed again as he looked at Doctor Allen. He glanced back towards Jason, who was still holding him by the neck. Jason, too, was looking at Sarah in shock.

The numbness within Sam dissipated as the power began to flow through his limbs. He brought his hand down and hit Jason's forearm. Jason dropped him to the ground and Sam hit him with an uppercut to the jaw. Sam hastily leapt towards Jason, who flew into the air. The two vampires grabbed each other tightly and Sam sent a headbutt Jason's way to loosen his grip. With Jason's hands no longer clenching Sam's shoulders, Sam kicked off of his thigh, elevating him, and came back down with a punch so strong he heard the crack in Jason's skull. Jason flew down to the ground and Sam came crashing down towards his chest. Jason managed to grab his feet, however, and sent Sam flying into a nearby tree. As soon as Sam stood up, he saw the dark red set of eyes charging towards him. Sam planted his feet solidly on the ground, bracing for the inevitable impact. Jason rammed into Sam and the pair exploded through four trees behind them. They rolled around in the dirt, exchanging punches back and forth, before Sam sent a kick into Jason's stomach, distancing the two of them.

"You're gonna die tonight," Sam said as he stood up and stared Jason down. Suddenly, a blue shine emerged from his feet and instead of shying away from the power, Sam embraced it. He looked towards the sky and waited for the blue shine to make its way through his body but Jason quickly picked up a fallen tree trunk and swung it at his head. The blue shine halted and Sam was sent ten feet into the distance.

"Get over here!" Jason called out to his vampires. "Stop him!" Sam could tell Jason was scared and smiled as they met once again. Sam landed one blow but Jason landed two before dodging a punch from Sam. Jason uppercut him and Sam flew into the air. He landed in the middle of a group of vampires and swung his fists widely at anything that moved. Once he found his bearings, he swiftly and gracefully moved through the collection of vampires before locking eyes with Doctor Allen, who was still standing over Sarah's body.

Sam let out a thunderous scream as the blue shine attempted to make its way through his body again. He kept his sights set on Doctor Allen, wanting more than anything to kill him, but a vampire came up behind him and knocked him to the ground, once again stopping the blue shine from spreading. From the ground, Sam saw the fear in Doctor Allen's eyes as he turned his back and fled the fight.

Sam rolled over, narrowly avoiding a kick from a vampire, before jumping back to his feet. Avoiding the kick was the least of his problems, however. The vampires had formed a rapidly closing circle around him, he was surrounded. He looked through gaps between the vampires, hoping to see Jason. He needed to get back to him, tonight was the night he killed him.

"Come at me!" Sam yelled at the approaching vampires. Sam swung his claws in all directions but there were too many of them. There was no way he was getting out of this. Sam could no longer see the night sky, his vision was overwhelmed by claws, fangs, and red eyes. Eyes of darkness. They grabbed a hold of his feet so he couldn't even escape into the air. Their claws began to rip into his flesh. He was powerless against the vampire assault. He looked down and saw the blood pouring from his stomach, just as it poured out of Sarah's. His vision grew blurry and the red eyes that were ravaging his body began to expand. Soon his whole world was red. A hand reached from out of the pile and grabbed Sam by the neck. His vision cleared up and he could see the female vampire, the one who introduced Jarek, standing in front of him. She lifted him high into the air and threw him out of the swarm of vampires.

Sam was relieved. He still felt the blood flowing out of his body at a rapid rate but thought he had a chance to escape now that he was out of the crowd. But he was mistaken. He turned over onto his back and saw his rival staring back down at him. Jason stepped on Sam's chest and stood proudly over the battered young man.

"You've been beaten," Jason said to him and Sam knew this was true. Jason sat on top of Sam, "Now it's time to end your suffering."

Jason sent his first punch into Sam's skull. "TONIGHT," Jason punched him again. "IS THE NIGHT," another punch. "YOU DIE!" Jason leaned upwards and held both fists high into the air, preparing to come down for the lethal blow.

A gunshot echoed through the forest. Jason stopped with his arms only halfway to Sam. More vampires approached Jason and more shots were fired. Sam watched two vampires' heads explode as they ran towards their master. Vampires continued to fall in rapid succession. Sam looked around but could not identify the shooter. Then an arrow flew by him and pierced through the skull of a vampire. He smiled. Only one girl could shoot a bow and arrow that well.

The chaos didn't stop Jason from picking Sam up, and he was still far too weak to fight back. A bullet had burst through Jason's shoulder, but he was still strong enough to lift Sam over his head. Jason dug his claws into Sam's neck, even deeper this time, sending blood cascading down his body.

"Now you di-" Another shot was fired. Jason dropped Sam and covered his ear with one hand whilst stumbling backwards. Upon removing the hand, Sam realized Jason's ear had been shot cleanly off, and now watched the blood pour out of him.

The shooter and the archer kept firing. Abe's assault rifle mowed vampires down faster than they could react. There were beings in black cloaks frantically moving in every direction. They were unorganized and their master was injured. Molotov cocktails were thrown, igniting bright fires in a previously dark forest.

"Retreat!" Sam heard as he laid on the ground. It was Jason's voice. He was still able to speak, still able to move, but he was scared. Sam could hear his voice trembling. Jason continued to call for a retreat, his voice growing more distant with each yell, as the vampires scattered in every direction of The West Woods. Soon there was no one attacking him, but there were still footsteps all around, there was still a sense of urgency.

Abe ran over to Sam and picked him up. Chelsea ran behind him and he locked eyes with her. However, his vision grew more blurry with each passing second. He tried his best to lift his arm and signal towards the cave. Chelsea looked behind her and smiled back at him, all the vampires were gone. He continued to point towards the vampire hideout. The cave, they needed to go back to the cave. Sarah was at the cave. But his vision waned until he lost sight of where he was. The looming West Woods transformed into a dark void.

He had been saved but he failed to save Sarah. She was destined to bleed to death in that dark void. He knew that even though they had temporarily escaped it, they would be flung back into it as well. This wasn't over. But for him, at least for now, it was. His vision was gone, all feeling in his body had fled him. All that remained was that emptiness, that numbness, the scariest feeling of all.

Darkness. Darkness surrounded him. He saw no light.

ACKNOWLEDGEMENTS

I'd like to thank Simon Ruscinski and Gabby Tomlinson, who spent countless hours editing this book. Without you, this book simply would not exist.

I'd also like to thank all of my amazing family and friends, who have supported me while writing this.

Lastly, Jack, the moodiest cat I've ever met who also had the biggest heart. He would sit on my bed everyday and watch me pace back and forth across my room, brainstorming story ideas. Black cats will always be good luck in my mind. Rest in peace, little guy.

ABOUT THE AUTHOR

Max Ruscinski was born in Hamilton, Ontario. Growing up, he loved nothing more than becoming immersed in fictional worlds, either through books, movies, or television shows. When he thinks of an idea, it's a BIG idea. Once that idea is in his head, he can't stop thinking about it. This led him to setting an immense goal of completing a novel in one year. From the moment he began writing, he knew it was his ultimate passion. Eyes of Darkness is his debut novel, and the first in a sprawling fantasy series.

www.ingramcontent.com/pod-product-compliance
Lightning Source LLC
Chambersburg PA
CBHW031624100726
47898CB00006B/1933